BREW UNTO OTHERS

BREW UNTO OTHERS

Sandra Balzo

**SEVERN
HOUSE**

First world edition published in Great Britain and the USA in 2024
by Severn House, an imprint of Canongate Books Ltd,
14 High Street, Edinburgh EH1 1TE.

severnhouse.com

British Library Cataloguing-in-Publication Data
A CIP catalogue record for this title is available from the British Library.

ISBN-13: 978-1-4483-1439-3 (cased)
ISBN-13: 978-1-4483-1490-4 (e-book)

All Severn House titles are printed on acid-free paper.

MIX
Paper | Supporting
responsible forestry
FSC
www.fsc.org   FSC® C013056

Typeset by Palimpsest Book Production Ltd., Falkirk,
Stirlingshire, Scotland.
Printed and bound in Great Britain by TJ Books,
Padstow, Cornwall.

Praise for the Maggy Thorsen mysteries

"Vividly drawn characters and dialogue crackling with wit"
Publishers Weekly on *French Roast*

"An inventive mashup of cozy subgenres"
Kirkus Reviews on *Any Pot in a Storm*

"Balzo's latest will keep readers on their toes . . . Solid cozy fare"
Booklist on *French Roast*

"The body count rises quickly as Balzo's quirky cozy turns darker than a freshly brewed espresso"
Kirkus Reviews on *French Roast*

"Lively, intelligent characters . . . make this stand out from the cozy pack"
Publishers Weekly on *The Big Steep*

"Connecting murders past and present provides a welcome challenge for coffeehouse cozy fans"
Kirkus Reviews on *The Big Steep*

About the author

Sandra Balzo built an impressive career as a public relations consultant before authoring the successful 'Maggy Thorsen' coffeehouse mysteries, the first of which, *Uncommon Grounds*, was published to stellar reviews and nominated for an Anthony and Macavity Award. She is also the author of the 'Main Street Murders' mystery series published by Severn House.

www.sandrabalzo.com

In grateful memory of Elaine Perez and Mary Michalek, whose That Coffee Place became my fictional Uncommon Grounds. We miss you.

ONE

'**E**dna was such a sweetheart,' the young dark-haired woman who had captured my hand told me earnestly. 'We'll miss her terribly.'

'As will we,' I said, while secretly coveting the black and gold scarf she was wearing over her simple black dress.

As the woman moved on to the casket in the front of the room, I elbowed my partner, Sarah Kingston. 'Do you think that was Hermès?'

'How in the hell would I know?' she growled.

Sarah and I owned a coffeehouse, but at the moment we were just inside the chapel door of Brookhills Mortuary and Cremation forming a very short receiving line. The occasion was the wake for Edna Mayes Kingston, Sarah's mother.

'I feel like a fraud standing in for your sister until she gets here,' I said. 'I've never so much as met Ruth – or your mother, for that matter.'

'I'm not convinced anybody here really has either,' Sarah said, her oblong face still scrunched in a scowl as she surveyed the small knot of people in front of the casket. 'Silly tradition, isn't it? People gathering around a closed casket. For all they know, the thing is empty.'

Valid, perhaps, but probably a discussion best left to another day.

'Who the hell *are* these people?' Sarah continued grousing.

I sighed, deciding to take her rhetorical question literally rather than listening to a continuing litany of bellyaching. 'Well, that woman who was just here – Melinda, I think? – volunteers at the county senior center where Edna played bridge.' I shifted onto my tiptoes to momentarily relieve the ache in my arches. Sarah and I had worked the Sunday shift at Uncommon Grounds before changing clothes – and shoes – for the wake/visitation. 'Everybody apparently loved her.'

'So they say. And see that guy there with the salt-and-pepper hair?' She chin-gestured toward a middle-aged man who had been cornered by a stoop-shouldered elderly man, his own hair dyed an unlikely shade of yellow. As we watched, Salt-and-Pepper broke away from Yellow Hair to shake hands with a younger man in a neat black suit. 'He swore he enjoyed meeting her when he did some work at the house.'

'You don't believe he worked for her?'

'No, I don't believe he enjoyed it. My mother put off maintenance endlessly, negotiated mercilessly and paid late, if at all. He's probably here planning to remind Ruth he's still waiting to be paid. Which, come to think of it, maybe why he's talking to Edna's lawyer at this very minute. He's getting on the list of creditors to be paid by the estate.'

'The youngish guy in the black suit is the lawyer?'

She snorted. 'Can't you tell? He and the funeral director out there,' she gestured to where the man stood in the entry vestibule greeting people, 'are the only males in black suits.'

'They're here as professionals,' I said.

'Carrion-eaters, feeding on the dead.'

Wow. 'Aren't we in a foul mood?'

'*Please* tell me that pun wasn't intentional,' Sarah said, glaring at me. 'I'm here mourning the death of my mother.'

'Oh, my God – no, it wasn't intentional,' I said, my heart dropping. 'I'm sorry if I'm being insensitive. I know you and your mother had a difficult—'

Sarah punched my arm. 'I'm just messing with you. My mother was a pain in the ass. Not that anyone here would come out and say it.'

'People don't like to speak ill of the dead.' At least most people.

Sarah scowled. 'And yet they come to their funerals.'

Yes, they did. Including me. 'These shoes are killing me.'

Sarah glanced down. 'I'm not surprised. If God wanted us to wear shoes like that, he wouldn't have given us toes.'

'They are pointy, aren't they?' The shoes had been stylish when I bought them a decade or two earlier. 'Think too pointy? I mean to be in style now?'

'Again, how would I know? Ask Arial when she gets here. If she gets here.' Sarah shifted to glance toward the door, nearly knocking the placard bearing her mother's photo off its easel.

Sarah's niece Arial, at least, I had met. 'Maybe Arial's plane was late. But what about your sister? Doesn't Ruth live right in town?' I sniffed and shifted my weight again. 'I don't mind filling in for them, but at this point I can't feel my toes.'

'They're together.'

'Absolutely squished,' I agreed, trying to slide my foot back in the shoe to gain more room. 'I'd slip off my shoe, but I'm afraid the toes will balloon like—'

'Not your toes,' Sarah snapped. 'Arial and Saint Ruth are coming here together. I could care less about your toes.'

That sentiment didn't surprise me, given my partner's legendary lack of empathy. But Arial and her mother riding in the same car did, at least from what Sarah had told me.

According to my partner, Ruth had gotten pregnant after an ill-fated fling with a married man and seemingly resented the baby from the day she had given birth to Arial some twenty-five years ago.

'There was no physical abuse or neglect,' Sarah had told me. 'More like . . . disregard. Both Ruth and Edna would say how they'd "done right by Arial." In front of her. Like it was the baby's fault and Ruth was noble for rising above.'

Hence Sarah's canonization of her sister to sainthood. And my partner's own bitter resentment toward Ruth and Edna. Sarah loved Arial and, if you had Sarah Kingston's love, you had it for life. For better or for worse.

'Maybe your mom's death will bring them closer together?' I ventured now.

'Fat chance,' Sarah said. 'Arial and Ruth barely speak, though that's kind of a tradition in my family. I hadn't seen Edna or Ruth for years until Edna got sick. And my father took off almost forty years ago, and we didn't hear from him until my auntie Vi called to say he was dead.'

I glanced sidelong at her. 'But you think he might have been bipolar like you.'

'Yeah. The jerk.'

This family didn't cut each other a lot of slack. 'He did leave you the depot.' Where our coffeehouse was located.

'He died and it went to my auntie Vi, who willed it to me when she died,' Sarah said. 'That's not the same.'

Still, I was grateful. 'About Arial, I don't want to put my foot in it when I meet Ruth. Is she aware of . . .?'

'The body you found in the house where Arial was dog-sitting? How could she not be? Brookhills is a small town. But I told Ruth that was on you, Maggy Thorsen. Arial just happened to be there.'

And had been coerced into helping dispose of a body. In the end, Arial had cooperated fully with the police and been sentenced to a year of probation. She'd spent the year at Sarah's and then celebrated its expiration by escaping to the Bahamas for a week to celebrate her twenty-fifth birthday. Which is where she'd been when her grandmother died. 'Did Arial get on any better with her grandmother than she does with her mother?'

'My sister and my mother are two peas in the same dried-up old pod,' Sarah said. 'Self-righteous, bitter and intolerant.'

'Amazing that you emerged from that same pod all empathetic and touchy-feely.'

'Right?' Sarah flashed a grin.

'Wrong. But you do try.' Sometimes.

'While the two of them just get – or got, as far as my mother goes – pettier.' Sarah glanced around to see if anybody was nearby and lowered her voice. 'Edna told me that she was cutting Ruth out of the will.'

I pivoted on my heels, forgetting my achy feet. 'You think she really did?'

'Time will tell.' Like a cartoon villain, Sarah was rubbing her hands together in gleeful anticipation. Or maybe it was to keep them warm given the cold air wafting in from the vestibule. 'I tried to get a read from Mr Jurisprudence when he came in, but he wasn't giving anything away until the reading of the will tomorrow.'

'Do you expect that your mom left something to you? I mean, I know things are tight with the kids heading off to college and all.' Sarah had adopted Courtney Egan and her brother Sam four years ago, when their mother Patricia – Sarah's best friend and one of my original partners in Uncommon Grounds – died.

'Left something to me? No way. I already inherited the depot from my father's side, remember? Ruth was ticked, and Edna told me flat out that I shouldn't expect anything from her.' She smirked. 'They were jealous that I was Auntie Vi's favorite.'

Whatever the reason, Sarah's inheritance had allowed us to

relocate our coffee shop to the historical Brookhills train depot when our original location in a strip mall was destroyed in a freak spring snowstorm.

'I suppose it's only fair that the house should pass to Ruth, since she lived there with Arial and took care of your mom as she got older.'

'That's one way of looking at it.'

'What's another?'

Sarah shrugged. 'That Ruth was sponging off her.'

I thought that was a little unfair, especially from the daughter who had left home and never had to look back. 'But at what cost to her own life? Ruth never married, never went away to school, like you did. She raised her daughter as a single parent—' I held up a hand as Sarah opened her mouth to object. 'Yes, I know – a bad single parent.'

'Poor Ruth.' Sarah was playing an invisible violin. 'She could have had a life. Could start one now, in fact, but I doubt she will. She enjoys playing the martyr too much.'

'Perhaps.' I closed one eye as I regarded my friend. 'But somebody had to take care of your mom when she got sick.'

'And it wasn't me, you mean.' Sarah ducked her head. 'You're right, of course. Martyrs like Ruth let the rest of us off the hook.'

I took a step back. 'Whoa. You really are giving this empathy and understanding thing a try.'

'I told you,' Sarah said. 'I'm the pea that mutated.'

I couldn't argue with that, though 'evolved' might have been a better word choice. 'But back to this will—'

'You're intrigued now, aren't you?' Sarah asked. 'Bet your feet aren't even hurting.'

'Because they've gone numb,' I told her. 'When was it that your mom mentioned changing her will? Recently?'

'June, I think.'

And it was now September, meaning that Edna had plenty of time to make the changes – or change her mind – before she died. 'Maybe she was just angry at Ruth and letting off steam.'

'My mother did more "righteous indignation" than anger,' Sarah said. 'Or at least she'd call it righteous.'

'But she didn't say what Ruth had done to make her . . . indignant? Or even tell her that she'd changed her will?'

'No, and I don't know.' Sarah wiggled her eyebrows at me. 'But I do find it interesting that Ruth is making nice to Arial all of a sudden. Offering to pick her up at the airport and all.'

Ahh. 'You think Edna hopscotched over Ruth and left her estate to Arial and Ruth knows about it.'

'Maybe. And Edna was of sound mind to the very end, so I'm betting she did make the change. And that it'll stick.'

In case Ruth contested the will, I presumed. 'Is there much beyond the house?'

'Edna's mother, my grandmother Gretchen, had a property on the Central Coast in California. Since Edna was an only child, I assume she inherited it when Gretchen died, but I don't really know that.'

'You said Edna and Ruth lived pretty modestly.'

'"Cheaply" was probably the word I used,' Sarah said. 'Or "miserly." My mother didn't spend a penny she didn't have to. Which means whoever does inherit the house will have to spend a good amount just to bring it up to date. Even to sell.'

'Maybe Edna left some cash?' I ventured.

'Maybe. Why don't you come to the will-reading with me tomorrow and find out?'

It was tempting. 'What time? I'm opening with Amy.' Amy Caprese was our star barista and, in fact, our only barista outside of Sarah and me. Who are not stars.

'Ten a.m.' Sarah folded her arms against another cold blast of air from the door. 'Brr. September twenty-third and it feels like winter.'

'My furnace went on last night,' I said. 'That's way early.'

'You probably keep it set at seventy,' Sarah said. 'Wimp.'

'Sixty-two,' I countered. 'And I am not a wimp.'

'You are a wimp. When I lived at home, my mother wouldn't let us turn on the furnace until Thanksgiving, no matter how cold it got.'

'You realize you're holding up your mother – who you just said was a miser – as a shining example of non-wimpness.'

'"Stop whining and put on a sweater,"' she parroted at me.

A sweater, in fact, would be quite welcome at the moment.

I rubbed my bare arms, wanting to be out of this reception line of two and closer to the casket, where presumably it was warmer. 'Can you see who just came in? Is that Ruth and Arial at last?'

Sarah cocked her head, listening. 'Just two old ladies, from the sounds of it.'

'Your mother was eighty-four. All her friends are old ladies.' I was feeling yowly. 'Don't you think you should try calling Ruth? Maybe you should have met Arial at the airport.'

'We were just closing up the shop two hours ago when her plane was due in,' Sarah reminded me. 'Besides, Ruth said she had it covered and there was no way I was getting in between those two.'

'But—'

'And if you'll take my advice, you won't start your "Ms Peacemaker" act when they get here. You'll only get burned.'

'I don't—'

'Please. You want everybody to like each other. And you especially don't like it when somebody picks on somebody that *you* like.'

I wasn't alone in that. 'Arial, you mean.'

'Exactly like Arial.' Sarah lowered her voice as the chatter from the vestibule got closer. 'But don't underestimate my niece. The daughter can give as good as the mother. Maybe better.'

'Fine. Consider me warned.' I turned gratefully from my crotchety partner to greet the new arrivals. 'Thank you so much for coming . . .' I started to say and then broke off. 'Sophie, Gloria. I didn't realize you knew Sarah's mother.'

Sophie Daystrom and Gloria Goddard were residents of Brookhills Manor, the senior living facility just a block from our coffeehouse. Along with Sophie's husband Henry, they were regular customers of Uncommon Grounds.

'I don't.' Gloria gave an eye-roll toward Sophie, apparently to indicate whose idea their attending was. 'But my Hank did a bit, from filling her prescriptions.'

Gloria and her late husband Hank, not to be confused with Sophie's Henry, had owned Goddard's Pharmacy, a few doors down from us in Benson Plaza, the original location of Uncommon Grounds.

'I haven't spoken to her for years,' Sophie said. 'But knowing the deceased is not the point of attending.'

'Attending a funeral?' Gloria was trying to extricate herself from her blue and purple cross-body pack, which had gotten tangled with her black cardigan. 'I think it kind of is.'

'Can I help you?' I asked, shifting the neck of her sweater to undo the strap and hand it to her.

'Thank you,' Gloria said, resettling it across the other shoulder. 'I forgot I had it on and put my sweater on over it.'

'And your coat,' Sophie reminded her. 'If you used it like a fanny pack, which was the way God intended—'

'It's not a fanny pack,' Gloria said, raising her chin. 'It's a sling bag. All the kids are wearing them.'

'Sure they are,' Sophie said. 'But this is your JanSport fanny pack from the Eighties that you've resurrected to wear to a wake, of all things.'

Sophie did have a way with words.

'Is not,' Gloria countered. 'And it was your idea to go to the wake of a woman we barely know.'

'Is, too.' Sophie patted her white curls. 'And I'm here to support the family.' She waved her hand toward the casket. 'Ellen could obviously care less at this point.'

'Edna,' Sarah corrected.

Gloria leaned in. 'I did want to see Fellowship Hall,' she whispered. 'I understand it's been remodeled since the new man took over from Mort Ashbury.'

'I assume that's where the light repast will be held.' Sophie was sniffing the air, presumably for signs of casseroles, gelatin molds and finger sandwiches. 'Do you need help getting things started?'

I turned to Sarah. 'Did you plan on food? We could have brought coffee and a tray of Tien's desserts.' Tien Romano was our baker and a local caterer.

'Ruth insisted we invite people back to the house after the visitation,' Sarah said. 'Though I presume my sister meant people she knew.'

This last was a direct shot at Sophie and Gloria.

I elbowed her. 'There are like fifteen people here total. Be grateful somebody came.' Especially given the portrait Sarah had been painting of her not-so-beloved mother.

Sophie was shaking her head sadly. 'The older we get, the fewer of our contemporaries are around to come to our funerals.'

'And the ones who do, come mostly for the food,' Gloria said sourly. 'Which is why Henry wouldn't come. He's too honorable to mooch food.'

'Socialization is important at our age,' Sophie protested. 'Henry doesn't understand.'

'Maybe because you're socializing in funeral homes?' I asked her.

'Not just funeral homes. Sometimes it's churches.' Sophie brightened.

'And today a house party at Saint Ruth's house,' Gloria added, not so brightly.

'You know Ruth then?' I asked, a little bewildered. 'And call her—'

'Saint Ruth? Everybody who knows Ruth calls her something like that.' Gloria stuck out a crooked little finger, like she was holding a cup. 'Hoity toity, Miss Latte-da.'

'It's lah-di-dah,' I said automatically. 'No coffee reference.'

'There is for me,' Gloria said, glaring. 'The woman had the nerve to call me over at the lunch counter and tell me her coffee mug had a lipstick smudge on the rim.'

Gloria's pharmacy lunch counter had been legendary for its egg salad sandwiches and bottomless cups of coffee, before the pharmacy was destroyed in the same storm that had taken down the old Uncommon Grounds.

'Did you check the color of the lipstick?' Sophie asked her friend. 'Bet it was the shade she was wearing herself that day. I wouldn't put it past her to try to sabotage you.'

'Oh, I don't think Ruth was trying to get us shut down by the health department or anything,' Gloria said. 'She just can't help but point out other people's mistakes, including that poor daughter of hers.'

'Defense mechanism,' Sophie said, nodding sagely. 'Nothing anybody did was ever good enough for Edna, so Ruth probably started to nitpick just to beat her mother to it.'

'They do say the apple doesn't fall far from the tree,' Gloria said.

'This apple did,' Sarah muttered.

'Miles away,' I agreed. 'I know from personal experience that you have absolutely no problem with a little smudge on a cup.'

'If it's gone through the dishwasher, it's clean. Get over it.'

'See what I mean?' I asked Sophie and Gloria.

'Polar opposite,' Sophie agreed. 'But then Sarah was older and went away to school. Maybe Edna wasn't as hard on her.'

'I do think you go one way or the other,' Gloria posited. 'Either you become your mother – or whomever – or you rebel and become the contrary.'

'That's me,' Sarah said, flashing a big toothy grin. 'Contrary.' From the horse's mouth.

'Anyway,' Sophie said, 'I can't wait to get to Ruth's house.'

'Check out her dishes and flatware.' Gloria was nodding.

'To eat,' Sophie countered. 'I'm starving. Isn't the visitation about over?'

Gloria was glancing around as the door opened again. 'And where is Ruth anyway?'

As if on cue, a petite young woman stepped in. 'That,' she said, shoving unruly fawn-colored hair out of her face, 'is exactly what I'd like to know.'

TWO

'Wait, wait,' Sarah said as she went to hug her niece. 'Are you telling me that your mother didn't pick you up from the airport? Why didn't you call me?'

'I snagged a rideshare,' Arial said, slinging an oversized duffel off her back. 'I don't know why I even expected her to show up. Making gelatin molds must have been more important.'

'Gelatin molds?' Sophie's nose was wrinkled in distaste. 'Hopefully not the one with grated carrots and crushed pineapple. Fanny packs I might be able to tolerate, but some things just need to be retired. I—'

'Now that can't be all the luggage you have,' Gloria interrupted, pointing at Arial's khaki duffel. 'Weren't you gone for an entire week?'

'I was,' Arial said, giving first Sarah and then me a hug. 'But you don't need much room for bikinis, shorts and tank tops.'

'Must have been such a relief after those orange jumpsuits,' Sophie said.

Arial rolled her brown eyes and grinned. 'Sorry to disappoint you, but orange was not my new black. I was on probation.'

'Ankle bracelet?' Sophie asked hopefully.

'I'm afraid not,' Arial told her. 'And I wasn't on house arrest, before you ask. I just couldn't leave the state and had to check in with my probation officer every month.'

'Arial flipped and turned state's evidence, Sophie,' Gloria said, leaning in to give the girl a peck on the cheek. 'You know that.'

'But exactly how?' Arial asked. 'I mean, exactly how does everybody know the details of my plea deal?'

'Small-town, big-mouthed coffeehouse.' I wrinkled my nose. 'Sorry.'

Arial sighed. 'Fine. But now can we all just forget it? I'm glad to have that chapter of my life over.'

'And we are proud to have a snitch in the family,' Sarah said. 'Or what's left of the family. We are here for a funeral, you know.'

'I'm sorry about your grandmother,' I told Arial. 'Why don't you take my place here next to Sarah, and I'll just—'

But Arial's auburn head was rotating. 'But where *is* Ruth?'

'Not here,' Sarah said. 'You're probably right that she got bogged down with gelatin molds and cutting chicken salad sandwiches into tiny—'

'Excuse me.' The funeral director was at my elbow, his voice low. 'We're at the end of our visitation period, so if the last of our guests to arrive would like to make their way forward to pay their—'

'Speak up,' Gloria interrupted, cupping her ear.

'It's not like you're going to wake the dead.' Sophie indicated the casket in the front of the room. 'And most of us here have a fair amount of hearing loss, I'd wager.'

'Certainly,' the funeral director said, raising his voice a notch. 'If we can all just pay our final respects to Mrs Kingston?'

'I think Ruth arranged for three hours of visitation – four to seven,' Sarah said, gesturing that Sophie and Gloria should precede us in following the funeral director. 'He's trying to close up.'

'Can you blame him?' I asked as we moved toward the casket. 'Not exactly the way I'd choose to spend my Sunday afternoon into evening.'

'Unless, of course, your best friend's mother had died,' Sarah said.

Yes, of course that.

'What's the name of the new guy?' I nodded to where the funeral director now stood, chatting with the stooped elderly man.

'I don't remember,' Sarah said.

'Not everybody can be as memorable as his predecessor,' I said. 'Mort Ashbury.'

'Shut up,' Arial burst out and then lowered her voice. 'That can't have been his real name. Mort, the mortician, Ashbury owned a crematorium? Really?'

'If he made the name up, you have to give him points for shameless marketing,' Sarah said, stopping dead in front of the casket. 'Now say goodbye to your grandmother, so we can go tell your mother what I think of her.'

Arial put her hand on the closed casket. 'Bye, Edna.'

She bowed her head and I waited until she'd turned back to ask, 'Sarah said you and your mom lived with your grandmother. Was that the same house they're living in now?'

The house she might be inheriting.

'Yup, the ancestral home,' Arial said, smiling. 'Though I spent more time at Sarah's or with friends than I did there.'

'More time?' Sarah said, cuffing her. 'You showed up at my door with your roller bag one morning and just didn't leave.'

'Really?' I asked Arial. 'How old were you?'

'Maybe fifteen?' the girl said, looking to Sarah for affirmation.

Her aunt nodded. 'You'd gotten up early and overheard your mother and grandmother in the kitchen.'

'Ruth was apologizing for getting pregnant and ruining Edna's life,' Arial said, turning to me. 'She was sobbing so hard she could barely speak.'

And Arial had heard this at fifteen. Most adults wouldn't recover from something like that. 'I am so sorry.' I glanced at Sarah, whose face looked murderous.

But Arial just shrugged. 'At least she finally said it out loud. She'd been acting that way since I could remember. Always shooing me away, telling me to be quiet, not to bother Grandma, not to leave even a single toy or book around.'

Nitpicking, as Sophie had put it, before Edna could?

'You sure made up for that at my house. Junk everywhere. And the noise.' Sarah rolled her eyes and shuddered.

I smiled at my friend. 'I bet you loved it.'

'Yes, but for ten years?'

Arial grinned. 'You're exaggerating. I went home occasionally. Or stayed with friends.'

'A few days or weeks here and there,' Sarah said. 'But mostly it was just us, the two musketeers, muddling our way through.'

Sophie had been trying to eavesdrop. 'There was family in California, did you know that? Edna moved here with Sarah and Ruth about the time you were born, Arial.'

I blinked. 'You weren't born in Brookhills, Sarah? I just assumed somehow that you were a local.'

The 'somehow' was because all of the marketing materials for

Kingston Realty, Sarah's career before she'd joined forces with me in Uncommon Grounds, had touted her local ties.

'Twenty-five years doesn't make me a local?' Sarah demanded. 'Besides, I didn't move to Wisconsin with Saint Ruth and Mommy Dearest. I was already here attending college in Madison.'

'Potatoes, potahtoes.' Sophie's stomach emitted an audible growl. 'So what now? Is there a funeral supper or should we head back to the manor for Salisbury steak, mashed potatoes and peas?'

Gloria groaned. 'I vote for Ruth's. She's probably unmolding the gelatin as we speak.'

'And didn't come to her mother's visitation?' I whispered to Sarah, as Arial snagged her backpack. 'That's odd, don't you think?'

'What I think is that you haven't met my sister.'

Yet.

Ruth wasn't picking up her phone, so we provided the address to the rest of the attendees and asked that they give us a half-hour head start before driving over. That way Sarah, Arial and I would be there to alert Ruth before the herd – a very small herd, albeit – showed up expecting to be fed and watered.

But when we arrived, the modest white brick ranch house was dark, and nobody answered when Arial climbed the steps to ring the doorbell.

Gloria and Sophie, not being the patient kind, had slipped into my Escape to ride with Sarah, Arial and me.

'There are no lights on,' I observed as I held the car door for the two octogenarians to climb out of the back seat.

'Like I said,' Sarah said as Arial returned to the car. 'You don't know Ruth. Or Edna. Probably saving on electricity.'

Arial lifted the tailgate of the Escape and pulled out her backpack. 'Do you have a key, Sarah? I'm not exactly sure where I put mine.'

'Ruth gave me one years ago, but it's at home somewhere.' Sarah went to the front door to push and hold the doorbell. 'Ruth should be here.'

'Did you hear the doorbell ring?' I asked, joining her at the door.

'No.' She was still holding it.

'Then maybe let it go and try again?'

She did, but I couldn't hear anything either. So I rapped.

'Maybe she's at the back of the house and can't hear us.' Sophie was standing with Gloria at the convergence of the walk leading to the front door and the one to the side driveway. 'Where is the kitchen?'

Sarah stepped back. 'At the rear of the house, as a matter of fact. Overlooking the back yard.'

'Like in most of these little ranches,' Gloria said, starting around.

'Wait,' Arial said, hurrying to intercept her. 'Let me go first. There's a fence along the driveway in back, so you have to go through a gate to get into the back yard. And there are no lights.'

It was barely seven thirty, but I agreed it was still too dark for a couple of seniors to be poking around. 'Sarah and I will go with Arial. You two stay here.'

'We'll cover the front door,' Gloria said, nodding.

'What?' Sophie said to her as we passed. 'You think Ruth's going to make a run for it?'

'It is dark back here,' I commented as we followed the driveway. 'Ruth should put in a motion detector light.'

'"And have that thing flashing on and off every time a blessed squirrel walks by?"' Arial was parodying her mother or grandmother, I assumed.

'"Damnable waste of money,"' Sarah continued for her.

'"Besides giving the thieves a good view of what there is to steal. Let 'em use their own flashlight."' Arial unlatched the gate as she and her aunt dissolved into giggles.

The two of them may not have spent much time around Ruth and Edna lately, but they sure had their imitations down pat.

Me, I really was concerned about the lack of light, but mostly because there was none inside the house where the kitchen should be. I hitched myself up to peer into the window next to the door, but all I could see were shapes and shadows. 'If Ruth was to pick up Arial and the two of them come directly to the funeral home, was somebody else staying here to prepare the supper?'

'You mean like a caterer?' Arial said. 'I doubt it.'

'Ruth said she was just doing cold things,' Sarah said. 'Salads and sandwiches.'

'Maybe she had car trouble or got in an accident on the way

to get me?' Arial was mounting the back concrete stoop to the door. 'She didn't answer any of my texts or calls.'

'Mine either.' Sarah's voice sounded worried in the dark. 'Is the door—'

'Unlocked. Some things never change.' Arial pulled open the door and stepped in, flicking on the wall switch. 'Hello?'

The overhead light now on, we could see packages of paper plates and plastic cups on the table, along with a roll of plastic wrap.

Sarah went straight to the refrigerator and pulled open the door. 'Deli cold cuts, tuna salad and . . .' She pulled plastic wrap off the top of a bowl, 'Ruth's bacon and tomato macaroni salad.'

'She probably made that last night,' Arial said. 'She always said it was better the next day.'

So there had been family mealtimes in the Kingston house. And maybe even parties.

I was glancing around. A bag of Dutchy-crust rolls and loaves of wheat and rye bread stood ready on the counter, but nothing was sliced or laid out. 'No sandwiches are prepared. Would Ruth have done all that and put everything in the refrigerator before she left to go to the airport?'

'Covered with the plastic wrap,' Sarah affirmed, picking up the rolls on the table.

'The car's not in the driveway,' Arial said. 'Maybe it's in the garage.'

'I'll go look,' I said quickly, having stumbled across a body or two in a garage.

I was out the door before anybody could argue the point.

Flicking on my phone light, I saw there was a side door into the garage from the yard. As I approached it, I couldn't detect the sound of a running engine. Not that it meant anything. Ruth was supposed to pick up Arial hours ago, which meant that an idling car might have run out of gas by now.

As I opened the door, there was only silence, and no smell of exhaust. I flipped on the light and approached the driver side of the SUV, holding my breath.

And let it out. Empty. I felt the hood of the car. 'And the engine's stone cold,' I said to myself.

I was relieved Ruth hadn't committed suicide on the day of

her mother's wake – unlikely anyway, given she'd purchased cold cuts and other groceries for the post-visitation supper. But still, the SUV's presence in the garage was worrisome.

'Maggy?' Sarah called from the door of the house, her voice sounding under-powered and hesitant.

'Car is still here in the garage,' I said, ducking back into the house. 'Empty,' I whispered to Sarah as I passed, just in case she'd been entertaining the same dark thoughts.

But Arial was standing hunched over the sink.

'Did she just get sick?' I asked Sarah, identifying the source of the stench. I put my hand on the girl's shoulder. 'It's OK, Arial. There's nobody in the car. Maybe your mom—'

'Check the bedroom.' Sarah's left hand was over her mouth as she gestured toward the hallway with her right.

There were three doors off the hallway – one to each side and another straight ahead. The door to my right was open, so I stuck my head in there first. The room smelled sweetly stale with a pong of bleach and disinfectant. Edna's room, judging by the hospital-style bed set on the opposite wall with a commode next to it. A dresser with a mirror above . . .

But no.

Despite my sense of urgency, I stopped to stare. The 'mirror' was actually a painting of the reflection of the dresser top at another time – a Tiffany lamp on a lace dresser scarf and a folded piece of ivory stationery, its envelope torn and cast aside, was painstakingly depicted where now only a discarded bedpan sat on the same white dresser scarf.

'Any sign of her?' Arial's voice called weakly.

Shaking off my moment of unintended art appreciation, I returned to the hallway and the opposite door.

'Ruth?' I called, knocking on the door perfunctorily before cracking it open.

The curtains were drawn, but I could see a shape in the bed.

'Ruth?' I said again, as Sarah and Arial entered the hallway behind me.

'She's sleeping?' Sarah asked, peering over my shoulder. 'What the—'

I held up a hand and crossed the room, my heart pounding in my ears.

Ruth Kingston was lying motionless on her stomach, head hanging partially off the bed. As I went to feel for a pulse, I registered the pool of vomit on the floor, along with coagulating blood from a two-inch gash on Ruth's right temple.

THREE

Turning away from Ruth's body, I stumbled to the window and slid it open, leaning my pounding forehead against the sash as I tried to get my breath. 'We have to get out of here.'

'Shouldn't we wake her first?' Arial was swiping awkwardly at her mouth. 'Is that blood, or . . . or . . .' She upchucked again, this time on the hallway floor.

Sarah tried unsuccessfully to dodge the spew as she got out her phone.

'We'll call for help outside,' I said, pushing them both ahead of me through the kitchen toward the back door. 'It's carbon monoxide – headache, disorientation.' I nodded to the sink. 'Vomiting.'

Sarah had her phone to her ear. ' . . . an ambulance. The address is . . . umm . . .'

I shoved them both out onto the grass and took the phone away from her. '138 Hawthorne Court. Fire department and EMTs. They'll have to come in the back. I think it's carbon monoxide poisoning and we can't—'

Gloria's head popped out of the very door we'd just escaped through. 'I thought you were going to let us in the front.'

'Get out here.' I was waving them out a little frantically. 'The house is filled with gas.'

'Gas?' she exclaimed, the two of them hurrying down the porch steps a lot quicker than I'd have expected at their ages.

'You mean like "going-to-explode" gas?' Sophie called from where they'd distanced themselves in the dark about twenty feet away.

'No, carbon monoxide, we think,' Sarah said, snatching her phone from me and switching on the flashlight so we could see.

Arial was leaning against the fence, breathing in slow breaths. 'How did you get in the front door?' she asked them.

'Senior discount card,' Sophie said, moving closer to show

us the plastic card in her hand. 'Ruth should really update the lock.'

'A deadbolt, at the very least,' Gloria agreed.

While I wished Ruth would have the chance, I wasn't hopeful. 'Did you leave the front door open?'

'Of course not,' Gloria said. 'But it is unlocked if you want to go in that way.' She wrinkled her nose. 'What—'

I held up a hand as a voice on Sarah's phone boomed, 'Five minutes out.'

The dispatcher was still on the line.

I reclaimed the phone. 'The front door is unlocked now. We'll meet the responders there.'

'Did you tell them I broke in?' Sophie asked when I clicked off. She appeared more proud than sheepish.

'I will when they get here, OK?' I promised, before handing Sarah back her phone. 'Sarah, take Arial around to the front. She should be checked over by the EMTs. You both should.'

'What about you?'

'Yes, me too,' I said, nodding. 'But Arial first.'

As Sarah and Arial went out through the gate, Gloria and Sophie hung back. 'Ruth?' Gloria asked.

I hesitated, but the two of them would find out anyway. 'She's still in her bed. I couldn't find a pulse, but that may have been because my own head was pounding. I'm nearly certain she was overcome by the carbon monoxide.'

'Was she cherry red?' Sophie asked eagerly. 'They say that's how you tell.'

'Oh, dear,' Gloria said, putting her hand to her face. 'When Hank and I went hunting and fishing up north, we had to be very careful with space heaters, lest we never wake up.'

'What would this be from, though?' Sophie asked as we rounded the corner of the house. 'The carbon monoxide, I mean.'

'Furnace, I'm betting,' Sarah said, as we joined them. 'I noticed it was warm when we walked into the house.'

'You think so?' I hadn't noticed.

'Warm by Kingston standards, she means,' Arial said, going to swing open the front door and switch on the porch light. 'And wouldn't Edna have a fit if she knew I had the door open while the furnace was on.'

'Letting out all the warm air,' Sarah said. 'Or poisonous gas, in this case.'

'It got cold last night,' I said. 'Maybe Ruth turned up the heat because she was having guests today.'

Arial squinted at me, seeming to try to orient herself. 'Is my mother dead, Maggy? The blood . . . Is that why you left her in there?'

'I . . . I don't know,' I admitted. 'I couldn't find Ruth's pulse and I was getting lightheaded and my head was pounding. I was afraid we were all going to end up on the floor, so I opened the window and . . .' I shrugged helplessly.

'The last thing we needed was all of you unconscious,' Gloria said, laying her hand on my arm.

'Though they do say carbon mo's the way to go,' Sophie said, mounting the steps to shove open the front door again. 'This keeps closing.'

We were all staring at her as she turned to come down.

'What?' she said, holding up her hands. 'A fireman I dated once told me it's not the worst way—'

'To die?' Gloria interrupted. 'How in the world do you find yourself in those kind of conversations?'

Especially on a date.

Sophie just shrugged. 'I'm easy to talk to. And not at all judgmental, like some people I could mention.'

The 'some people' tutted. 'It's probably not the best time to be talking about that sort of thing.' She threw a sideways glance at Arial, who was staring at the ground, hands folded, knuckles white.

Sirens could be heard in the distance now, finally. 'I should call Pavlik.' Brookhills County Sheriff Jake Pavlik was my fiancé.

'Can you please stop?' Sarah snapped at me. 'This isn't your typical body-as-usual.'

Sarah called me the corpse-stumbler, given my propensity for happening upon murders. But this was different, of course. Despite the dysfunctional family dynamics, Ruth was Sarah's sister, Arial's mother. And this was obviously a sad accident, not murder. In fact, we didn't know for sure that Ruth was dead.

Which probably was why I hadn't quite known what to do when I'd found her. Most of my bodies were as obviously dead as the proverbial doornail. Fixed pupils, sometimes lividity and even rigor mortis. Pretty easy to tell somebody's dead at that point. But with Ruth, I hadn't even been sure about the pulse.

'I'm sorry,' I said, my voice coming out in a bit of a croak. 'But a fire rig and sheriff's squad are always sent out with EMTs. Since somebody from the sheriff's department will have to attend, I thought a familiar face might be reassuring for Arial.'

'Because she's a parolee,' Sophie ventured.

'Ex-probationer,' Arial corrected automatically as she collapsed onto the porch steps, her head in her hands. 'I can't tell you how many awful things I was wishing on Ruth for not picking me up. And here she was . . .'

'Never woke up this morning by the looks of it,' Sarah said, settling down next to her.

'But the blood,' Arial said in a whisper. 'I did really see that, right?'

'She may have started to get up, been woozy and hit her head,' I told her. 'Do you know if the furnace was cleaned and checked regularly?'

'No clue,' Arial said. 'To be honest, I didn't even know they had to be.'

Yet she'd known the macaroni salad was best made the night before. Which probably meant furnace maintenance wasn't high on the list of must-dos at the Kingston house. 'You're supposed to do it every year before heating season, but I admit I'm not faithful about it. I guess this could have been any of us.'

'But . . . oh, damn,' Sarah said, twisting her head to look down the lane. 'I forgot about the rest of the vultures.'

Six or seven cars and a panel truck were chugging up the road toward us, each pulling over in turn to allow first the EMTs and then a fire engine to pass.

'We'll handle them,' Gloria volunteered, waving for Sophie to come join her.

'I know they enjoy being in the know and lording it over everybody,' I said, watching the two seniors flag down the cars to direct them to park on the opposite side of the street. 'But they do have a good heart.'

'One between the two of them.' Sarah nodded. 'I'll agree to that.'

The EMTs had turned into the driveway and were hustling to get out of the truck and grab their gear.

'Where is the victim?' a young ponytailed EMT in a black jacket called, as the fire truck parked on the street.

'The hallway off the kitchen, the room on the left,' Arial told her. 'Please hurry. She—'

'There's carbon monoxide,' I cautioned quickly. 'I opened the bedroom window, but we didn't stay long enough to check if the furnace was still on and pumping it out.'

'Good for you, getting out,' the EMT said. And then, *sotto voce* as she turned away to consult with one of the firefighters climbing out of the truck, 'Not so good for the person you left inside.'

'I felt for a pulse,' I called after the EMT.

She turned back. 'And you're an expert?'

'More so than the rest of us,' Sarah told her. 'But the fact is that we all were feeling the effects of the gas. If Maggy hadn't hustled us out—'

'It absolutely wouldn't have been safe for you to do anything beyond what you did,' the firefighter – a lieutenant – said, giving the EMT a glare as he pulled on his own respirator. 'Vacate the building and call us. That's the protocol for EMTs as well.'

The EMT looked like she wanted to argue, but the lieutenant waved her off as a Brookhills County Sheriff's department squad car pulled up on the street. Not Pavlik, but Deputy Kelly Anthony, one of his senior people.

She climbed out of the car, adjusting her heavy leather belt. Somehow she didn't look surprised to see me. 'Maggy.'

'Kelly,' I said, holding up a hand in greeting. Before the deputy could ask how it was that I was involved in yet another . . . unfortunate incident, I added hurriedly, 'The house belongs to Sarah's sister, Ruth. You remember Sarah, don't you?'

'Of course.' Kelly was getting out a notepad. 'And is the victim inside your sister, Sarah?'

'Yes. We were concerned when she didn't show up for our mother's wake.'

'And these other people?' Kelly swept her hand toward the occupied cars still idling on the opposite side of the street. 'They were concerned, as well?'

'My mother was hosting a buffet after my grandmother's wake,' Arial said, standing up and wiping her hand on her pants before putting it out to shake. There was a slight tremor. 'I'm Arial Kingston.'

'The dog-sitter, I know. Your probation must be about over.' Her expression said the time didn't match the crime.

'Arial did help the prosecution,' I reminded her, as the pony-tailed EMT sidled closer to listen. On my glare, she withdrew a half-step toward their vehicle.

'And got a deal in return,' Kelly said with a pasted-on smile. 'Now Arial, did you see your mother today before you left for the wake?'

'No,' Arial said, the pallor of her face going pink. 'I . . . I don't live at home. My mother was supposed to pick me up at the airport at about three thirty, but she didn't show.'

'And where were you coming from?' Kelly's pen was poised above the pad.

'Nassau,' Arial said.

'She left after her probation was up,' Sarah said, frowning. 'And before that she stayed with me.'

'A post-probation vacation, how nice,' Kelly said, staring at Arial just long enough to be uncomfortable before turning away.

'Can't you give the kid a break?' Sarah snapped, hiking her thumb toward the house. 'Her mother . . .?'

Kelly lifted her chin. 'Do we know the condition of Mrs Kingston?'

This last was directed to the lieutenant we'd spoken to. He was just coming out of the house, pulling off his respirator. 'They're bringing her out now. We've shut down the furnace and opened the remainder of the windows, but it'll take a few minutes before it's safe to go in without a mask.'

As he spoke, firefighters emerged from the house carrying Ruth on a gurney, her face covered by an oxygen mask.

'We've got a faint pulse,' one of the men was saying as they passed us to load her into the ambulance.

The EMT threw me a triumphant glare.

My heart dropped, though I was happy Arial's mother was alive. 'Oh, my God,' I said, feeling sick myself now. 'I just left her in there.'

'We missed the pulse the first time, too,' the lieutenant told me. The tag on his jacket read 'Arsen,' but I wasn't sure if that was his last name or specialty.

'Thanks for saying that,' I said, 'but—'

'But there was also the head wound to consider,' he continued. 'Dragging the victim off that bed and through the house wouldn't have been advisable, even if you, yourself, weren't already feeling the effects of the carbon monoxide. You were taking enough of a risk staying to open the window.'

'I saw the head wound as she came by,' Kelly said. 'What's your thought? She fell as she was overcome by the gas?'

'I'm no medic,' the firefighter said, shrugging off the oxygen tank on his back. 'What I can confirm is the presence of carbon monoxide and an unconscious victim.'

'She wasn't cherry red,' I said involuntarily, and belatedly put my hand to my mouth. 'I should have known she was alive.'

'Despite what you may have heard,' the lieutenant said, 'that red flush is only seen in two to three percent of symptomatic carbon monoxide poisoning.'

'Most often seen at autopsy,' the EMT interjected. 'So, by leaving her there, you—'

'Don't you have a job to do?' Kelly Anthony snapped, gesturing toward where two other EMTs were preparing Ruth for transport.

I looked at Kelly quizzically and she shrugged. 'I hate know-it-alls.'

'Thank you. But I do feel terr—'

'Well don't,' Kelly said, putting her hand on my arm. 'How did you know there was a carbon monoxide leak?'

'When I leaned to feel for a pulse, I realized my head was pounding and I stumbled when I straightened up. Meanwhile out in the kitchen . . .' I nodded at Arial.

'Our canary in the coal mine here was throwing up in the kitchen sink.' Sarah slung her arm around her niece as the doors of the ambulance closed and the siren started up.

'We should follow,' Arial said, as the vehicle pulled out of the driveway.

'We will,' Sarah assured her. 'But they won't be able to tell us anything for a while.'

The look she shot me over Arial's head said whatever they told us wouldn't be good.

Kelly, apparently realizing she'd been insensitive with Arial, given the circumstances, cleared her throat. 'I am sorry for the loss of your grandmother. I hope your mom will be OK.'

Arial nodded mutely at the peace offering.

'An apology,' she said as Kelly moved away. 'That was unexpected.'

'Kelly is good people at her core,' I said, as the siren on the EMT transport started up.

'She just plays being a hard-ass?' Sarah said sarcastically. 'She should give it a rest.'

Given both Sarah and Arial seemed to be struggling to balance their dysfunctional relationship with Ruth with their concern for her, I thought Sarah's criticism of Kelly might be a little unfair.

As the vehicle wailed away, an engine started up on the street and we turned to see first the panel truck and then a blue sedan pull away, each driver in turn – the man with salt-and-pepper hair and the young woman with the Hermès scarf – raising a hand in sympathy to us as they passed by.

'At least some people have the grace to take their leave,' I said, turning to scan the cluster of people from the funeral who'd left their cars to talk to Sophie and Gloria. Edna's lawyer was one of them, and as I watched, he lifted his head and crossed to us.

'I am so sorry,' he said to Sarah. 'What's your sister's condition?'

'We don't know yet,' Sarah told him. 'I don't think you've met Maggy Thorsen, Charles. And this is Arial, Ruth's daughter.'

'Good to meet you both.' Cokely nodded to me and then turned to Arial.

'This is your grandmother's attorney, Charles Cokely,' Sarah told her niece.

The lawyer took Arial's hand. 'I've heard a lot about you. I'm so sorry to meet under these circumstances.'

'Me, too,' Arial said, but she seemed puzzled. 'But who told you about me? Edna?'

'Yes, your grandmother Edna,' he affirmed, holding her hand between the two of his. 'But I'd planned on talking with you about that and about her will tomorrow. I don't know if that's still something you want to do given . . .' He let it drift off.

Sarah glanced at Arial, who shrugged. 'Up to you.'

'I think we should still meet then,' Sarah said. 'Your office, Charles?'

He bowed his head. 'Or I'm happy to come to you. Where are you staying, Arial? I assume that the house is . . .' He let that go, too.

'Not an option,' Sarah finished for him. 'She'll be with me at my place in Brookhills Estates. It's—'

'The cream and rose Victorian,' he said. 'Beautiful home. Shall we say . . .?'

'Ten,' Arial said, when Sarah hesitated. 'Is that OK with you, Sarah?'

'Sorry,' Sarah said, blinking. 'Yes, of course. But I'm just wondering how you knew which house was mine?'

'I represented the family who lived there before you bought it. The Chambers?'

'Lauren and Peter,' Sarah said. 'But I don't recall you handling the closing.'

'Oh, no, no, that was best left to the real estate attorneys,' Cokely said. 'I was in charge of their quite extensive estate.'

Well, lah-di-dah. Or *latte-da*, as Gloria would say.

'I will absolutely understand,' Cokely continued, 'if you'd prefer to delay our meeting, given what's happened with . . .'

'My mother,' Arial supplied. 'Though if *you* need to delay, given her . . .' This time she was the one who let it ride.

'I do wish her the very best,' he said, and put his hand on Arial's arm. 'But your grandmother's estate should not be effected by Ruth's unfortunate . . .'

With that, he took his leave.

'Does that man ever finish a sentence?' Arial asked, swiping at where his hand had been. 'But I don't get why he's fawning over me. You and Ruth are Edna's heirs.'

'We'll know more tomorrow about the will,' Sarah said, cutting off any further discussion. 'And hopefully Ruth's condition.'

'Thought the rest of them would never leave, the busybodies,' Sophie was muttering as she and Gloria came to join us. On the street, car doors slammed and more engines roared to life.

'A couple of them had the grace to leave immediately,' I said, grateful for the diversion from the will. Telling Arial that her mother – whose life hung in the balance – had been written out of the will in favor of Arial herself was probably best left to another day.

That day apparently being tomorrow.

'That woman from the county senior center was one of them,' I ventured to make conversation. 'She seemed very nice.'

'What woman?' Sophie demanded.

'Melinda – young brunette, wearing a gorgeous black and gold scarf,' I said. 'Edna played bridge there apparently.'

'That would be a trick, since there is no senior center in Brookhills County,' Gloria said. 'Hasn't been for a decade or more.'

'Well, I thought she said Brookhills,' I said. 'But the truth is I wasn't listening very closely. Maybe she meant Milwaukee or Wauwatosa.'

'I doubt it,' Arial said. 'My grandmother didn't drive.'

'Maybe Ruth took her then,' I suggested. 'Or a friend.'

'Edna didn't *have* friends,' Sarah started, but both Sophie and Gloria had their heads on swivel in the negative.

'She did have friends?' I guessed.

'Not many,' Sophie said. 'But I know the woman you're talking about. She told me she did Edna's hair.'

Gloria pursed her lips. 'And me, that she knew Edna from church.'

'She's lying?' Arial asked, frowning.

'Apparently so,' Sarah said.

'That's a little judgmental, don't you think?' I asked. 'For all we know, Melinda is a hairdresser who goes to Edna's church and volunteers at a senior center . . .' I wound up lamely. 'Somewhere.'

Sarah wasn't having it. 'My mother – Arial's grandmother – didn't like to be "fussed over" by strangers. She did her own hair, or Ruth did it. Same with nails.'

'And she quit the last church I remember going to years and years ago,' Arial said. 'When I was little.'

'Probably wasn't hell and brimstone enough for her,' Sarah said. 'Edna never was much on salvation.'

'Then how did this woman know Edna?' Melinda might be long gone, but I couldn't help glancing in the direction she had driven. 'And if she didn't, why was she here?'

'Funeral crasher,' Sarah said, waving us all toward the Escape. 'Now shall we go see if my sister is going to live or die?'

FOUR

'Ruth is in a coma,' I told Pavlik later that night. 'They don't expect her to come out of it.'

Sheriff Jake Pavlik has tousled dark hair that curls at his collar and gray eyes that could go to nearly blue or nearly black, depending on his mood. We were sitting on the couch in the living room with our two dogs, sheepdog Frank and chihuahua Mocha, stretched out on the floor between the couch and the coffee table. Mocha was using Frank's paw as a pillow. In other words, life was good.

Except for our subject matter.

'Prolonged exposure to carbon monoxide,' Pavlik said, leaning down to give Frank a scratch. 'Even if Ruth does make it, there could be impairment.'

'I should have dragged her out of there.' I'm into self-flagellation.

'You had the presence of mind to open the window, despite feeling the effects of the carbon monoxide yourself.' Pavlik pulled me close. 'I'm just glad I didn't lose you, too.'

'It's just all so . . . odd feeling,' I told him. 'Both Sarah and Arial are pretty much estranged from Ruth and Edna, so I'm not sure they know how to act.'

'Why should they "act" at all?'

I felt myself flush. 'They shouldn't. I mean, they shouldn't pretend to feel something they're not. But then . . .'

'Family is family,' Pavlik finished for me. 'They did go to the hospital, right?'

'Of course,' I said. 'I had driven everyone to Ruth's, so first we had to drop Sophie and Gloria off at the manor—'

'The dynamic duo didn't insist on going to the hospital with you?' Pavlik knew the two of them.

'They tried, but Sarah wasn't having any of it. After dropping them, we went straight to the hospital and I let Sarah and Arial out at the emergency room door. By the time I had the car parked and went in, they'd only gotten as far as the admissions office where they were being grilled about insurance and healthcare directives. Sarah was fit to be tied.'

'Annoying in an emergency, but necessary.' Pavlik was a measured man.

'Thing is,' I said, sitting up, 'Sarah and Ruth had barely spoken until Edna started to fail and Arial hadn't lived at home for years. Neither of them had the faintest idea what kind of health insurance Ruth had or even what her wishes would be regarding life support and all.'

'At least Ruth must have had insurance cards.'

I nodded. 'In her purse at home, so Arial and I went back to get it. The fire department investigators were just packing up to leave for the night.'

'Did you eventually get to see Ruth?' Pavlik asked, reaching down to give Frank a scratch somewhere in the proximity of his ear under all that fuzz. The sheepdog responded by rolling over for a belly rub, too, burying Mocha.

'Not me, but Arial and Sarah did, briefly,' I said, as the chihuahua gave a muffled snarl and belly-crawled out from under Frank. I tucked my feet up under me so she had space on the floor.

'Is Ruth on a ventilator?'

'Yes. The doctor apparently said something about using a hyperbaric chamber, if the carbon monoxide levels in her blood don't go down fast enough with just the oxygen.'

'Did they say anything about brain function?'

'The EEG showed brain activity but obviously they're monitoring that.'

'No way of telling if there's damage at this point probably.'

'Not for sure until she wakes up. If she wakes up.' I sighed. 'We stayed for a while but since there was nothing to be done, we left and I dropped them both at Sarah's.'

Pavlik was eyeing me. 'It's not your fault. Lieutenant Arsen told you that.'

So that was his name. 'Ironic name for a firefighter.'

'I'm sure people have mentioned it to him a time or two, but his name is spelled with an "e" not an "o."'

I closed my eyes. 'Sheesh, I didn't even register the difference in spelling when I saw the name on his uniform at the scene. I thought arson – with an "o" – might be his area of expertise. Glad I didn't say something to him about it. He'd think I was an idiot.' Who couldn't spell.

'Just shows that you were a little out of it,' Pavlik said, rubbing the back of my neck. 'Did the EMTs check you?'

'Yes, and Sarah and Arial. Arial seemed the most affected, but we all felt fine by then.'

'You were all lucky.' Pavlik was watching me. 'You're thinking about something else, though.'

'Caught me.' I grinned. 'It's just . . . Edna died on Tuesday, so it's been barely five days and now this? And did you hear that Ruth had a head injury? Don't you think it's odd?'

'I wouldn't go looking for connections just yet.'

'But—'

'But it got cold last night for the first time this heating season,' Pavlik said. 'The furnace – a faulty furnace, from the sounds of it – came on and Ruth was overcome by carbon monoxide. She probably woke up during the night feeling sick and tried to get up. Hit her head. It's not a mystery.'

I'd said the very same thing to Arial. 'Did I tell you about this Melinda person? She showed up for the wake but told everybody a different story about how she knew Edna.'

'You did tell me,' Pavlik said. 'Maybe the woman was homeless and just wanted to come in out of the cold. How was she dressed?'

'For a funeral. And wearing a silk scarf that was either a Hermès or a good knockoff.'

'Would I recognize one?' Pavlik said, wrinkling his nose. 'A Hermès, I mean. You've mentioned them before.'

'Because I covet one,' I said. 'They're made of the most beautiful silk. Many of them have equestrian themes, stirrups and saddles, because the Hermès family got its start making leather harnesses and such in 1837.'

'Interesting,' Pavlik said, looking like it was anything but.

Fine. I sighed. 'Anyway, Sophie thought she might be a crasher, too, but I think it's possible this Melinda did know Edna. Or at least knew *of* her. What puzzles me is why she didn't just say so. Why did she think it necessary to give each of us a different story about how she and Edna met?'

Pavlik cocked his head. 'Telling each person what she thinks they want to hear. Sociopaths often lie just because they enjoy it. It's a game.'

'Well, I expect more from my sociopaths,' I said. 'Pick a story and commit. She told me she knew Edna from playing bridge; why not stick with that?'

'Maybe because she thought it was boring,' Pavlik suggested. 'Or maybe because the senior center story was too risky with people who were seniors themselves like Gloria and Sophie.'

Hmm. I leaned over to retrieve my phone from the coffee table and nearly fell onto the dogs in the process.

Pavlik pulled me back from the brink. 'Either you're going to have to move the table closer or get up to reach it.'

I unfolded my legs and stood, being careful not to trample Mocha. 'We move the table closer to the couch and Frank can't fit on the floor by our feet. Which means the two of them will be up here with us.'

'Good point.' Pavlik was watching me as I settled back onto the couch. 'I assume you're going to search for this Melinda online. Do you have a last name?'

'No,' I said absently, not looking up from my phone. 'I guess I can text Sophie and Gloria and see if she gave them one. Or more than one.'

'Which might be fake.'

'I know.' I was typing in Edna Mayes Kingston. 'But first I wanted to pull up Edna's obituary. See if there's anything that might interest a predator of some kind.'

'Like "died at the age of eighty-ish of natural causes, leaving behind gold bullion in her closet and a genuine Monet on the wall"?' Pavlik suggested.

'Exactly.' I was reading. 'Hmm, here's a story about Edna's death in a paper called the *Carmel Cypress*.'

'Carmel, Indiana?' Pavlik's chin had settled on the top of my head.

'Uh-uh,' I said, reading. 'California.'

Pavlik's head lifted. 'As in Carmel-by-the-Sea, where Clint Eastwood was mayor?'

'You mean *Dirty Harry* Clint Eastwood?' I asked absently.

'Who else?' Pavlik said. 'But the man is so much more – on

both the acting and directing sides. Think *Mystic River, American Sniper, Sully.'*

'And four academy awards.' I turned my head to kiss his cheek. 'You don't have to tell me. But my favorite role was Rowdy Yates in *Rawhide* reruns. I had such a crush.'

'*Rawhide* was back in the Sixties.'

'And *Dirty Harry* from the Seventies.' One of the many things that Pavlik and I shared was a love of old movies and TV shows. 'All masterpieces.'

'I'm not sure *Paint Your Wagon—*'

I held up a hand as I enlarged the article. 'Listen to this. The headline is "Local Artist Edna Mayes Dies." Then, "Pacific Grove native Edna Mayes Kingston died yesterday in Brookhills, Wisconsin at the age of eighty-four of natural causes. The Mayes family home in Pacific Grove is where Kingston spent her formative years, growing to fame on the peninsula for her landscape paintings of the area as well as her still lifes and . . ."' I broke off.

'What?'

'There was this great still life in Edna's bedroom. One of those "fool the eye" thingies?'

'*Trompe-l'œil*,' my renaissance man supplied.

'Yes.' I tucked my feet under me on the couch. 'I may have been a little loopy from the carbon monoxide, like you said, but I actually thought it was a mirror at first.'

'Just a blank mirror?' Pavlik asked. 'And you had no reflection?'

I laughed. 'That really would have freaked me out. But no, it was painted to reflect the contents of the same dresser top at some point in time – none of it there anymore, of course. In fact, the only things that are left in the room now are a hospital bed, that dresser and a bedpan.'

'Remnants of Edna Mayes Kingston's life,' Pavlik said. 'The painting sounds nice – maybe it reminded her of her younger days.'

'It was better than nice, though,' I said, sitting up straight. 'I didn't think to check for a signature at the time.'

'Given the carbon monoxide and all.'

Yes, that. 'But given this obituary, it makes perfect sense that it would be one of hers.'

'Edna Mayes Kingston. Did you say the family home was in Pacific Grove? Is that near Carmel?'

I clicked on a link. 'Looks like it's the north tip of the Monterey Peninsula. Kind of between Monterey and Pebble Beach. And just past Pebble Beach is Carmel-by-the-Sea.'

'Not bad company,' Pavlik said, leaning down to give Frank another scratch. 'But can I assume there's nothing in the article that would draw vultures?'

'Not that I can see,' I admitted. 'It does mention her marrying Kevin Kingston of Denver. Sarah said that didn't last long.'

'Divorced?'

'I assume so,' I said. 'Sarah and Ruth were young. I think he may have had mental health issues, but regardless, he just up and went one day.'

'Then he wasn't at the wake?'

'He's dead. When Sarah was diagnosed as bipolar, she thought about finding him, but just about that time her aunt called with the news.'

'Too late, huh? Is the condition inherited?'

'I don't think it's as simple as if your parent has it, you get it. But genetics do enter in, from what little she's told me.' Sarah basically tried to ignore the disorder but did take her meds for the most part.

I set down the phone. 'The *Cypress* is the only publication that has anything about Edna's past life. Otherwise, it's Edna Kingston lived in Brookhills and then she died. No Edna Mayes, no Pacific Grove, no Kevin Kingston, no Denver, no early hopes and dreams – realized or otherwise.' I gave an involuntary sniffle.

Pavlik pulled me toward him to look over my shoulder. 'Somebody had to give the funeral home the information for the obituary. Sarah maybe? Or Ruth?'

'It sounds more like Sarah,' I admitted, chewing on my lip. 'Very cut and dried. But from what I've heard about Ruth, I'd have expected the information to be more comprehensive.'

'Keeping public information to a minimum is a good thing these days,' Pavlik said. 'Have you heard about obituary pirates?'

I shook my head.

'They target a death – especially one that's been in the news –

and create false content. A simple accidental death becomes a suspected murder.'

'Sarah would call me an obituary pirate,' I muttered.

'You just have a suspicious mind,' Pavlik said with a grin. 'Oftentimes rightly so, which is why I pay attention to your suspicions.'

'And the pirates?'

'Make up stories to get hits. The more salacious and sensational, the more hits.'

'At the expense of ordinary people,' I said. 'That sucks.'

'It does, and these pirates can be anywhere in the world. Plus, they're using artificial intelligence to write the supposed news stories, so an anonymous lone actor can do a lot of damage.'

'When I just searched Edna's obituary, if I'd pulled up articles speculating about her death, I'd certainly be tempted to search further.'

'Most people would,' Pavlik said, shrugging. 'Which means the name, tied to whatever accusations are being made, moves higher on the search engines. To make matters worse, there was a study a few years back that showed that false news is shared or retweeted seventy percent more than the truth. I doubt that's changed.'

Since I'd been known to search for . . . let's say unsavory information about people, I was starting to feel like part of the problem. 'That's horrible,' I said again. 'But there's no sign of it with Edna's death, unless some troll wanted us to believe she was a painter, when she wasn't.'

'*That*, I doubt,' Pavlik said. 'Though somebody must have notified the Carmel paper of Edna's death.'

'The Mayes might be – or have been – a prominent family, so they'd have information on file to pull when an obit was needed.' I was reaching for my phone again. 'If Edna's paintings are valuable, maybe her death would draw vultures, as you put it, instead of pirates.'

'You're thinking of your mysterious Melinda?'

'Sure. Maybe she came here in the hopes of snagging one of Edna's paintings before the art world knows she's dead.'

'But you said she took off yesterday as the first responders arrived.'

'Not quite,' I said, thinking back. 'It was after the ambulance transporting Ruth to the hospital left.'

'She wouldn't necessarily know who was in the ambulance, would she?'

'When the guests from the funeral home started arriving, Sophie and Gloria went down to the street to fill them in,' I said. 'So yes, she definitely would have known.'

'Then if Melinda came to the house hoping to talk to Ruth and the rest of the family about Edna's work, she'd have been disappointed. Maybe that's why she left.'

'Maybe.' I looked up from my phone where I had been searching 'painting' and every iteration of Edna Mayes Kingston's name I could think of. 'But that doesn't mean she'll give up.'

Pavlik eyed me. 'You really do think she's up to something?'

'I don't know. Maybe I'm just reading too much into it.' I set down the phone. 'I can't find anything online about Edna's paintings. As for Melinda, I suppose she can still try to contact Sarah or Arial.'

'Couldn't she have done that earlier at the funeral home?'

'True, though Arial got there late, and Sarah was in a foul mood.' I shrugged. 'Maybe Melinda just thought bringing it up at the wake was in poor taste.'

'But making up stories wasn't.' Pavlik's phone trilled and he pulled it out of his pocket. 'Hang on a sec. This is the fire inspector.'

When he hung up, he was shaking his head. 'Damn shame. People just can't be bothered, I guess.'

'About what?' I asked. 'Cleaning and checking the furnace? I know I should call—'

'No worries, I had it checked last month.'

Showed you what I knew.

'Thank you,' I said, laying my head against his shoulder. 'Have I told you how much I appreciate you?'

'Not today yet, but I figure there's still time.'

I grinned. 'So you meant it's a damn shame about Ruth? Did she—'

'No, there's no update on her condition. But the inspector did say it appears the heat exchanger on the furnace is cracked and the venting incomplete. To make matters worse, the house had two carbon monoxide detectors, but they didn't have batteries in them.'

'They weren't wired into the house's electrical?' The two we had in our house had batteries, but only for backup in case the electricity went out.

'No, Ruth's house is pretty old, as is the wiring,' Pavlik said. 'Both the smoke and carbon monoxide detectors are powered by batteries that have to be changed regularly.'

'And they chirp when they get low, like our backup batteries?'

'Yup. It's meant as a safety feature, but unfortunately most people's first instinct – especially in the middle of the night – is to take out the failing battery to shut them up. They figure they'll put in a new battery the next day or whenever they can.'

'Except Ruth never got around to that.'

'And it may very well cost her life.' Pavlik got to his feet and held out his hand to me. 'Like I said, damn shame.'

FIVE

Amy and I opened Uncommon Grounds the next morning. At one time, the depot where our coffeehouse was located was a stop for long-distance passenger trains heading both west to Seattle and east to New York, via Chicago. Now, though, it was the origin for commuter trains running between Brookhills and downtown Milwaukee, some fifteen miles east on the shore of Lake Michigan.

This meant that weekdays at the shop were busier than weekends and our hectic periods coincided with the morning and evening business rush hours. Between those times, we were fairly quiet, with just our locals stopping by for a cup and conversation.

'You can go now if you want,' Amy told me, setting aside the rag she'd been using to wipe the tables and glancing up at the clocks. 'It's nine thirty.'

The original three clocks that marked the time here in the Central Time Zone as well as Pacific and East Coast times remained in place above what had been the station's ticket windows. They were now our service windows. The East and Pacific clocks worked in fits and starts, but our Central clock – in both time zone and position – was always dependable.

As was Amy, our multiply pierced barista who had only recently given up dying her short hair in stripes of blue, pink, and whatever other color took her fancy that day. I wasn't sure what we would do without her.

'I will go, if you truly don't mind,' I said, circling behind the counter to take off my navy Uncommon Grounds apron and hang it on a hook by the office. 'And remember that I'm happy to take a shift for you next week.'

'You need to support Sarah and Arial. Besides,' she said, shaking out her now blonde hair, 'you pay me for the hours I work. You don't have to make up the time.'

'I know,' I said, going to hug her. 'But I'm leaving you on your own.'

'*After* the rush. I think I can survive, even if a horde of soccer moms or the gang from Brookhills Manor should descend on us.' She handed me my purse and pushed me out the door.

'We need to give Amy a raise,' I said, when Sarah opened her door to me.

'You've been feeling guilty about leaving her alone the entire way here, haven't you?' she said, stepping aside to let me in.

'Of course. Luckily it was a short drive.' Sarah's home was in sharp contrast to Sarah herself. Where Sarah was all beige trousers and baggy jackets, her house was all bright florals and white-painted woodwork.

'Has the hospital called?' I asked her quietly. 'Anything new on Ruth?'

Sarah shook her head as we moved toward the parlor. 'We ran over there first thing this morning to catch the doctor during rounds. The oxygen seems to be clearing the carbon monoxide from her system, but she remains in a coma.'

'Brain damage?' I asked, stopping short of the doorway.

'They're not committing one way or the other,' Sarah said, waving me into the room.

Arial was sitting side-saddle in an overstuffed reading chair in rose red and clear yellow, her back to one armrest, legs hanging over the other.

I gestured for her not to get up. 'It's just me.'

She smiled. 'I'll be a lady when the lawyer arrives, but I love nesting in this chair.'

'Thing's so big you'll look like Edith Ann if you sit in it the regular way.' Sarah paused in the doorway leading to the kitchen. 'Coffee?'

We both nodded in the affirmative and Arial waited until Sarah was gone to ask, 'Edith who?'

'Edith Ann. It was a character Lily Tomlin played on *Saturday Night Live*. She'd sit in this giant rocking . . .'

Arial's eyes started to glaze over, so I gave up.

'Never mind.'

The young woman let out a laugh. 'I know who Edith Ann is, Maggy. Just messing with you.'

'Thank God.' I took a seat on the couch across the coffee table from her. 'Sarah told me you went to see your mother this morning.'

'More the doctor than Ruth. Ruth is just . . . there.' She took a deep breath. 'At least her body is. She looks so helpless lying there, I feel guilty for all those years of . . .'

'Resenting her?' I tried.

'That's putting it charitably,' Arial said, shifting in the chair to face me.

'You had your reasons,' I said quietly.

'Yes, but it feels like ancient history, all of a sudden. Edna is dead and now my mother . . .' She shrugged.

'Speaking of Edna,' I said, wanting to lighten the mood, 'you have to look at what I found.'

I handed her the phone with the Carmel obituary for her grandmother on it.

She read it, her eyes widening. 'Edna was a famous painter? I had no idea.'

I took the phone back. 'Famous in her hometown, at least. Did you know she was born in California?'

'I think I probably heard something,' Arial said, as Sarah came in with a tray laden with a French press pot and cups and saucers.

'About what?' Sarah set the tray on the coffee table so Arial could offload it.

'About Edna's family coming from California originally,' Arial said, pairing delicate porcelain cups with their saucers. 'Somewhere on the coast, but not Los Angeles.'

'Monterey Peninsula.' Sarah pulled the press pot toward her so she could press the plunger. 'On the central coast about ninety miles south of San Francisco. Town called Pacific Grove.'

I punched up the map to show Arial as Sarah poured the coffee.

'Next to Pebble Beach,' Arial observed. 'Sounds pretty chi-chi.'

'Not as chi-chi as Carmel,' Sarah opined.

Arial leaned forward to claim her cup. 'You've been there?'

'My grandmother Gretchen – Edna's mother – had a house in PG. We spent every summer and most school holidays there when I was young. This was after my father left.'

PG, Pacific Grove. 'Edna would visit, too?'

'And did she paint there?' Arial asked eagerly.

'Edna came for at least part of the time,' Sarah said, sliding a cup to me and claiming her own. 'I don't remember her painting, but then Ruth and I weren't around much. We would take off with the local kids. Ride bikes, swim at Lovers Point, go to Cannery Row for candy or ice cream. I loved the sea lions and keeping watch for sea otters and whales.' She was smiling in a way I'd seldom seen my partner smile. 'It was the best part of the year.'

'Sounds amazing,' Arial said, putting her cup on the table. 'Why did you stop going? Did they sell the house?'

'No, but I went away to college and wasn't interested in spending my school breaks with my sister and mother at my grandmother's house.'

'What about Ruth and Edna?' I asked, as the doorbell rang.

'They went another year or so, but it pretty much ended when Ruth got pregnant, and they moved to Brookhills.'

'And here I come again,' Arial said. 'Ending all joy and sunshine with my illegitimate presence.'

'I'm sure it wasn't about you,' I said.

'No.' Getting up, Sarah smacked her niece in the arm. 'I think there may have been some sort of rift between Edna and her mother. As far as I know, nobody went back there again except to see Gretchen safely in the ground.'

'Sheesh.' I exchanged looks with Arial as Sarah left us to go to the door.

'Dysfunctional families, thy name is Kingston,' was Arial Kingston's assessment.

'I'm very sorry there's no improvement in Ruth's condition,' Charles Cokely said, taking a coffee cup from Sarah. 'Such a senseless accident to happen on the heels of Edna's death.'

'Senseless for sure,' I said.

'*And* an accident.' There was a warning look in Sarah's eyes.

'Of course, an accident,' I said. 'I didn't mean—'

'You know, Maggy, you do have a reputation.' Charles Cokely had an eager gleam in his eyes as he settled on the couch next to me. 'It wouldn't have been appropriate to mention it yesterday, but I was very interested to see you there.'

I held up my hands to stave him off. 'I know that things seem to happen when I'm around, but—'

'Things,' Sarah said to Cokely. 'People are murdered is what she means.'

'But not in this case,' I hastened to add.

'In fact, Maggy may have saved my mother's life by finding her and opening the window to ventilate the room,' Arial pointed out.

'Absolutely,' Cokely said. 'Ruth's unfortunate accident aside, I find what you do fascinating, Maggy.'

His eyes were open wide, regarding me with a touch of fear. But instead of distancing himself, Cokely seemed to be leaning closer to me on the couch.

'You mean, serving coffee?' Sarah asked dryly.

'No really,' he said, turning to her. 'You both are the talk of the courthouse, what with the deaths in and around your coffee-house and then your trip up north just a couple of months ago, with that . . . well, practically a serial killer.'

'Believe me, Ruth's carbon monoxide poisoning was just a sad accident. Senseless, as we all said, because Pavlik . . .' I turned to Charles Cokely. 'The sheriff.'

'And your fiancé,' he said. 'I know. I am such a fan of you both.'

This guy was creepy. But at least today, he seemed to be finishing his sentences. 'Anyway, he told me there were carbon monoxide detectors in the house.'

'Then why didn't they go off and wake her?' Arial asked.

'Yes, why?' Charles Cokely asked, edging closer.

I retreated an inch, realizing too late that I should have discussed this with Arial and Sarah first, without the presence of Chucky here.

'No batteries,' I said, trying to be offhand. 'Ruth must have removed them and not gotten around to replacing them.'

'An accident as you say then.' Cokely glanced at his watch, apparently losing interest in something so mundane. 'Now as to the will. While I would have been happy for Ruth to attend this meeting, as I told you yesterday, it wasn't necessary.'

Sarah and I had our eyes on Arial, knowing what was coming.

'No?' The girl shifted uncomfortably. 'I don't understand why.'

Cokely leaned down to unlatch his brown leather briefcase and slipped out a two-page document. 'The will is quite simple, really, and doesn't involve Ruth Kingston because Edna Mayes Kingston named—'

Arial's head swung expectantly toward her aunt.

'—Arial Kingston as her sole beneficiary.'

'Me?' she sputtered. 'But even if Edna bypassed Ruth for some reason, what about Sarah?'

'I inherited the depot from my father's side,' Sarah told her. 'Which is why I assumed anything my mother left would go to Ruth.'

'Especially since Ruth took care of her,' I contributed.

'But . . .' Arial started.

Cokely cleared his throat to get our attention. 'Edna Kingston did provide for Ruth. She designated that Ruth have a life estate in the house, meaning she could live in the Brookhills property on Hawthorne Court until she died—'

Which could be any minute.

'The Brookhills house, itself, is held in a trust,' Cokely continued. 'Arial Kingston is sole beneficiary of the trust, of which I am trustee.'

'Are you also executor?' Sarah asked.

'Yes.'

'Thank God.' She let out the breath she'd apparently been holding. 'I was afraid she'd named me. Or Ruth, with me as backup.'

'Mrs Kingston felt it was . . . cleaner like this, I believe,' the attorney explained.

'She didn't trust us, you mean,' Sarah said. 'But I'm fine with that. Serving as executor of an estate is a pain in the butt.'

'You're telling me.' Cokely seemed surprised he said it out loud.

'At least you get paid for it, right?' Arial asked.

'I do,' he said, 'but any executor can charge the estate for their time.'

'Which is subtracted from the estate they may be inheriting,' Sarah pointed out. 'So they normally don't charge much – certainly not what an attorney charges.'

'True that.' Cokely again.

Arial was moving on. 'Edna's trust. Is it—?'

Cokely waved her off. 'I should have been clearer. There are actually two trusts. Edna's trust holds this house, while Gretchen Mayes's—'

'Wait.' Arial's face was screwed up, trying to understand. 'That was your grandmother, right, Sarah? The one in California?'

'Yes,' Sarah said. 'But I didn't know there was a trust. I assume Edna was the trustee?' This last was directed to the attorney.

'Trustee, yes,' Cokely affirmed, digging out another document, this one much longer. 'But Gretchen Mayes named Arial sole beneficiary, with the assets to be held in trust for her until the age of twenty-five.'

'What?' Arial said, looking to Sarah. 'I never knew any of this.'

'I didn't either,' Sarah admitted. 'I knew about the house in California, but not what happened to it. If Arial was named in her trust, shouldn't she have been notified when Gretchen died ten years ago?'

'She was,' Cokely said. 'At least, a notification was sent out. But with Arial being a minor at the time, I can't say whether—'

'My grandmother and mother actually gave it to me?' Arial said, indignantly. 'That's ridiculous.'

'It is. If that's indeed . . .' He shrugged regretfully.

The fanboy was gone. The lawyer was back, artfully obfuscating.

'I'm telling you that's what happened,' Arial said. 'I didn't even know about Gretchen or even that she died, much less that I was her beneficiary.'

I was reflecting. 'You turned twenty-five on the nineteenth, the day after your grandmother Edna died.'

'I know when my birthday is.' Arial's eyes widened and her brows lifted. 'Are you saying it's a good thing I was out of the country when she died?'

'Why?' Sarah demanded. 'Because Arial had a reason to kill Edna, or somebody had a reason to kill Arial?'

Either. Both. But it was interesting. I turned to Cokely. 'Who would have inherited, if Arial hadn't reached twenty-five?'

If Cokely was a dog, his ears would have perked up. 'Let me see here.' His lips were moving as he read. Then he set the document down, disappointed. 'Oh, dear. I'm afraid it's nothing sinister.'

He was the first lawyer I'd met who preferred 'sinister.' Or at least admitted it.

'Who is Gretchen's secondary beneficiary?' Sarah asked impatiently.

'Beneficiaries, plural,' he corrected. 'Two organizations – animal rescues.'

'I'd be OK with that,' Arial said.

'You'd be dead,' I reminded her.

'Oh, yeah.'

It was Sarah's turn to look to Cokely. 'You said Edna's trust contains the Brookhills house. What assets are in Gretchen's trust? The PG house?'

'PG, umm . . .' He was scanning again. 'Yes, Pacific Grove on the Monterey Peninsula.' He looked up. 'We'll need to get it appraised if you intend to sell it. Given the location, I'm thinking it will bring well upwards of a million. Perhaps closer to two.'

'Dollars?' Arial clarified.

'Oh, yes.' He delved back into his bag and laid out photocopies of both trusts and the will. 'You'll want to look through this, but I think you'll find it's all in order.'

He stood and took Arial's hand. 'Please call me with any questions and congratulations on your inheritance. You're quite a wealthy young woman.'

I was a little puzzled at the attorney's quick exit, but stood along with Arial, as Sarah ushered him to the door.

'Do you have Ruth's will on file, as well?' I heard her ask the attorney as she opened the door. And then in a lower tone. 'Just in case.'

'Oh, my God,' Arial murmured, putting her hand to her forehead. 'That's the last thing we need.'

I wasn't sure if she was talking about her mother dying or yet another will handled by Cokely.

'I'm afraid I wasn't asked to do an estate plan for your sister,' we heard the attorney say. 'You might want to check the house, assuming it's safe to go back in. The hospital will want a healthcare directive and perhaps there's a durable power of attorney as well. Her will – or at least the name of her attorney who might have it on file, might be there. Hopefully, she won't die intestate.'

Arial was frowning as Sarah came back. 'Intestate?'

'Without a will,' I told her.

Sarah slung her arm around her niece's shoulder. 'It's OK to be happy about your inheritance. Your mother . . . well, we can't control what happens there. And please don't worry about me.'

'I'm not.' Her face reddened. 'I mean, yes, I do feel a little guilty. I still consider the house Ruth's and have no desire to live there, whether she comes out of the coma or not.'

'But the house in California?' I asked.

'That sounds lovely,' she admitted. 'God knows I can use the money and a new start. But don't you think it's odd that neither of us knew anything about Gretchen's trust? Or that Cokely was Edna's attorney, but not Ruth's?'

'I think Cokely is a little odd in general,' I said. 'Bit of a ghoul.'

'Aww,' Sarah said, releasing Arial to elbow me. 'If you're a star, you have to expect fans.'

I ignored that. 'But to Arial's question, I do think it's odd you didn't know about the disposal of Gretchen's estate.'

'To be fair,' Sarah said, flopping down in a chair, 'I kind of lost touch with that side of the family. I went to Gretchen's funeral with Edna, but—'

'Ruth didn't go?' Arial asked. 'I don't remember even hearing about it.'

'I think she was working,' Sarah said. 'Edna didn't say really.'

Probably because Sarah didn't ask.

'As far as Cokely being Edna's attorney, but not Ruth's,' Sarah continued, 'I'm not sure what legal work Ruth would have needed.'

'A will, for one thing.' Arial was stacking the cups and saucers. 'And the healthcare directive the hospital was asking about.'

'I hate to say it, but she might not have either,' I said. 'I mean, she's not that old—'

'She's in her forties,' Arial said.

'Those of us in our forties don't consider it all that old,' I pointed out, settling on the couch.

Arial turned to survey us. 'And I suppose neither of you has a will?'

'Of course I do,' Sarah said. 'But then I have Courtney and Sam to think of. And you.'

'And I have Eric.' My son was at college in Minneapolis, a five-hour drive west of Brookhills.

'Well, my mother had me, too,' Arial pointed out.

'And I'm sure she made provisions,' I said reflexively.

Arial and Sarah just stared at me.

'Or not,' I said lamely. 'I'm sorry. But the woman is in a coma.'

'Doesn't make her a saint,' Sarah said.

'No, you've already done that,' I retorted. 'Sarcastically, of course. But I'm just saying—'

'Don't fight on my account, kids,' Arial interrupted, picking up the tray to take back to the kitchen. 'Whatever my mother's failings, I always had Sarah.'

'Lucky girl,' Sarah called after her.

'You know, you say that lightly,' I told her, 'but Arial is lucky. I was astonished how quickly you adjusted when you adopted Sam and Courtney, but I guess you'd already had practice being a surrogate mother for Arial.'

'And a great one, for which I'm very grateful,' Arial said, coming back into the room. 'Do you think we can get into the house now? Cokely's right that it's the most likely place for any papers Ruth had, including the health directive.'

'It would be good to know her wishes about . . .' I glanced at Arial, ' . . . life support and such.'

'At what point she would want us to pull the plug, if it comes to that,' Arial said, leaning down to retrieve her purse. 'That would be a good thing to know.'

It would, unfortunately.

'I'll check with Pavlik to see if they're done at the house,' I said, pulling out my phone to text him. 'I . . .' I stopped, staring at my phone.

'What?' Arial asked.

'It's from Pavlik.' I held up the phone. 'Your house on Hawthorne Court was broken into last night.'

Arial's own phone pinged in the depths of her purse, and she pulled it out. 'It's the sheriff's department, telling me the same thing. They want me to come to the house so I can tell them if anything's missing.'

'It's been years since you really lived there,' Sarah said. 'Will you know if anything is missing?'

'Probably not,' Arial said, chucking her phone back into the purse. 'But I have every intention of going to snoop anyway. Coming with me?'

SIX

Arial didn't have to ask twice. I made a quick apologetic call to Amy, but when she heard there had been a break-in, she had no problem with manning the coffeehouse. As long as I reported back.

As we pulled into the driveway of Ruth's – or Arial's, depending on how you looked at it, house – we saw a Brookhills County squad car parked on the street. Kelly Anthony came out of the front door to watch from the porch as we climbed out of the car.

'I didn't know I was going to get the whole family and a plus-one when I asked you to come by,' she told Arial.

'The whole family, minus my mother,' Arial reminded her, no doubt to shame the deputy.

It worked. 'I'm sorry,' Kelly said, stepping aside for us to enter. 'How is your mother doing?'

'No change in her condition,' Arial said. 'I wanted Sarah here because she's been in the house more recently than I have . . .' She hesitated. 'Discounting yesterday, of course.'

'And Maggy just shows up everywhere,' Sarah added.

As I passed the wooden doorjamb, I took a second to examine it for signs of forced entry.

'They came in the back,' Kelly said, knowing full well what I was doing.

I nodded and stepped through.

Arial was already standing in the center of the living room. 'You know, it has been years since I actually lived in the house. But I'm not sure anything has changed in here, at least.'

'Old people,' Sarah said. 'They never move anything.'

'Ruth was younger than you,' I said.

'But it was my grandmother's house,' Arial reminded me. 'And her view was if it ain't broke don't fix it.'

'Apparently even if it *was* broke . . .' This last was from Kelly who had the grace to blush. 'Sorry. I was just thinking about the furnace.'

'The furnace was definitely the source of the carbon monoxide?' Sarah asked.

I had mentioned the battery-less carbon monoxide detectors in front of Cokely, but then had clammed up about the rest of what Pavlik told me last night. Which meant that Sarah and Arial didn't know about the cracked heat exchanger.

So I let Kelly tell them.

'According to the fire inspector, the heat exchanger on the furnace is cracked,' she said.

Sarah shook her head. 'That would explain it.'

'Back to the break-in last night,' Kelly said. 'I understand that it's difficult, but can either of you tell if anything is missing or disturbed in here?'

'Like I said, even the drapes are the same,' Arial said, facing the front picture window. 'Couch has always been there, with the end-tables on each end. Two ottomans.'

'Lamps are the same, too,' Sarah said, walking over to switch one on. 'Matching.'

'Books on one table and magazines or tabloids on the other,' I observed.

'Book side was my mother,' Arial said. 'Gossip magazines, my grandmother.'

Interesting. I was imagining the two, side by side on the couch, night after night, feet up, books in hand. It wasn't a bad image, though it did leave out Arial.

'Nice big TV,' I observed, turning to the wall opposite. 'Sixty-five inch?'

'Seventy-five,' Sarah said. 'My present to my mother last Christmas.'

Arial's nose wrinkled. 'That certainly couldn't have been cheap. Wouldn't thieves take that first thing?'

'Depends,' Kelly Anthony said. 'It's pretty big to sneak out.'

I glanced toward the kitchen. 'They came in the back door, you said. And flat screens don't weigh much these days.'

'But it would take two people to carry one this big,' Arial said. 'And first they'd have to get it off the wall.'

She was right. The thing looked like it would snap in half if mismanaged. 'Is there any jewelry in the house?' That would be a whole lot easier to steal.

'Edna incinerated her wedding ring,' Sarah said. 'And neither of them was much for jewelry.'

Like Sarah herself.

'Anyway,' Arial said, leading us through the kitchen, 'if Ruth or Edna did have anything valuable to them, they'd stash it in their bedrooms. In the drawer below the underwear drawer.'

As we reached the bedroom hallway, I couldn't help but notice a smoke detector on the ceiling and the carbon monoxide detector on the wall, its cover hanging askew.

'Some things never change,' Sarah said, stopping at the door of the room where we'd found Ruth. The door was open, but crime scene tape crisscrossed the doorframe. 'Can we go in?'

'Just lift the tape and duck under,' Kelly said.

The linens had been stripped from the bed where we found Ruth, leaving a wet spot visible on the mattress. I stepped closer, examining a dark blotch about a foot above the mattress on the headboard. 'Is that blood?'

'Yes,' Kelly said. 'We assume that's where Mrs Kingston struck her head.'

'You'd best call her Ruth,' Sarah told her, coming over. 'She, Arial and I are all Ms Kingstons. Only Edna was a Mrs, but it's still all too confusing.'

'It is,' Arial agreed, leaning in. 'You're sure it's my moth— Ruth's blood?'

Arial's habitual use of her mother's first name seemed to be slipping a bit.

'Who else's would it be?' Kelly asked, surprised.

'I don't know,' Arial said, moving toward the dresser. 'But I presume you people don't just assume these things.'

I suppressed a smile as I went to join her. 'You said the drawer below the underwear drawer?'

'The idea was that thieves always searched the underwear drawer,' Sarah said.

'But nobody looks in the one below that?' I asked. 'And how would they know which was the underwear drawer – or the drawer beneath the underwear drawer – without checking.'

Arial grinned. 'Because underwear is always in the top.'

'Of course,' Sarah said, sliding out the next one down. 'And stockings, back in the day, below it. It was their way, for as long as I can remember.'

'It was Edna's way, to be fair,' Arial said, shifting a tangle of nude and suntan-colored pantyhose to lift out a small jewelry box. 'Ruth just went along with it.'

'It was Edna's house,' I said. 'I suppose Ruth respected that and let her have her way.'

'Or she just has no backbone,' Sarah said, running her hand along the inside of the drawer. 'There's a gold necklace and diamond earrings in here.'

'Real?' Kelly asked, as Sarah passed them to Arial.

'These diamond studs are,' Arial said, holding them up to the lights. 'I know because I asked to wear them, and Ruth wouldn't let me.'

'Maybe they were a gift,' Sarah said. 'But if so, it was a long time ago. Ruth let her pierced ears close up when I was still in college.'

'Probably my fault, too,' Arial said, replacing the jewelry and closing the drawer with a bang. 'She had me and gave up on life.'

'Wah-wah-wah,' Sarah said, pulling out another drawer. 'And punching holes in your earlobes is hardly life.'

'Having nice things, I mean. And going places to wear them.' Arial's voice went a little hoarse and she had to clear her throat before she continued. 'Should we check Edna's room?'

The girl obviously wanted out of the room, and I didn't blame her.

Back in the hall, Arial swung the opposite door open. 'Edna had the larger of the two rooms.'

Now that I was standing inside the room with the hospital bed – and not sucking in carbon monoxide – I realized Arial was right. Edna's room was half again the size of Ruth's, though it seemed even larger with a front-facing window and just the bed and dresser for furniture.

'Wait,' I said. 'Where's the painting?'

'Over there,' Sarah said, pointing at the opposite wall, where four wide swatches of paint – one yellow and three shades of blue cut through the otherwise white wall. 'Not sure how you could miss it.'

'This room was lavender as long as I can remember,' Arial mused. 'Now it's primed, and Ruth was already deciding on colors.'

'She didn't waste much time after Edna died.' Sarah sniffed the air. 'Stinks of bleach and—'

'No, I said the painting,' I interrupted impatiently. 'As in the *trompe-l'œil* that hung over the dresser. I saw it there yesterday.'

'Tromp who?' Sarah asked.

But Kelly was already examining the wall where the painting had hung. 'There's a nail hole here and it hasn't been filled in preparation for painting. When exactly did you see it, Maggy?'

'Just yesterday when we couldn't find Ruth. This door was open, and I glanced in here first before I opened the opposite door and found Ruth on the bed.'

'This . . . whatever you called it. Was it valuable?'

'*Trompe-l'œil* is just a style of painting. It means "fool the eye." I didn't stop to check the signature, but I think that Edna may have painted it herself.'

Kelly cocked her head, one hand resting on her belt. 'Now why would you think Edna Kingston painted the picture you saw?'

'I'm just guessing,' I admitted. 'But Edna was an artist – a painter – when she was younger. The image felt very . . . personal. Like maybe it depicted her dresser at another time in her life.'

Sarah's face was screwed up as she thought. 'You know, I do remember a painting there. It was like a painting of a dresser hung over a dresser. Weird.'

'Exactly,' I said. 'I thought it was a mirror at first because it showed items on the dresser top – or actually the backs of items on the dresser top.'

'The way the mirror, if it were real, would reflect them,' Kelly said. 'That's very clever.'

'That's what I thought,' I said, nodding. 'The panes of the Tiffany lampshade, the lace of the dresser scarf – I felt like I could reach out and touch them.'

'Hence the *trompe-l'œil*,' Arial said. 'I remember it, too, though I never really looked at it. Seemed really old.'

'Any idea of the painting's value?' Kelly asked, jotting down notes. 'I assume you would be able to identify it?'

'Sounds like Maggy can identify it better than either of us,'

Sarah said. 'But you might want to ask Edna's attorney, Charles Cokely. He may have a dollar value for it if it was an original.'

'Original Edna Mayes,' I said.

Kelly cocked her head. 'Edna Mayes being Edna Kingston's maiden name, I presume?'

'Yes.' I decided to trot out my latest theory. 'Did Pavlik tell you about this Melinda woman, Kelly?'

A single nod was my answer.

'Nobody seems to know who she really is or why she came to Edna's funeral. But if Edna's paintings are valuable, especially now that she's dead, then maybe . . .' I shrugged.

'Then maybe what?' The deputy was apparently trying to be obtuse.

'Then maybe the painting above the dresser was worth stealing. Especially since it apparently has been stolen. Which we've discovered while we were here looking for things that were missing because the house has been broken into.' My voice was getting more strident, so I toned it down. 'Just a thought.'

'Uh-huh.' Kelly made another note. 'If you can provide a photo of the painting, that would be helpful.'

'We'll look.' Sarah's tone indicated she didn't expect to find anything.

I gave up and moved on. 'Did Edna die here in this room?'

'Yes, in her sleep Monday night,' Sarah said, rubbing her hand across the yellow stripe. 'Ruth found her Tuesday morning and must have started planning the redecoration the moment her body was toted away.'

Whenever Sarah is particularly snide or unkind, I feel the need to argue. 'You don't know that. Maybe Ruth had already primed it and they were choosing colors together so Ruth could paint it. For Edna.' Rather than post-Edna.

'Because nothing brightens a dying woman's day more than a room full of paint and bleach fumes,' Sarah muttered.

'There is jewelry in this dresser, too.' Kelly had the second drawer from the top open. 'A string of pearls in a tube sock. And they look genuine, too.'

'Her engagement ring should be in there,' Sarah said.

'I thought she destroyed her wedding ring,' I said.

Sarah shrugged. 'The engagement ring has a diamond.'

Apparently there was a dollar limit to Edna's wrath.

'It certainly does.' Kelly had turned the sock inside out and came up with a yellow gold ring set with a fair-sized diamond. 'Any half-decent thief should have found these and taken them.'

'Unless they came here focused on stealing something else in particular,' I argued. 'Something that—'

'They could have been disturbed,' Arial interrupted.

'By who?' Kelly asked. 'We didn't know the house had been broken into until the fire investigators called in at eight this morning. They arrived to finish up and found the back door hanging open, but nobody was here.'

'That they saw,' Arial said. 'The investigators would have come in the front, wouldn't they? The intruder could easily have snuck out the back.'

'It's not exactly a mansion,' Kelly said doubtfully. 'There's a small living room and an even smaller kitchen between the front and the back doors.'

'If the thief was in Edna's room,' I said, 'there's a window facing the street. They could have seen the unit from the fire department pull up.'

'Grabbed the painting and run, huh?' Kelly said. 'Is that your idea?'

'From what we can tell, it's the only thing missing.' I was not going to let go of this bone. 'What's your theory?'

Kelly just shrugged.

'Are there any other paintings around that you remember?' I asked Arial. 'Maybe stored somewhere, instead of hung up?'

'Sorry, Maggy, but no,' Arial said, before turning to Sarah. 'Did you know anything about Edna being this great *artiste*? I'm starting to feel like I knew absolutely nothing about my own family.'

Sarah shifted uncomfortably. 'When Edna was younger and had a glass or two of wine, she'd get all dramatic. Talk about giving up "her art" for the family. I figured it was just the typical maternal guilt trip.'

'Right,' Kelly said, opening the lower drawers. 'Nothing but clothes in these.'

'But it might be important,' I protested, pulling up the obituary on the phone and shoving it in front of Kelly. 'Edna did have some renown as a painter.'

But Kelly wasn't going to let me have this one. 'Or so says her hometown newspaper.' She pulled open the bottom drawer of the dresser to the sound of paper ripping. 'Damn, this one is stuffed full.'

'Careful,' Arial said, plucking out the snagged paper and setting it on the dresser. 'What are you looking for?'

'I'm not sure,' Kelly admitted. 'Signs that somebody rifled the drawer searching for something? Cash? Stock?'

'I'd be willing to bet that the mess in that drawer is of my mother's own making.' Sarah had my phone now and was going over the article more closely. 'Edna's painting must have pre-dated meeting my father and moving to Denver. Why give it up?'

'Maybe she didn't,' I said. 'Maybe she got married thinking she could have a family and keep up her work but found that it was too much.'

'Her dreams beaten out of her by life,' Kelly muttered and then glanced up self-consciously.

Sarah set down my phone and cocked her head to regard the deputy. 'Are you speaking as somebody who knows?'

'Who me?' Kelly glanced up from the drawer, embarrassed. 'No, not really. But we all make our choices, don't we? Can't have it all, no matter what they tell us.'

'Well, I can't speak for Edna's success as a painter,' Arial said. 'But her family certainly turned out to be a disappointment to her. Daughter gets knocked up on a one-night stand and she's stuck helping to raise her bastard grandchild.'

Kelly closed the drawer and picked up the paper Arial had set on the dresser top. 'Could taint one's outlook, I suppose.'

Sarah cleared her throat. 'Ah, a little sensitivity please?'

'What?' Realization struck as the deputy straightened. 'Oh, Arial is the bast— Sorry.'

'Not as sorry as I am, I'll wager.' Arial flashed her a grin. 'What do you have there?'

Kelly flattened out the paper. 'It's an estimate for replacing a cracked heat exchanger on the furnace.'

'Or, alternatively, the purchase and installation of a new furnace,' Arial read over her shoulder.

'Any indication the work was done?' I asked, trying to get a look myself.

'When was this?' Sarah pushed in.

'End of March,' Kelly was tucking the paper into her notebook. 'Given the current state of the furnace, I doubt anything further was done, but I'll turn this over to the fire inspector and they can check with this JM Services.'

'If something went wrong with the furnace at the end of the last heating season,' Arial said, 'Ruth and Edna probably just turned it off.'

'Deferred maintenance,' Sarah said.

'But this is Wisconsin,' I said. 'March isn't the end of the heating season. We've had snow in April and even May.'

'Doesn't matter,' Sarah said. 'I told you. When I lived at home, the furnace went off at Easter or thereabouts and—'

'On at Thanksgiving,' Arial supplied. 'You'll be thrilled to know that tradition was continued after you.'

Brr. 'Was there anything else interesting in that drawer?' I asked Kelly.

'Nothing pertinent to the break-in or Ruth's asphyxiation, as far as I can tell.' The deputy shifted her heavy gun belt as she got to her feet. 'I'm going to check out the kitchen.'

'No oil paintings in here,' Sarah's voice echoed. She had her head inside Edna's closet. 'By Edna or anybody else.'

'How do you know Edna painted in oil?' I asked curiously. 'That wasn't in the obituary.'

Sarah thought about it, frowning. 'I honestly don't know, I just said it.'

'It does smell like that in here, doesn't it?' I said, sniffing. 'Mingling with the bleach. Oil paints have a distinctive odor. I should have recognized it yesterday when I came in. Kind of sweet and . . .'

'Oily.' Sarah's nose was wrinkled. 'We should check the attic, too. If there are paintings here that neither Arial or I have seen, they might be up there.'

'There's an attic?' I'd seen just the three doors leading off the short hallway. A bathroom, Edna's bedroom and Ruth's bedroom. Which made me wonder. 'Where did you sleep when you lived here, Arial?'

'Shared a room with my mother when I was younger,' she said, following us into the hallway. 'But the couch mostly.'

'Which is why she's so comfortable flopping on the couches of her friends or dog-sitting clients when she's not with me,' Sarah said.

'Wherever I can lay my head, especially if there's a puppy to snuggle.' She shook her head. 'Kind of weird to think that I now own two houses, presumably both with bedrooms.'

'One of which you might sleep in,' Sarah suggested.

'I might, though probably not here,' was Arial's answer.

I was glancing around the hallway. 'Are you sure there's an attic?'

'Look up,' Sarah said, pointing to a rectangular cut-out in the ceiling.

'A pull-down attic door.' I hadn't noticed it.

Nor, apparently, had Arial. 'I had no idea this went to an attic,' she said. 'I would have made a room for myself if I had. How do you get up there?'

'There's a ladder attached to the door,' Sarah said. 'Once you pull it down.'

'But how do we do that?' I was surveying the two-by-four-foot flat surface that theoretically should pull down at an angle, allowing access. 'Usually there's a string or chain or something.'

'It was a rope, and it got torn off years ago, I think,' Sarah said.

'And it was never fixed?' More deferred maintenance. 'So how did you get up there?'

'I never did, after I helped them move in,' Sarah said. 'I was living in Madison, I told you. The University of Wisconsin dorms at first, and then my own apartment with a friend.'

'But when you helped move Ruth and Edna's things in, did you see—'

'Gilt-framed oil paintings?' Sarah finished. 'No, but I have to admit I wasn't looking for anything like that.'

Arial had ducked into the kitchen as we spoke and now re-appeared with a chair. 'I'm going up.'

'Careful,' I said, putting a hand up to steady her.

'She's a twenty-five-year-old climbing onto a kitchen chair,' Sarah snapped. 'I think she can handle it.'

'Sarah has always been a sink-or-swim kind of nurturer,' Arial said with a grin. She was now solidly planted on the chair, working her fingers around the crack between the door and the molding. 'I think I'm going to need—' She broke off as Kelly Anthony followed her in from the kitchen.

'Attic?' she asked quite reasonably.

'There's no pull on the hatch,' Arial told her. 'But the wood is splintered, like somebody pried it open.'

'They'd have to,' Kelly said. 'Without a rope, wedging in a crowbar or big screwdriver is the only way you'd get your hand in to pull it down.'

'I'm finding that out,' Arial said. 'I didn't even realize there was an attic.'

'What did you think that was?' Kelly pointed to the panel in the ceiling.

'Access panel to something mechanical, I guess. If I ever thought about it.'

'How old are the gouges in the paint and the wood?' Kelly had shifted position to see better.

'I never noticed them before, obviously,' Arial said, running her hand along the crack between the door and the ceiling. 'But I see why you're asking. These look like fresh splinters. Certainly since the ceiling was painted, whenever that was.'

'Ceiling and hall, about a year ago maybe,' Sarah said. 'I don't know why Ruth didn't reattach the rope right away.'

'Maybe she didn't want anybody going up there,' I ventured.

'Like who?' Sarah asked. 'It was just her and Edna and, though my mother did OK on steps, I don't see her crawling up an attic ladder.'

'I doubt Ruth even thought about access,' Arial said, pulling at the splinters with her fingers now. 'You couldn't get her to go into the basement, much less an attic like this.'

'A repair person maybe?' I asked. 'Is the furnace up there?'

'Furnace is in the basement,' Kelly told us before Arial or Sarah could answer. 'Would there be a crowbar down there?'

'The tools are in the garage,' Arial said. 'There should be a crowbar hanging on the wall next to the toolbox.'

As Kelly left to get it, I craned my head to peer up at Arial. 'You don't know the house has an attic, but you know exactly where a crowbar is?'

'I spent hours in the garage fixing things and tinkering back in middle school. It was a great way to stay clear of Edna and Ruth before I moved out.' Arial stepped down off the chair, my hand involuntarily hovering to spot her. 'I'm pretty sure nobody has touched the tools since I left.'

We heard the back door open, and Sarah put her foot on the seat of the chair as Kelly returned with the crowbar. 'Give it to me. I'll get it.'

'No, you won't,' Kelly said, and held the crowbar out to me. 'But you can hang onto this while I look at the damage to the wood.'

I hesitated.

'Don't worry,' Kelly said, thrusting it into my hand. 'If we find blood on it, I'll testify as to why your fingerprints are on it.'

Reassuring.

'It may have been used to break in the back door,' Arial said.

'Doubt it,' the deputy said, as she climbed onto the chair to examine the edges of the attic door. 'It was practically stuck to the wall with dust and grime.'

'Told you,' Arial said. 'Ruth wouldn't know a diagonals from a needlenose.'

Neither did I. 'What—'

'Types of pliers.' Kelly was brushing her hands off as she stepped off the chair. 'You're quite handy then,' she observed to Arial. 'You like taking things apart?'

'To see how they work,' Arial acknowledged. 'I've learned from books and videos, mostly.'

'Interesting,' Kelly said.

Sarah and I exchanged uneasy looks.

SEVEN

'You're not thinking that Arial tampered with the furnace, are you?' I asked.

'Way to go, Maggy,' Sarah muttered under her breath. 'If she wasn't, she probably is now.'

'Don't be silly,' Arial said. 'According to that estimate you found, the heat exchanger has been cracked since March. That's certainly not something I could have done with my handy little tools.'

'No, it's not,' Kelly said.

There was an uncomfortable silence.

To break it, I held the crowbar out to Kelly. 'Did you want to open the door?'

'Arial is right about those gouges in the wood appearing fresh,' Kelly said. 'I think we'll get forensics in here before we go any further.'

'Couldn't we just take a peek?' Arial asked hopefully. 'See if anything's been stolen?'

'How would you know?' Kelly asked, shaking her head. 'You've never been up there, remember?'

True. 'Maybe Sarah would. She helped them move in.'

But my partner was shaking her head. 'Twenty-five years ago. You think I'm going to remember?'

'We could see if there are scuffs in the dust, at least,' Arial suggested. 'Or voids where something was moved.'

'Our forensic team can check that as well as you can,' Kelly said, dragging the chair back toward the kitchen. 'We'll let you know.'

'Can we check out the basement then?' I asked, following her to set the crowbar on the counter.

'Not yet.' Kelly pushed the chair under the kitchen table and stopped to survey the room. 'I didn't see any signs that whoever broke in was interested in this room.'

'You didn't see the attic door either,' Sarah said under her breath.

Kelly ignored that. 'Is there anything out of place here in the kitchen?'

'Same white refrigerator,' Arial said, tapping the freezer compartment. 'Same turquoise stove.'

'I didn't know they made turquoise stoves,' I said.

'Probably about the time they made that green toilet of yours,' Sarah told me.

'You have an avocado toilet?' Arial asked, eyes wide. 'That is so cool. Nineteen Seventies, right?'

It was the Seventies, but the toilet was not cool.

'We just took it out,' I told her and then, to lessen the blow, 'it was cracked.'

An outright lie, of course. The thing was like a cockroach. It would outlive all of us.

'That's a shame.' Arial opened a cabinet and slid out a brown cardboard accordion file. 'This is where Ruth would keep bills and household papers.' She set it on the countertop to thumb through. 'I'm not seeing any estate documents, though.'

Kelly's eyebrows rose. 'Like a will? That's jumping the gun, isn't it?'

'Like a healthcare directive or power of attorney,' Sarah said darkly. 'My sister is unconscious. Somebody has to make decisions for her.'

'Of course,' Kelly said, her face reddening. 'Sorry.'

Arial came up with a blue pocket folder. 'Subaru – these look like purchase documents.'

Sarah held out her hand. 'Let me see.'

'I am an adult, you know.' Arial had unfolded the documents and was paging through. 'Ruth is the buyer.'

'Give me.' Sarah snatched the folder. 'I want to see if there's a lien on the car.'

The girl knew about pliers, but apparently not finances. 'Lien?'

'A bank's legal claim to the car,' I told her. 'It means there's a loan.'

'Ahh,' Arial said, nodding. 'That would be a good thing to know, I guess.'

'You've never bought a car?' Kelly opened another of the upper cabinets.

'I have a car,' Arial said. 'Just not a new one.'

'Calling that thing you left in my driveway a car is a stretch,' Sarah said. 'It's an oil spill with a roof.'

'Don't badmouth Gertrude. She runs just fine.' She paused. 'Just so long as she starts.'

'Like I said.' Sarah gestured with the papers. 'This Forester is probably in the garage, assuming Ruth took delivery when she did the paperwork.'

'It is,' I told them. 'I saw it when we were looking for Ruth yesterday.' Though I hadn't noticed much about the vehicle other than it was an SUV.

'The vehicle is titled in her name,' Sarah continued. 'If Ruth dies intestate, it will have to go through probate.'

Again, that seemed to be rushing things. But then Sarah was a great believer in expecting the worst. 'What if Ruth has a will?'

'Then only if her assets total more than fifty thousand dollars.'

'The house alone . . .' I stopped as I remembered. 'That's right. The house wasn't hers, it was Edna's.'

'And now Arial's,' Sarah said.

Kelly, who had been opening drawers and quietly eavesdropping, stopped and turned to Arial. 'Your grandmother left this house to you directly?'

'Along with a house on the Monterey Peninsula,' I said. 'Place called Pacific Grove.'

Both Sarah and Arial glared at me.

'What?' I asked them. 'Kelly can find out easily enough, anyway.'

'I can,' Kelly said, turning to rest her butt against the cabinets. 'I can't imagine it was easy for Ruth to hear that her mother had bequeathed the house she was living in to you, Arial. Especially since it sounds like the two of you had a . . . prickly relationship.'

'That's putting it mildly,' Arial said, seeming unperturbed as she opened the cabinet under the sink and slid out the wastebasket.

'My sister doesn't know the contents of my mother's will,' Sarah told the deputy. 'And before this morning, neither did Arial, before you ask.'

But Kelly just rubbed her chin.

Sarah, though, had gotten Arial's attention. 'Are you saying you knew about Edna's will and didn't tell me?'

Sarah ducked her head. 'Edna told me in June that she was changing it – taking Ruth out in favor of you. But I didn't know for sure that she'd actually done it until Cokely told me at the funeral.'

'Cokely?' Kelly asked.

'Charles Cokely, my grandmother's lawyer?' Arial reminded her. 'And no, I have no intention of kicking my mother out of this house. I hate it, and I've always hated it.'

'Arial couldn't make Ruth leave even if she wanted to,' Sarah said. 'Edna granted Ruth a life estate.'

'Meaning?'

'Edna willed the house to Arial,' I explained, 'but stipulated that Ruth could stay in the house as long as she lived.'

'Which may not be much longer, as it turns out.' Kelly turned to Arial. 'And you had no idea of the terms of your grandmother's will when you arrived back in the country?'

Arial's eyes narrowed, but she kept her voice pleasant. 'Sarah just told you that. And if you want to check, I went through customs in Fort Lauderdale yesterday morning and got a connecting flight to Milwaukee. I didn't land there until just about three thirty p.m., when Ruth was supposed to pick me up and never showed for obvious reasons. She'd been asphyxiated in her sleep before I even left Nassau.' She smiled. 'Is that clear enough?'

'Crystal.' Kelly smiled back, seeming to enjoy the game. 'Do we know what the terms of the original will were?'

We all looked to Sarah.

She grimaced. 'Edna told me she revised it when my aunt – that's my father's sister,' she said for Kelly's benefit, 'left me the train depot a few years back.'

'The building Uncommon Grounds is in?' the deputy clarified.

'Correct. She said that she thought it was unfair to Ruth, but she'd "balance the inequity" in her will.'

'You took that to mean she'd left everything to Ruth back then.' Kelly had the damned notebook out again.

'Or at least most of it,' Sarah acknowledged. 'I didn't know if she'd made any arrangements for Arial, but I doubted it.'

Kelly glanced up. 'Because you assumed Ruth's inheritance would pass on to her daughter?'

'Because they both barely tolerated me,' Arial told her.

Kelly tapped the pen on the pad, once, twice, three times. 'Yet Edna left everything to you. How do you explain that?'

'I can't,' Arial said simply.

Kelly made a show of flipping back in her notebook and then forward again. 'Sarah, you're sure your mother didn't tell Ruth she was changing her will in Arial's favor?'

'If she did, neither of them told me,' Sarah said.

'Or maybe you told her?' Kelly pressed. 'I mean, both of you had been passed over. There was no feeling of . . .'

'Camaraderie?' Sarah filled in, her lips tight. 'Hardly. I didn't expect anything and haven't for years. And, like I said, I can't tell you what Ruth did or didn't know about my mother's estate.'

Sarah wasn't handling Kelly's questioning as well as Arial was, getting unnecessarily defensive. But to me, Kelly's interrogation, if you wanted to call it that, was following a pattern.

'Are you training for detective?' I asked the deputy curiously. 'Your questions are very good.' And straight out of a book.

'Thank you,' she said, flushing a little. 'Did the sheriff tell you?'

I held up my hands. 'He doesn't discuss personnel stuff. I'm just assuming from your line of—'

'If you two are done fraternizing,' Sarah said, tossing me daggers, 'maybe we should get going?'

'I'm not sure Kelly is done,' I told her and turned to the deputy. 'You're wondering whether Ruth might have been depressed, am I right?'

Kelly nodded. 'Her mother, who she had cared for and lived with for many years, is dead. Then she finds out that same mother had betrayed her and left everything, including the roof over her head, to Arial. She'd be angry, but she'd also be—'

'You think Ruth was suicidal?' the girl asked, frowning.

'It honestly crossed my mind, too,' I told her. 'That's why I checked the garage when Ruth didn't answer the door yesterday.'

'Carbon mo's the way to go,' Arial muttered. 'You might have been right, but you had the wrong location.'

'But why buy a new car if you're planning to off yourself?' Sarah asked. 'Unless you wanted to do it sitting in your new leather seats.'

'I don't know. When she called me, Ruth seemed to be more conciliatory than despondent.' Arial was shaking the wastebasket. 'Like insisting on picking me up from the airport.'

'That was unusual?' Kelly asked.

'My mother being maternal? Yes.' Arial had reached into the wastebasket and now came up with two blue and black rectangles. 'Batteries.'

'Nine volt,' I said, with a little shake of my head. 'Must be the ones Ruth took out of the carbon monoxide detectors.'

'And purposely didn't replace?' Arial said.

Kelly cleared her throat. 'OK, well, thank you for coming by. Best leave those batteries where you found them, Arial, for forensics.'

'Forensics?' I asked. 'Not the fire investigators?'

She dipped her head. 'Just in case there's more to this than meets the eye, and Ruth's death is not ruled an accidental death. They'll already be here, anyway, looking into the break-in.'

'We still need to find Ruth's personal papers,' Arial said, sliding the wastebasket back under the sink. 'The healthcare directive and a will if she had one.'

'Give me a few hours with the crime scene people,' Kelly said. 'If I see anything that resembles what you're looking for, I'll send them over. Otherwise, you can get back in to look when they're done.'

Kelly pushed the door open for us to leave.

'We need to get into the attic, too,' Sarah said as she and I stepped out onto the back stoop. 'And the basement.'

'As soon as the forensic team and fire investigators finish, it'll be all yours,' Kelly promised.

'Arial,' Sarah called back. 'You coming?'

'Don't rush her,' I told Sarah. 'If Arial needs time—'

'No worries.' Arial ducked out the door. 'I'm fine.'

Kelly gave her a longish look and went to push the door closed. It swung open again.

'The latch is broken,' Arial reminded her. 'Why don't I get a hammer and nails out of the garage so you can secure it temporarily?'

'No need,' Kelly said. 'The rest of the team will be here soon. I'll just wait for them.'

'But—'

'Can we look in the garage?' I interrupted. 'Check out the new car?'

'You do that,' Kelly said, seeming done with us. 'I'll be in touch.'

'Thank you,' Sarah said, waving a congenial hand as she led us to the garage. Opening the back door, she stepped in before saying, 'Now tell me why you two wanted into the garage suddenly?'

'I'm still searching for paintings or art supplies,' I said.

'Yada, yada, yada. They were on the shelf in Edna's closet.'

'What?' I whirled on her. 'Why didn't you tell me?'

'Relax.' She elbowed me. 'No works by the master. Just a wooden kit with tubes of oil paint, brushes, palette knife and pencils. You know.'

No, I didn't know, thanks to her. 'Sounds kind of amateurish, considering . . .'

'Edna was the great artist? That's what I thought, too, when I saw it. But maybe Ruth bought it for her, thinking she might want to take painting up again while she was sick. You know, therapeutically, like people do paint-by-number.'

'Nice thought,' I admitted. 'Could you tell if it had been used?'

'Maybe once or twice,' Sarah said and turned to Arial. 'And you? What made you so hot to get into the garage?'

'The new car.' She laid a hand on the gray Subaru Forester that stood in the center of the garage. 'This is way cooler than I'd have expected for Ruth.'

'I still think she didn't know the will had been changed,' Sarah said. 'Picking paint colors for Edna's room is one thing. But this? It screams, "My mother died, and I just came into money."'

It kind of did, I thought as I glanced around the garage.

'The doors aren't locked,' Arial said, opening the driver's side. 'And the key is on the dash. Obviously, our thief didn't come in here or he or she could have helped themselves.'

Or maybe there wasn't a thief at all.

A framed canvas leaned against the far garage wall, facing away from us. 'Is that the painting that was above Edna's dresser?'

Getting not so much as a spark of interest from my compatriots, I circled the truck and turned the canvas, squinting to get a better look. 'It is the *trompe-l'œil*.'

'So the fire guys probably moved it,' Sarah said, shoving past me to open the passenger door of the SUV and lean in.

'They should have been more careful then,' I said. 'The paint is damaged.'

But the SUV was a bigger, shinier object.

Arial was sitting in the driver's seat.

For her part, Sarah was busy peeling a small packet of folded papers from inside the lower front windshield. 'Here's the temporary registration. I didn't look at the date on the purchase contract.'

She unfolded it. 'September twentieth – what was that? Friday?'

'Thursday,' Arial told her, climbing out of the SUV. 'And Edna died on Tuesday.'

'That is awfully quick,' I said, setting the painting back where I'd found it. 'You'd think Ruth would have more pressing things to do than to buy a car. Like arrange the funeral.'

'Maybe her old car gave up and she didn't have a choice.' Arial had abandoned the SUV to search through the workbench snugged beneath a window to the back yard.

'Edna's funeral was prearranged, anyway,' Sarah said. 'There wasn't much to do but meet with the funeral director to sign the papers and order copies of the death certificate. We did that on Wednesday.'

'You were there, too?' I said, a little surprised. 'At the funeral home you made it sound like Ruth had made most of the arrangements.'

'Ruth insisted I come. I just made sure I got there late, left early and listened to virtually nothing.'

Now *that* didn't surprise me. Hopefully Sarah wouldn't have Ruth's funeral to arrange, or the poor woman might never get into the ground.

Arial had lifted a pile of rags. 'Painting supplies here.'

I joined Arial at the workbench. 'Quart paint cans, the colors Ruth sampled on the wall.' Along with pans, rollers and brushes.

'Edna painted canvases and Ruth painted walls,' I mused. 'I wonder if Edna ever encouraged her to . . .'

'Paint in her footsteps?' Sarah continued before I could. 'I doubt it. Even if Ruth had tried, Edna would have belittled her efforts and destroyed her spirit.'

Deflated myself, I glanced around at the spartan garage. 'Nothing else here.'

'Except for the car,' Sarah said. 'Which is probably worth far more than that old oil painting.'

Arial closed the last drawer and picked up her purse. 'Let's go.'

'Kelly might know when we can come back,' I suggested, hearing the deputy with someone – likely her forensics team – in the back yard.

Arial opened the door and stepped out into the yard. 'Nothing interesting in the garage,' she called to Kelly. 'And the new car is still here.'

The deputy gave a thumbs-up and ducked into the house after the techs.

'I suppose we could wait?' I said to Arial and Sarah. 'The papers—'

'They can wait,' Arial said. 'I need caffeine. A latte might be just the thing.'

Sarah and I exchanged looks as we followed her around the house to my car.

'Is she up to something?' I asked.

'Most definitely.'

EIGHT

'What's with the urgent need to get coffee?' I asked Arial, as we drove to Uncommon Grounds.

'I was just thinking of you, Maggy,' she said from the back seat. 'And Amy, of course. Aren't you supposed to be relieving her?'

'Oh, damn.' I glanced at the time on the dashboard. 'It's already past one.'

'You're welcome,' Arial said, sounding an awful lot like her aunt.

'What did you take from the house?' I asked curiously. 'You were in there a little too long.'

'Yeah,' Sarah said. 'And if I'm not mistaken, I saw you stuffing something into your pocket as you came out the back door.'

'Can't put anything past the two of you.' Arial passed two nine-volt batteries wrapped in paper towel up to Sarah. 'I tried to palm these when I put away the wastebasket, but they were too big, and I could only get one. I went back for the other.'

'Why would you want the dead batteries that Ruth took out of the carbon monoxide detectors?' Sarah asked, holding them out on her own open palm. 'That's on the creepy side of sentimental.'

Given that the non-functioning detectors had contributed to Ruth's asphyxiation, it did seem a little macabre. And I usually appreciate macabre. But I thought Arial had more to tell us and I wanted to let her do it in her own time.

'I suppose they're a good reminder not to put off routine maintenance,' I offered inanely. 'Useful, as mementos go, I guess.'

'Have you lost your mind?' Sarah demanded, twisting back in my direction. 'What's she going to do with them? Create a shrine? Put them on her Christmas tree, come December? Hey, maybe she can use the cracked heat exchanger, too.'

'I was just—'

'Please stop,' Arial said. 'I just wanted to give the two of you the opportunity to appreciate my ingenuity. I thought I managed it pretty slick.'

'Stealing things from the trash baskets at your own house?' Sarah asked. 'Brilliant.'

'I have to admit I didn't see her put anything in her pocket,' I told Sarah. 'That was a good catch on your part.'

'Thanks, I—'

'I patted my pocket to see if Sarah would notice,' Arial said smugly. 'I'd already secreted them in my purse.'

'She's playing us,' Sarah told me. 'And doing it well. There must be a point to all this.'

'There is. I also grabbed this from the workbench in the garage.' Arial leaned forward to dangle a rectangular red box by its red and black wired leads.

I snuck a glance sideways. 'What's that?'

'Watch it,' Sarah cautioned as the car in front of me stopped short.

I stepped on my brakes hard, throwing my passengers forward but averting catastrophe. 'Sorry.'

'You're a terrible driver when you're distracted,' Sarah said. 'Let me ask the stupid questions.'

'Fine,' I said, starting up again. 'You're better at it anyway.'

'*This* is a battery tester,' Arial said, bouncing the red box up and down. 'Sarah, can I have the batteries back?'

Sarah threw me a sideways glance, as she complied. 'You're going to test the batteries to make sure they're dead?'

'That's exactly what I'm going to do,' Arial said. 'I just need to hold—'

'Damn.' The guy in front of me had slammed on his brakes again. 'It's not me, it's him.'

'Then you might want to give him some room, so you don't set off the airbags when he does exactly what you know he's going to do.'

'You might want to shuddup,' I muttered, doing what she'd advised.

'Actually, Maggy,' Arial said, 'would you mind terribly pulling over? This battery tester doesn't have alligator clips, so I have to hold the leads on both terminals to—'

'No need. We're here,' I told her, zipping right to snug the

Escape to the curb in front of the coffeehouse. 'In fact, why don't you wait until we get into Uncommon Grounds. It'll be easier at a table and—'

But aunt and niece were already fully engaged in the project.

'I'll hold the battery on the center console here,' Sarah said, swiveling in her seat to face Arial.

'Use the paper towels,' Arial said. 'We don't want more fingerprints on them than necessary.'

'Why would that—' I started.

'Got it,' Sarah was saying. 'You touch the leads to them.'

Getting my way was difficult enough when I just had Sarah to deal with. Two Kingstons were one too many. Two too many, some days. I switched off the ignition and turned to watch.

Arial already had the black wire on one of the two contacts on top of the battery and went to touch the red to the other.

'Wait,' I said. 'Are you sure you have the right wires to the right contacts?'

'Good thought,' Sarah said, the small rectangular battery she was holding in the paper towel shifting just a bit. 'Wouldn't want to blow me up.'

'It's a nine-volt battery, not a bomb,' Arial told her. 'Though it is possible to start a fire if something like tin foil or a paper clip crosses both terminals. Did you know that?'

'Start a fire, like in a drawer?' I asked, wondering what my spare batteries were keeping company with in my junk drawer at home. 'That's horrifying.'

'You never heard that? They teach you how to make a fire with steel wool and a nine-volt battery in survival school,' Sarah said, repositioning the paper towel and steadying her hand again. 'Try now.'

'Survival school? When did you go to—' I started.

'So long ago that I'll need a refresher before the apocalypse,' she snapped. 'Now can we get on with this?'

Arial grinned and handed me the red meter, retaining custody of the attached wires. 'To answer your question, Maggy, red is positive. Black is negative. But even if I had them reversed, the meter would still read the voltage, just as a negative number. Can you turn it so I can see the readout?'

I obeyed. 'What's the purpose of negative and positive on the meter then? I mean, I assume a battery can't be drained below empty, so why have a negative—'

'You heard Arial,' Sarah snapped. 'It tells you that the leads are right.'

This is what happens when I try to learn.

'It's more complicated than that,' Arial said, still playing peace-maker, 'but I'll spare you the details right now. Ready Sarah?'

'It's this damn paper towel,' Sarah groused.

'I know.' Arial touched the two leads to the battery terminals, making sure to keep them separated. 'Just as I suspected.'

'Dead?' I asked.

'Nope.'

I turned the meter so Sarah and I could see it from the front seat.

Nine volts. Even I knew that meant fully charged.

'Let's try the other one,' Sarah said, setting the one battery carefully on her lap and picking up the second with the paper towel.

She set it on the console, and Arial touched the leads to it.

'Also nine volts,' I read. 'Both batteries are good.'

'So maybe Ruth took them out early?' Sarah suggested. 'They tell you to change the batteries in your smoke alarms and carbon monoxide detectors on your birthday – or some other significant day – every year so they don't die or start chirping.'

'Arial's birthday was last week,' I reminded them.

'I think my mother preferred to forget my birthday,' Arial said skeptically.

'Rather than commemorate the occasion with the changing of the batteries?' Sarah asked, with a little grin. 'I think I agree.'

'Besides,' Arial said, 'you wouldn't go to change them if you didn't have replacements, right? You would wait.'

'Can you tell if the batteries were used for a few months?' Sarah asked her niece, wrapping the batteries back up in the towel. 'I mean, would they still read nine volts on the meter? Or would the voltage go down incrementally?'

'Good question. That depends on the type of battery.' Arial had taken the batteries from Sarah and was examining them. 'Lithium batteries, for example, hold a steady charge longer, but then they just drop off. They usually don't recommend using them in smoke and carbon monoxide detectors for just that reason.'

'They're in cahoots with the battery manufacturers?' Sarah guessed.

'Maybe,' Arial said, suppressing a grin. 'But, no. They want there to be a longer warning period, so people have time to change out the batteries in the detectors before they stop working completely.'

Sarah's niece seemed to know an awful lot about the subject. 'And these are lithium, I assume? That means they could have been in the detector for a while and still show fully charged, right?'

'No and no.' Arial held up a battery to show me. 'These aren't lithium or even alkaline. These are regular heavy-duty carbon zinc batteries. That means the voltage would have gone down gradually and, if they had been in the detector for months, as Sarah said, we'd see some signs of decline.'

'Maybe instead of throwing out the old batteries, Ruth accidentally threw out the new . . .' I stopped, seeing the very obvious flaw in my logic. 'If she did have two sets of batteries – one old and one new – she'd have put one set in the detectors before throwing out the other two batteries.'

'Because why would you remove two perfectly functional batteries from the carbon monoxide detectors and throw them away if you didn't have replacements to put in?' Arial asked.

'Yes,' Sarah said, turning back. 'Why?'

With a start, I realized the question was directed to me. 'Why are you asking me?'

'Because you're usually the first one to suspect all things nefarious when there's a death,' Sarah said. 'Except in this case apparently.'

I shifted uncomfortably. 'We're talking about Arial's mother. And your sister.'

'People drop like flies around here all the time,' Sarah said, folding her arms. 'Friends, relatives, lovers. Never stopped you before, even when you were trying to pretend you were being sensitive.'

I was sensitive compared with Sarah. But that admittedly was a low bar.

'Please, Maggy.' This was from Arial. 'What do you think?'

'I'm sorry, Arial,' I said, meeting her eyes. 'But Kelly Anthony was already asking questions about your mother's state of mind, and I told you I'd wondered the same thing.'

'What does that have to do with the batteries?' she asked. 'If she committed suicide . . .'

'Maybe she didn't want to be disturbed,' I said quietly.

Arial sat back in the car seat, dropping the batteries in her lap. 'Disturbed.'

'Carbon monoxide detectors' alarms are loud and annoying, especially if you're just trying to drift . . .'

'Off,' Arial said. 'On a sea of deadly gas?'

I nodded. 'Disabling the detectors would also eliminate the chance of a neighbor hearing the alarm and calling the police.'

'But disabling the detectors – that would be the easy part.' She carefully tucked the paper towel around the batteries. 'What about the furnace? That would have to be malfunctioning in the first place to send carbon monoxide throughout the house.'

'We saw the estimate from the HVAC guy,' I reminded her. 'Ruth may have known the heat exchanger was cracked.'

'Supposing she did,' Arial said. 'I'm not sure she'd even realize what that meant.'

'Arial is right,' Sarah said. 'I was always the one who was more mechanically inclined between Ruth and me. Arial obviously inherited my skill.'

'Your skill,' I repeated.

Sarah bristled at my tone. 'I've kept a 1975 Firebird running all these years.'

My partner had trouble putting new receipt tape in the cash register. 'Your mechanic has kept the Firebird running. It's not like you're swapping out spark plugs or changing the oil on your driveway.'

'I'll have you know that Sam and I work on the Firebird together,' Sarah said defensively.

I glanced at Arial, who nodded. 'The deal is that if he wants to drive it, he has to know how to take care of it.'

'That's really smart.' I was genuinely impressed.

An uncharacteristic tinge of pink rose in Sarah's face. 'But about Ruth and suicide. I'm not sure I buy it. Like I said to Kelly – the car, trying out paint colors. Insisting on picking Arial up from the airport.'

'You think she was looking forward to a fresh start,' I said.

'Or trying to,' Arial said, biting her lip. 'I'm not sure I was as . . . enthusiastic as I could have been when she suggested picking me up. Maybe I should have been more receptive to her—'

'You weren't receptive because you've had a lifetime of not being able to count on your mother,' Sarah said. 'And, as it turned out, she didn't show up. Again.'

'Because the woman was in a coma,' I reminded her. 'You might have to give your sister a pass on this one.'

'Sure,' Sarah said. 'But it doesn't forgive the rest. It doesn't make up for the way that she and my mother treated Arial all these years.'

'Maybe once Edna was gone, Ruth realized—'

Sarah snorted. 'The error of her ways? I doubt it.'

'But even if she was depressed – about Edna dying, about the inheritance, whatever.' Arial's tone was hushed. 'There are less complicated ways to commit suicide.'

'But maybe not as . . .' I felt stupid saying this, ' . . . peaceful-seeming? At least in her mind?'

'Carbon mo's the way to go,' Sarah repeated softly. 'Maybe Sophie isn't the only one who believes that.'

'Maybe,' Arial said. 'But what's the point of all this window dressing, if that's what it is? Why not chuck the new car and the paint samples and just run a hose from the exhaust in through the window of the old Chevy.'

'Because that would have been an obvious suicide,' I said. 'It was the first thing I thought of, at least.'

'True,' Sarah said. 'Plus somebody could have heard the car running. A neighbor, like with the alarms.'

Arial was watching me. 'That's not what you mean, though.'

'It's just that . . . maybe Ruth wanted you to believe her death was an accident. She didn't want you to think—'

'That I wasn't enough to live for now that Edna is gone?' Arial's eyes were angry under the sheen of tears. 'But I already knew that.'

Sarah reached back and touched her arm. 'Ruth was a shit mother, but I believe underneath it all she loved you.'

'Which is why she wanted me to be the one who found her?' Arial asked.

'Why do you think—'

Arial didn't let me get the question out. 'If what we're saying is true, how else do you explain her offering to pick me up? She probably knew I'd get mad when she wasn't there and take a taxi or rideshare home.' She flopped a hand. 'And there she'd be.'

I'd opened up a can of worms by mentioning suicide. But then they had asked my opinion.

'I am so sorry,' I said, back-pedaling on my theory. 'I'm just speculating, like always. That's why I didn't want to do this, didn't want to treat your mother's CO poisoning like an investigation. It's far more likely that it is exactly what it seems. A terrible oversight.'

'Maybe Ruth wasn't trying to hide her suicide from *us*,' Sarah interrupted, as if she hadn't heard a word I'd said.

'Well, Edna was already dead.' Apparently, Arial wasn't paying attention to me either. 'Who else is there?'

'Herself,' Sarah said. 'Ruth and I were taught that suicide is a mortal sin.'

'Sure,' I muttered under my breath. 'Why not burden people who are already struggling in life, with threats of eternal damnation? That'll cheer 'em up.'

'I agree with you,' Sarah said. 'But if Ruth did want to die, maybe sleeping with the disabled carbon monoxide detectors and cracked heat exchanger was her way of rolling the dice.'

Which landed her not dead, but in a coma. 'Like ultimate risk-takers who get more and more reckless in their exploits. You almost wonder if they have a passive–aggressive death wish.'

Arial was shaking her head. 'I do see what you're both saying. But if it's true, I think it's more likely she was protecting her reputation. Saint Ruth and all that.'

'Does Ruth have an insurance policy?' I asked, perhaps a little abruptly.

Sarah blinked. 'Why? Now that we've unleashed the beast, your new theory is that Arial tried to kill Ruth for an insurance payout?'

'The beast being me?' I asked.

'The beast being your imagination,' Arial said. 'At least that's what I assume Sarah means.'

'You *have* gone from attempted suicide to attempted murder in the blink of an eye,' Sarah pointed out.

'An insurance policy doesn't mean Arial tried to kill her,' I told her. 'She wasn't even in town, as far as we know.'

'As far as we know?' Arial repeated. 'You want to see my boarding passes?'

'Of course not,' I said. 'My point is that Sarah would be the better suspect.'

My partner was unfazed. 'If Ruth has an insurance policy, my mother is probably the beneficiary. Or was.'

'To provide for Edna's care, if Ruth died,' I surmised. 'That would be very considerate of Ruth.'

'If the policy exists, it was probably my grandmother's idea,' Arial said. 'Most likely she paid the premiums too.'

'Self-interest,' Sarah agreed. 'Runs in the family.'

I wasn't going to touch that one. 'I never asked. What does Ruth do for a living?'

'Took care of my mother mostly,' Sarah said. 'At least the last few years.'

'Edna had a heart attack, right?'

'About five years ago. They put in a stent, and she recovered just fine for a while. Not that she didn't make the most of it.'

'She did have Ruth trained,' Arial said, with a twisted grin.

'Did you help out?' I asked Sarah curiously.

'Sarah is *not* as well-trained,' Arial said, with a grin. 'Me neither, to be fair. Once Edna was out of the hospital and home, though, Sarah is right. She really didn't want or need help.'

Besides Ruth. 'So was it her heart that finally killed her?'

Arial nodded. 'She was diagnosed with congestive heart failure.'

'Docs gave her weeks,' Sarah said. 'But the old bird hung on for almost a year.'

Until last Tuesday.

'Anyway,' Arial said. 'To answer your question, Ruth worked as an accountant at that tax firm in Benson Plaza before it fell down.'

Where the original Uncommon Grounds was, as well as

Goddard's Pharmacy. No wonder Ruth had spent enough time at Gloria's lunch counter to annoy her.

'What about Edna?' I asked curiously. 'Did she work after she gave up painting?'

'Not that I saw,' Arial said. 'But before now, we didn't even know she painted.'

'Edna's family had money,' Sarah said. 'How much and how long it lasted, I don't know because we never talked about it. Edna considered it *déclassé*.'

Presumably because she had it. The rest of us seemed to talk about it incessantly. 'The reason I asked about a life insurance policy isn't that I suspect either of you in Ruth's death. I just thought it might be a reason for Ruth to try to disguise her suicide as an accidental death.'

'Life insurance companies don't pay out for suicides?' Arial looked skeptical. 'I thought that was only in bad detective novels.'

'Good or bad detective novels, it's based on truth,' I said. 'Sometimes suicide is still excluded. But most likely it's covered after the policy has been in place two or three years before the death.'

'Makes sense,' Sarah said. 'Don't want people taking out life insurance policies and throwing themselves out of buildings willy-nilly.'

No, we don't. 'When we go back to the house, we can check for any insurance policies – Ruth and Edna's.'

'It would be so much easier if Cokely was my mother's attorney, in addition to Edna's,' Arial said. 'He'd have everything.'

'Maybe. But my lawyer doesn't know anything about my insurance policies. I keep that sort of thing in my safe-deposit box at the bank.'

'Mine's in my safe,' Sarah volunteered.

'You have a safe?' I asked.

'Sure, where do you think I keep my gun? I do have kids, you know.'

Teenagers, but that made the safe even more important. 'I hate that you own a gun.'

'That's not what you said when I saved your life with it.' Sarah made a gun of her hand and pointed it at me.

'I know,' I said, uncomfortably, 'but—'

Bam, bam, bam.

I jumped and turned to see Amy's face scrunched grotesquely against my window, her hand clenched in the fist she had just used to pound on the glass.

'Are you coming out,' she said in a menacing tone, 'or am I going to have to come in to get you?'

'So, somebody threw out new batteries and the CO_2 detectors were empty.' Our barista was sitting at a table with Arial and Sarah, while I made an I'm-sorry-for-getting-back-late iced latte for her. 'Couldn't that be two separate incidents?'

'CO,' Arial corrected, taking a sip of her cappuccino. 'CO_2 is carbon dioxide.'

'What's the difference again?' Amy nodded her thanks as I sat down and slid her drink to her.

'One oxygen atom,' Arial said, swiping her tongue across her upper lip to catch the foam from her cappuccino. 'Both carbon monoxide and carbon dioxide have one carbon atom – that's the "c." But carbon monoxide has one oxygen atom, dioxide has two. Which is why the "O" – for oxygen – in the dioxide formula has a two next to it.'

'Can someone explain that in English instead of science?' Amy asked with a grin.

'Sure,' I said. 'Carbon monoxide is the one that kills you in your sleep, while carbon dioxide is what we breathe out.'

'And what plants need for photosynthesis,' Arial contributed. 'It's also dry ice when you freeze and compress it.'

'Oh, right.' Amy was nodding, the three earrings in her right ear tinkling faintly. 'I always get that turned around.'

'Probably not a big deal until you want to kill yourself or freeze ice cream fast,' Sarah assured her. 'And then you can always google it first.'

'And your search will tell you that it's liquid *nitrogen* you use for freezing ice cream,' Arial said, exasperated. 'Haven't any of you had a basic chemistry class?'

'A long time ago in a galaxy far, far away,' Sarah told her niece. 'But back to Amy's initial question, could the batteries in the wastebasket just be a coincidence and have nothing to do with the disabled carbon monoxide detectors?'

I raised my eyebrows 'You do know what Sherlock Holmes said about coincidence.'

'Please spare us,' Sarah said.

No chance. 'It was in an episode of the TV series, but not in the Conan Doyle books. At least I haven't found the reference in the books.'

'Good,' Sarah said. 'So—'

'It's the Benedict Cumberbatch *Sherlock*,' I continued. 'BBC. Set in modern London. Not to be confused with *Elementary*, the American show on CBS that was set in modern New York. Both are great, but I think it was *Sherlock*'s series three—'

Amy groaned. 'You're not going to stop until you tell us, are you?'

'Absolutely not.'

Arial suppressed a smile. 'Go ahead then.'

'"What do we say about coincidence, Sherlock?"' I asked, quoting Sherlock's brother Mycroft. '"The universe is rarely so lazy."'

'Good one.' Sarah turned back to Amy and Arial. 'But setting aside the batteries for now, literally . . .' She eyed Arial, who had been tapping the two nine volts – now taped into their paper towel covering – on the table.

Arial set them down.

Sarah slid them away from her. 'There's the question of the furnace and whether it was already dangerous when it was turned off last spring.'

'Presumably,' Arial said. 'We know it had a cracked heat exchanger and that's nothing to mess with.'

'But did Ruth know that?' I said. 'The company that did the repair estimate may be able to tell us – or Kelly – that.'

'The estimate was for replacing the heat exchanger or replacing the furnace?' We'd filled Amy in on the day's developments and our various theories.

'Yes,' Arial said. 'Either or, prices for each.'

'With the new furnace being much costlier obviously,' Amy said.

'But more cost-efficient in the long run,' Sarah said. 'I'm not sure that's the way Edna would look at it.'

'She was dying,' I reminded her. 'Probably not doing a lot of long-term planning.'

'Well, what about that?' Amy asked. 'Could they have done some sort of short-term repair, that didn't . . .' she was searching for a word, ' . . . take?'

'No reputable firm would do a repair on a heat exchanger,' Sarah said. 'They always replace, which is likely what Edna found out when she got the estimate.'

'The inspector also said the venting was incomplete,' I reminded them.

Arial cocked her head. 'The venting. If Ruth did know about the heat exchanger and wanted to make sure the gas got up into the house, she might mess with that.'

'You really think she'd know how?' Sarah asked.

Arial just shrugged. 'She could always get a video off the web.'

'The fire department was checking the furnace,' I told them. 'I can ask Pavlik if there are signs of a repair or tampering.'

'We should look ourselves,' Arial said, standing. 'The inspectors should be done by now. Let's go check.'

I glanced at Amy. 'The store is still open.'

She rolled her eyes. 'Go ahead. But, as always, keep me informed.'

'Minute by minute,' I said, going to give her a hug.

'Arial,' Amy's voice followed us to the door as we prepared to leave. 'Were you planning to stay at your mom's house while you were in town?'

She turned. 'No, at Sarah's.'

'Did your mother know that?' Amy persisted, coming to the door.

'I think she'd have presumed it,' Arial said, preceding us out onto the porch and turning back to Amy. 'Why?'

'One of your theories was that Ruth knew the furnace was faulty but decided not to do anything and let the universe decide her fate.'

'Playing Russian roulette,' Sarah said.

'Well, yes.' Amy seemed uncomfortable. 'But she'd only do that if she was sure Arial wasn't staying there. Obviously.'

'Obviously,' Sarah repeated as the door closed, leaving Amy in the shop and the three of us on the porch.

Sarah lowered her voice, as Arial went down the porch steps

to the sidewalk. 'Ruth insisted on picking Arial up at the airport. Could she have intended to convince her to stay?'

'To do what?' I whispered back. 'Kill her, too?'

'Well, I—'

'Excuse me,' Arial was standing by the car. 'I can hear every word you whisper. And if you're suggesting my mother plotted a murder/suicide, with me in the co-starring role, there's only one problem.'

I tweeted the car open. 'Just the one?'

Arial swung the door wide to slip into the back seat again. 'It's a very slipshod way to do it. So much so that she ended up in a coma before getting a chance to implement it. Or even pick me up.'

'Very true,' Sarah said, getting into the passenger seat as I went around to the driver's side. 'Ruth would be more precise.'

'Precisely,' came from the back seat.

NINE

These Kingston women were hard-core. At least my clan pretended to like each other on the odd occasion that we got together.

'Let me get this straight,' I said from the driver's seat of my Ford Escape. 'The only reason you're discounting Ruth trying to kill Arial is that murder by carbon monoxide is . . . slipshod?' In their words.

'Not just that,' Arial said, as I wound my way back to her mother's house. 'I mean, Ruth had no reason to kill me other than not liking me very much.'

'Don't forget that Ruth would likely inherit the house and Edna's money if you were dead,' Sarah reminded her.

'But it sounds like the real money is in Gretchen's estate,' Arial argued. 'Even if Ruth intended to murder me before my twenty-fifth birthday, she'd get nothing. Those lovely animal rescue organizations would benefit.'

'Maybe we should look into them,' Sarah said. 'Dog people can be wackadoodle about protecting their furry friends. Look at Maggy.'

'Because dogs are nicer than people,' I said.

'Except for licking their butts,' Sarah said.

'Don't tell me we wouldn't do that if we could,' I said, flashing my best human friend a big ol' grin. 'But let me remind you both that Arial did make it to her twenty-fifth birthday. And if Ruth had planned a murder/suicide, by definition she'd be dead, too.'

'Leaving Sarah as Edna's sole heir,' Arial said. 'That's a good theory, Maggy. I like it.'

'Slipshod plot,' Sarah repeated. 'I'm better than that. If I wanted you dead, you'd be dead.'

I believed that. 'I'm shocked that neither of you is making Ruth out to be a mass-murderer,' I said as we rounded the last corner to Ruth's house. 'She did invite us all over for post-visitation dinner, after all.'

'And it might have happened,' Sarah said, twisting to regard Arial in the back. 'If we'd come through the front door and gathered in the living room, a few of the old folks might have bought the farm before we figured out what had happened.'

'The old folks did come in the front door,' Arial reminded her. 'They were just fine, while I was throwing up in the kitchen sink.'

'Gloria and Sophie are indestructible.' I pulled the Escape to a stop in front of the white brick ranch since there was a fire investigation van and a squad car filling the driveway.

'They're still here. We're not going to be able to get in—' I broke off, adjusting the visor against the glare of the lowering sun.

'Pavlik can't tell them to let us in?' Sarah asked.

'No way he would do that. Not if the technicians are still—' I broke off again, peering at a car halfway up the block. 'Is that a blue sedan?'

'Maybe.' Sarah was squinting as the car pulled away from the curb. 'Like the one that Melissa . . . whoa!'

This last was because I'd stomped on the gas pedal to follow the sedan as it took a quick left onto a side street.

Arial was leaning forward, hanging onto the headrest of Sarah's seat as we turned, too. 'Who's Melissa?'

'She means Melinda,' I told her, scanning for the blue car. 'You know, the one who keeps changing her story about how she knew Edna.'

'Melissa, Melinda – what's it matter?' Sarah groused. 'It's a fake name anyway. Turn here, turn! Damn, you missed it.'

'Turn which way?' I demanded.

'Right, I pointed right.'

'I can't see which way you're pointing,' I said. 'I'm driving.'

'Is that what you call it? You've already lost her. Three blocks into a twenty-mile-an-hour car chase that would have made OJ proud.'

'Shaddup,' I said, pulling over to the curb.

'Are you two done?' Arial asked from the back.

I looked at Sarah. 'Pretty much.'

'So why were we following her?' Arial asked. 'And do we know for sure that it was Melinda in the first place?'

'No clue to the first and no to the second,' Sarah said. 'You, Maggy?'

'Taking the last question first, I'm pretty sure it was Melinda. I noticed as she pulled away yesterday that the car had Illinois plates. Also, it was a blue Corolla, which is a pretty common rental if she flew into Milwaukee or Chicago and rented a car.'

'Not bad,' Arial said appreciatively.

'Thank you,' I said. 'As for why I was following, I just wanted to talk to her. See if we can find out who she really is and why she's nosing around.'

'Got the handcuffs and rubber hoses in the trunk, do you?' Unlike Arial, Sarah had a low opinion of my abilities.

'I'd follow her to wherever she went next,' I said. 'Then we'd park inconspicuously and "accidentally" run into her at her hotel or a coffee shop or whatever.'

'That's perfect.' Arial was nodding. 'We could thank her for coming to the wake and ask her last name, at least.'

'She'll lie, of course,' I said. 'But at least it's a starting point.'

Sarah had perked up. 'I know how we can find out her last name and where she's from. Without the wild car chase.'

'And how is that?' I asked.

'Drive back to Brookhills Road and take a right,' she said, snapping on her seat belt. 'I will *verbally* point the way.'

'The funeral home,' I said, turning into the parking lot. 'But why – ah, the guest register. Do you truly think Melinda signed it?'

'I know she signed it.' Sarah was already getting out of the car, looking very pleased with herself. 'Because I saw her do it in the vestibule while I tried to ignore your non-stop whining about your feet.'

'She'll have lied, of course,' Arial said, trotting after her to the entrance. 'Like Maggy said.'

'Of course.' Sarah rattled the door. 'Damn. Locked.'

'Push the buzzer,' Arial said. 'They're probably in the back, pumping embalming fluids into veins or incinerating people.'

I obeyed. 'Doesn't mean they'll answer – oh, hello,' I said as the funeral director from Edna's funeral opened the door. 'We weren't sure you were here.'

'Death, sadly, does not keep to a schedule,' he said, stepping back to let us in. 'How can we help you and your departed loved one?'

'You already have,' Sarah said. 'I'm Sarah Kingston. You buried my mother yesterday, remember?'

'Edna, of course. I do hope there wasn't a problem.'

'Not yesterday,' Sarah said. 'But—'

'I don't think I introduced myself yesterday,' Arial said, offering her hand. 'I'm Arial Kingston. We were hoping to pick up my grandmother's guest book. There are a few people we couldn't place, and we certainly don't want to miss them when we write thank you notes.'

'That is so considerate of you,' he said, covering her hand with his. 'So often these days young people don't send notes. It's all electronic now, you know.'

'I know,' Arial said, sucking up. 'Convenient, but so terribly impersonal.'

'Quite so,' the man said, and gestured to a small, serenely appointed conference room opposite the vestibule from yesterday's viewing room. 'Would you like to step in here while I retrieve the guest register? I believe Edna's death certificates have come in as well.'

'Thank you so much,' Arial said, and then turned to Sarah. 'I hate to say it, but we probably should discuss prearrangements for Mother, assuming he has the time.'

'She's in a coma,' I explained.

'Oh, dear,' he said, seeming shocked but not ungrateful for the two-fer. 'I'm so sorry, but of course I have the time. Can I get you anything? Coffee? Water?'

'Bourbon?' Sarah suggested.

Arial grinned. 'We're fine, thank you.'

'They dropped Edna, you know,' Sarah said in a low voice as the man scurried away.

'No, I didn't know,' Arial said. 'You mean the casket or—'

'Her body as they were taking it off the bed,' Sarah said. 'Ruth told me.'

'Then it was the mortuary who picked up Edna's body at the house?' I asked.

'Instead of the coroner, you mean?' Sarah sensed where I was going with this. 'Edna was under a doctor's care and her physician signed the death certificate.'

'So, no autopsy,' I said.

'No autopsy and no mystery,' she confirmed. 'Which I know is unusual in your corpse-strewn world.'

'Nicely put,' I told her.

Arial's forehead was wrinkled. 'I mentioned prearrangements, but do you think Ruth would be OK with the same people who dropped Edna managing her own funeral?'

'Tough luck if she isn't,' Sarah said. 'She was only too thrilled to take the oops-we-dropped-her discount for our mother.'

I was starting to see why Arial gave her family a wide berth.

'I should remind him about it,' Sarah continued.

'You think he'd forget something like that?' I asked.

'I'm not sure, but if Ruth dies, she deserves the same cut-rate deal she negotiated for Edna. He—'

'We still don't know the man's name,' I interrupted, hoping to put the discount discussion to bed.

'Here.' Arial pointed at a framed degree on the conference room wall. 'Ian Barrymore.'

'I. Barrymore,' I repeated and turned to Sarah. 'How on earth could you forget that?'

She just shrugged.

'Stiff competition for Mort Ashbury?' I tried.

'Please don't,' Arial said, choking down a laugh as Mr Barrymore rejoined us.

'You're sure I can't get you some water?' he asked, concerned, as she started to cough.

'No, no, I'm fine.' Arial was trying to catch her breath. 'Is that the guest book?'

'It is.' He slid the ribboned presentation box onto the table.

'Oh, it's lovely,' Arial said. 'You didn't have to go to all that trouble, Mr Barrymore.'

We could have taken a photo of the page in question and been done with it, but it was pretty for a book of death. Which reminded me, 'You mentioned Edna's death certificates?'

'Here,' he said, taking an envelope from his jacket pocket and handing it to Arial, who was apparently his favorite. 'And please call me Ian.'

'Ian, then.' Arial smiled.

'Now, your mother,' he said, gesturing for us to sit and taking the chair across from Arial. 'This is Ruth you're talking about? You say she's in a coma? But I just saw her yesterday.'

'Day before,' Sarah said. 'She didn't make it yesterday. Coma.'

I thought more explanation might be in order. 'We found her at home unconscious when she didn't show up at the wake.'

'On the same day her own mother was buried,' Ian said. 'I am so sorry. But that's the way it is in families sometimes. With longtime mates, as well. One half of the couple goes and the other follows soon after. Is her condition improving at all?'

'We haven't had any updates since first thing this morning,' Arial said, involuntarily reaching for her phone.

Sarah reached over to stay her hand. 'The doctor said that at this point we should consider no news good news. Remember?'

'Ruth must have missed her mother terribly,' the funeral director said.

Arial nodded with a little sniffle, seeming to waffle between grief and . . . well, I wasn't quite sure. Relief? Disinterest? Practicality?

Whichever, it seemed to run in the family, given Ruth's paint preparations and the new SUV she'd purchased at Edna's passing. 'Terribly,' I echoed.

'Now we will hope for the best, but prepare for the . . . well, we all do die.' He flipped open a leather-bound notebook placed strategically on the glossy wood table. 'Do we know Ruth's wishes?'

'Not to be dropped,' Sarah said in a stage whisper.

Ian cleared his throat. 'For example, would she prefer burial or cremation?'

Sarah and Arial looked at each other.

'She did request burial for her mother,' Barrymore prompted.

'Edna had strong feelings about resurrection and such,' Sarah said. 'But I'm not sure if Ruth shares them.'

'Or just went along with them, like she did everything else,' Arial said, rallying. 'We'll consider cremation, but I'd also be interested in seeing what you have in eco-friendly caskets. Pine, perhaps? Bamboo?'

'Cardboard?' Sarah added.

'Of course, of course,' Ian said, getting up. 'Let me just go . . .'

The moment he was out of the room, Arial had the ribbons untied and the box open. 'Here,' she said, running her finger along the page, '"Melinda" . . . I think it's "Pagrovian." Weird name to make up.'

'Not Smith or Doe, at least,' Sarah said. 'The woman has imagination.'

'Maybe it's her real name,' I said, watching Arial take a photo and then slip the book back into its box. 'We don't need to be furtive. Aren't we taking the book with us?'

'Yes, but I didn't know he'd have it ready,' Arial said. 'And besides, I'm not lugging the thing around with me. A photo is easier.'

Because everything is best kept on our phones. Until we lose them.

'Anyway,' Arial continued, 'Melinda is obviously not a master criminal. She kept changing her story and she was pretty obvious in her surveillance of the house.'

If surveillance was what she was doing. But what else could it have been? Casing the joint? 'We should check with Caron and see if a Melinda Pagrovian is staying at the Morrison.'

My former partner in Uncommon Grounds, Caron Egan, had purchased an historical hotel with her attorney husband Bernie. The Hotel Morrison was the best hotel in Brookhills and not just because it was the only hotel in Brookhills.

'Can you text her?' Arial asked.

'I can, but she won't tell me over the phone,' I said, standing. 'Privacy issues.'

'But she'll tell you in person?'

'Only because Maggy will torture her until she does,' Sarah said, getting to her feet.

'So best done in person.' Arial picked up the box and the envelope with the death certificates. 'I get it.'

'Now, we do intend to bring in representative samples of our natural options,' Ian said, returning to the room with his laptop. He seemed surprised to see we were all standing, but went with it, setting up his computer on the end of the table and punching up a website. 'But for now, they're probably best viewed online. There's the proverbial pine box, of course, but also bamboo and wicker. And while the cardboard isn't much to look at, it's completely biodegradable and can be decorated with writing or photos of the loved one and—'

'They really have cardboard?' Sarah said, giving him a little nudge so she could see the screen. 'I was just messing with you.'

'Oh, yes,' Ian said. 'And very affordable, as you might expect.'

'You wouldn't even need a discount,' I told her.

'It's a coffin-shaped shoebox, essentially,' Sarah said. 'I like it.'

'A non-bleach whitening process is used,' Ian said, warming to his subject. 'And no metal, of course, because that won't degrade. The casket is constructed using a starch-based adhesive.'

'I'm afraid we've had a call from the hospital and need to go,' Arial fibbed, rounding the table to him to hand him a card. 'For now, could you send me the link to that website, and we'll finish another time?'

'Of course,' Ian said, getting up to follow us to the foyer. 'I do hope the call from the hospital isn't bad news about your mother.'

'I hope so, too,' Arial said, as he opened the door for her. 'But if so . . .'

Barrymore slipped a card from a silver cardholder and gave it to her. 'We'll just need a phone call from you. We'll pick up your mother's body at the hospital, you can make a few decisions and leave the rest to us.'

'Thank you so much.' Arial stepped out onto the porch and shifted the guest book to the other side so she could shake hands with him. 'You've been very helpful.'

'You have,' Sarah said pleasantly. 'Despite dropping my mother.'

Ian's hands went up and his voice dropped. 'I am so sorry. I had a new man on. Believe me, nothing like that will happen to . . . Ruth is your sister, correct?'

'Yes.' Sarah smiled at him. 'And I know it won't. But . . .'

He cleared his throat. 'And, of course, I will offer you the same discount on whatever you choose for your dear sister.'

Sarah just waited.

'And . . .' he said uncertainly, ' . . . umm, any other members of the family who might pass this year—'

She cleared her own throat.

'Or . . . ever?' he croaked.

Sarah shook his hand.

'That poor man,' I told Sarah as Barrymore closed the door behind us. 'And I thought Cokely was a ghoul. *You*, my friend, have him beat.'

Arial was regarding her aunt suspiciously as we moved to the car. 'Just how many of us do you expect to bite the dust?'

'This year?' Sarah was waiting for me to unlock the car. 'None of us, hopefully, which is why I pressed for the lifetime discount.'

But whose lifetime? 'Just how many of you are there anyway?' I asked, pushing the key fob to unlock. 'I was getting the impression that the two of you are it.'

'I honestly don't know. As you can tell, we're not exactly close-knit.' Sarah swung open her door to get in once more. 'If you like, I can sneak you in on the discount. Who's going to notice one more?'

'Thanks, but I'll pay my own way,' I said. 'That woven bamboo one on the website was very affordable.'

Arial held it up. 'That is nice, isn't it?'

'The wicker, too,' I said. 'And ye ol' pine box. Nothing wrong with simplicity.'

'Are you two going to get in?' Sarah asked.

'Door's still locked,' Arial said, trying the handle.

'Sorry, Arial. Here you go.' I popped the unlock a second time and went around to the driver's side.

'Why do you lock it anyway?' Arial asked, climbing in. 'This is Brookhills, and we're parked at a mortuary.'

'Yeah, Maggy. If somebody wanted to steal a car, they'd take one of those nice big black ones with room for storage.' Sarah was pointing at the fleet of hearses, of course.

'It's not entire cars they take,' I told Arial. 'We have a band of catalytic converter thieves operating here. One of my friends had three of them stolen off her Prius.'

'Well, all the door locking in the world isn't going to stop that,' Arial said as I turned the ignition. 'All they have to do is climb under.'

'I know,' I said. 'It just messes with my sense of security, I guess.'

'And the cavalcade of murders that dances through your life doesn't?' Sarah sniffed.

'You know,' Arial said, leaning forward earnestly, 'I threw out the eco-friendly casket idea on a whim, but I think that's what we should do for Ruth, if she passes.'

'Absolutely,' Sarah said. 'I'm especially jazzed about the cardboard coffin idea. I might get one for myself.'

'Now?' I asked.

'Sure, why not? Gives me time to decorate it. And when I feel like I'm about to go, I'll just lie down in it. You all can slap the lid on and shuffle me off to the mortuary.'

'Tidy.' Putting the car in drive, I noticed a paper snagged under the windshield wiper. 'Damn advertising flyers. Even in a funeral home's parking lot.'

'I'll get it,' Arial said, hopping out to pluck the paper off the windshield. 'Where should we head nex— Hmm.'

'Something wrong?' Sarah asked, as her niece got back into the car, studying the flyer.

'Or in poor taste?' Like a bury-one-get-one-free offer.

Arial passed it up to her aunt.

'"If you want the truth,"' Sarah read, '"don't cremate her."'

TEN

'"Her," meaning my mother?' Arial said, as we pulled away from the curb. 'Obeying the note isn't going to be a problem, since Ruth's not dead.'

'They can't mean Edna,' Sarah said. 'She's already in the ground.'

'She is?' Given the visitation was just last night, you'd normally expect the private burial to be today. And Sarah and Arial to be there. But given the circumstances . . . 'You aren't having something graveside?'

'Per Edna's wishes, as relayed by Ruth,' Sarah said. 'A closed-casket visitation and then immediate internment by the funeral home.'

'You don't think that's a little . . . perfunctory?' I asked.

'Sarah wants to be buried in a cardboard box,' Arial said. 'Doesn't get more perfunctory than that.'

'I'm all for simplicity and eco-friendliness,' I said, twisting to glance back at Arial. 'But it was Ruth who planned Edna's funeral and they were both kind of old style. Yet there wasn't even a service—'

'Watch the road.' Sarah smacked my shoulder. 'Yes, just a visitation, which is what Edna wanted and Ruth arranged.'

I turned back to the road in time to make a quick left onto Brookhills Road. 'But I thought they were both religious. You know, Saint Ruth and the whole suicide is a sin thing.'

'Being "holy" and being "holier than thou" are two different things,' Arial muttered. 'Did you want to stop at Uncommon Grounds?'

'No, I'm going straight to the Morrison,' I told her as we passed the coffeehouse. 'If Melinda left that note, I want to find her sooner rather than later.'

'Good thought,' Arial said, settling back. 'You know, whoever left that note thinks Ruth is dead.'

She was right. But it was Edna's quick interment that was

bothering me just this second. Had it really been the older woman's choice? Or was Ruth in a hurry to put her mother in the ground for some reason? But if so, why not cremate Edna's body? As the note hinted, it was a great way of keeping secrets.

Maybe we should be looking into the deaths of both the mother and the daughter.

'I suppose Edna didn't want to be cremated?' I asked idly, turning the car into the Hotel Morrison's parking lot.

'Can't be resurrected if you don't have a body,' Sarah sing-songed.

'And yet they weren't religious.' I drove up one aisle of the parking lot and circled to the next.

'There's a spot there,' Sarah pointed out.

I kept going.

'Don't try to make sense of it, Maggy,' Arial told me as I turned up the last aisle. 'Edna was eclectic in her beliefs.'

Her aunt groaned. 'If by "eclectic" you mean Edna used whatever Bible verse was convenient to bludgeon us into submission, you're right there. Hey, watch it!'

I had made a quick right into a space and slammed on the brakes. 'Parking spot.'

'There are lots of spots,' Sarah grumbled, unbelting. 'You couldn't have parked up near the—'

'Sorry.' I pointed to the car next to us. 'Blue Corolla.'

'Way to go, Maggy,' Arial said, hopping out to peer into the Toyota. 'Black and gold scarf in the back seat.'

'Melinda was wearing that at the visitation,' I said, shading my eyes to look. 'This has to be hers.'

'Which means you're right.' Sarah was rubbing the back of her neck. 'You didn't have to give me whiplash to prove it.'

'Sorry,' I said again, even though I wasn't. 'Now let's find Caron and see if we can convince her to tell us what room Melinda is in.'

Arial was already at the front entrance, looking back toward the street. 'Wow, I haven't paid much attention, but the Morrison's grounds and entrance are looking amazing.'

Caron and Bernie had spent a fair amount of time and money renovating the lobby and were gradually updating the rooms and the exterior.

'It does look good, doesn't it?' Stepping past Arial and through the revolving doors into the lobby, I looked to see who was staffing the front desk. 'Bingo.'

'Caron?' Sarah asked, following me in.

'Better,' I said. 'Bernie.'

At the sound of his name, attorney-by-day and hotelier-by-night Bernie Egan lifted his round, mostly bald head and beamed at me. 'Maggy. You just missed Caron. A vase went missing from the third-floor elevator lobby and she's on the warpath.'

'A guest stole it?' Sarah asked.

'Given the size, Caron thinks it's more likely one of the housekeepers broke it and is afraid to own up to it.'

Having worked with Caron, I didn't blame said housekeeper.

'Is it valuable?' I asked, going in for a hug over the counter.

'Unlikely,' he said. 'But you know Caron. She's not going to let it go.'

'I still bet it walked out of here packed in a guest's oversized suitcase along with a towel or ten,' Sarah said, raising a hand in greeting to Bernie. 'You know my niece Arial, don't you?'

'Of course, I do,' he said.

Arial grinned. 'Bernie was kind enough to give me legal advice when I got caught up in that . . .'

'Business,' Bernie supplied, circling the desk to hug her, too. 'And I believe all I did was recommend a good criminal attorney.'

'And tell me to find better friends,' Arial said. 'Both excellent bits of advice.'

'I think I gave you the same advice on the friends,' Sarah said. 'Several times.'

'Sometimes it just takes getting arrested for something to sink in,' Arial said, and turned to Bernie. 'This place looks terrific. I would have barely recognized it from the street.'

'Because now you can see the hotel from the street,' he said. 'Standard maintenance, according to our groundskeeper, but—'

'You have a groundskeeper?' I asked, suppressing a smile. 'How very civilized of you.'

Bernie grinned and glanced around to see if anyone was listening – most probably his wife. 'It's Caron's idea, calling him that. It feels a bit *Downton Abbey*, but Jackson thinks it's funny. He—'

'Jackson?' Sarah interrupted. 'And you didn't make him the butler?'

Bernie grinned. 'He'd probably make a great one. Truth is, though, he can do a little bit of everything. As far as I'm concerned, his real value is keeping the hotel chugging along. I'm not great with my hands and a hotel is only as good as its showers are hot and its sheets are clean.'

'Wait.' I was holding up a hand. 'Doesn't that make him a Ja—'

'Please don't say a Jack-of-all-trades,' Sarah said, elbowing me. 'Or I'll have to kill you.'

'Not in the lobby,' Bernie warned, raising his hand in greeting as a man in coveralls passed through from the elevators. 'Speak of the devil, there he is now.'

'That was Jackson?' The man seemed vaguely familiar. 'Jackson what?'

'Morrison,' Bernie said. 'He's a third cousin or something to the former owners.'

Even that vaunted last name didn't help, but then I wasn't sure if I knew many Jacksons at all. Or any Morrisons.

'We'd be lost without the man,' Bernie continued. 'He played here as a kid, so he knows every foot of the place.'

'Why did the Morrisons sell?' Arial asked.

'Ahh, you know. The hotel business is tough and the four Morrison kids – or really great-grandkids of the founders now – were brought up here and are pretty much over it.'

'They preferred eight-hour-a-day jobs rather than twenty-four/seven?' Sarah guessed.

'That, and I doubt the hotel made enough money to support all four families,' Bernie said.

'Had to go out and get real paying jobs, huh?' Sarah slapped him on the shoulder.

Bernie gave her a good-natured shove back. 'Believe me, if I didn't have my day job as a lawyer, we would be struggling.'

'Renovations don't come cheap,' Sarah said. 'This building has to be eighty years old.'

'It is. Though there have been some improvements over the years. And luckily the grounds haven't cost too much. The plants and trees were there, just so overgrown you could hardly see the building. Jackson recommended we cut back some things, transplant others and *voilà*.'

'So not a ton of investment beyond labor,' Sarah, the former real estate guru said. 'That's good.'

Arial sighed, taking it all in as she sank onto the plushy lobby couch. 'I considered going into hospitality. You know, run a bed-and-breakfast or something.'

'Like Sarah said, it's a twenty-four/seven business,' Bernie warned. 'Not much time to sit on the couch.'

Arial laughed. 'Just knowing I owned the couch I slept on would be enough.'

'You own significantly more than a couch now,' Sarah reminded her niece and turned to Bernie by way of explanation. 'My mother left Arial a property in California as well as the house here.'

Arial was shaking her head. 'It's like after a quarter of a century on this planet, I suddenly crash-landed into adulthood.'

'Just be grateful you didn't inherit any kids,' Sarah told her. 'It ages you.'

'Don't listen to her,' Bernie told Arial. 'If anything, "inheriting" Sam and Courtney when Patricia died has kept Sarah young.'

'Young, huh?' Arial was grinning at Sarah.

'Childlike, at the very least,' was my contribution. 'Did you know Edna Kingston, Bernie?'

'Not really, but Caron told me she'd died,' Bernie said. 'And we heard about Ruth's accident just this morning. How is she doing?'

'She's in a coma,' Sarah said. 'Apparently severe carbon monoxide poisoning can do that. Whether it's what they call a prolonged coma or she'll come out of it – with or without neurological damage – we just don't know at this point.'

Bernie shook his head and turned to Arial. 'You told me that the relationship between you and your mother was difficult, but I am sorry. It can't be easy having your grandmother gone and your mother hospitalized within the space of a few days.'

'Thank you,' she said. 'We can't do anything to help Ruth, but at least we can try to figure out what happened.'

Bernie's eyes narrowed now and shifted sideways to me. 'Meaning what?'

I held up my hands. 'This is not on me. Ruth was poisoned

by carbon monoxide from a faulty furnace. I didn't suggest anything else.' My voice got small. 'Until asked.'

'I don't believe it was an accident,' Arial told him flatly.

'Why?'

'Well, for one,' she folded her arms, 'the batteries were taken out of the carbon monoxide detectors.'

'But lots of people forget to replace their—' Bernie started.

'The detectors didn't have batteries in them, yet two perfectly good nine-volt batteries had been thrown in the trash,' Arial said.

'Because a mysterious killer removed them?' Bernie asked, frowning. 'That seems a stretch.'

'Or my mother could have taken them out herself,' Arial said. 'We're not ruling out the possibility that she committed suicide.'

'In fact, it seems the most logical explanation at this point,' Sarah said.

'But don't forget the paint and the new car,' I said. 'They don't fit.'

Bernie just cocked his head, waiting for an explanation.

'My mother bought a new SUV two days after my grandmother died,' Arial explained. 'And she had primed my grandmother's room and was already trying out paint colors.'

'Then shouldn't you be looking into whether your mother topped your grandmother?' The words were out of Bernie's mouth before he could apparently stop them. His eyes got big. 'Sorry.'

'Don't be sorry,' Arial said.

'But probably don't search that online,' I interjected, given what Pavlik had told me about pirates.

I got blank stares from all three of them.

'It just can lead to pirates . . . well, never mind,' I finished lamely. 'I'll tell you another time.'

'Aye, matey,' Sarah said, before turning back. 'I don't blame you for asking the question, Bernie. In fact, Maggy has been making noises about how quickly Ruth wanted Edna in the ground.'

It did seem . . . expedient. And if we were looking for a reason to explain why Ruth might have wanted to kill herself, a fit of sudden remorse at shoving her mother through death's door was right up there. But so many other things didn't make sense. 'Edna's doctor signed off on the death certificate. And with her already buried . . .' I shrugged.

'C'mon, Maggy,' Sarah said. 'Where's that let's-exhume-the-body can-do attitude we've come to know and loathe?'

Bernie snorted. 'You're a fine one to talk, Sarah. You're right in there with her. Maggy couldn't have found a better partner after Caron bowed out.'

'Well, thank you.' Sarah blushed. 'I do save the day quite often.'

Arial rolled her eyes. 'What Bernie is really saying is that you're as cray-cray as Maggy. You realize that, don't you?'

'Of course,' Sarah said. 'What's important is that Maggy knows that if she wants to dig up my mother, I'll be right there handing her the shovel. Unlike Caron.'

'And for that I'm eternally thankful,' Caron's husband said, shaking his head.

'No worries,' I said. 'We're still fact-finding at the moment. In particular, we're trying to identify a woman who came to Edna's wake yesterday – someone we didn't know.'

'I didn't know pretty much everybody,' Sarah said. 'To be fair.'

'But this someone gave three different stories about how she knew my grandmother,' Arial told Bernie. '*And* she's been following us. We saw her in a car parked outside my mother's house just now. We think she left—'

I cut her off before she could fish the note out of her pocket. 'She left her car in your parking lot.'

Bernie closed his eyes and groaned. 'I knew this wasn't a social call.'

I cocked my head. 'I don't make a lot of social calls.'

'You don't make any social calls,' Bernie said, circling back behind the desk. 'Do you have the license plate number?'

I recited it for him and added, 'Blue Toyota Corolla.'

'Are you allowed to just give us her name?' Arial asked curiously, as Bernie tapped on the computer keys.

'Absolutely not, but Maggy will get it somehow anyways,' Bernie said, and punched one last button. 'Melinda Springbok.'

Springbok, not Pagrovian. But then, she would have had to present a credit card or ID checking in, so lying would be more difficult. 'Room number?'

'Now that I can't give you,' Bernie said. 'Privacy and safety issues.'

Arial wrinkled her nose. 'But you just—'

'I know, I know,' Bernie said. 'I gave you her name, which is also invading her privacy. But she did show up at your grandmother's funeral.'

'Good point,' I said, weighing how much I should tell Bernie in the quest to squeeze more information out of him. 'We also think she left a threatening note on my car.'

'Which means she's virtually asking to be found, doesn't it?' Arial added.

'It does,' a voice said, and we whirled to see the young dark-haired woman. 'And here I am.'

We were sitting now, rather than standing, in the lobby of the Hotel Morrison. Arial and Melinda were seated on the couch while Sarah and I had taken the two armchairs across the coffee table from them. Bernie had supplied coffee and there was an awkward silence as we waited for the waiter to finish pouring the last cup – Melinda's – from the French press.

'Thank you,' the young woman said, lifting the cup to take a sip. I thought I detected a slight tremor in her hands.

'Who are you?' Arial asked, leaving her cup untouched as she watched Melinda. 'Why did you come to my grandmother's funeral and why are you stalking us?'

'I'm not stalking you,' Melinda said, setting down the cup. 'You really should try the coffee. It's delicious.'

'We own a coffeehouse,' Sarah said crossly. 'We don't need coffee recommendations from the likes of you.'

'Apparently not,' the woman said, holding up her hands. 'Sorry.'

Silence.

'It really is good coffee,' I said, making a try at conversation. 'Caron and Bernie – they're the owners of the Morrison – specifically do press pot because we don't have it at the shop. Caron was my former partner at Uncommon—'

'She doesn't need your life story,' Sarah snapped. 'We need hers.'

'I'm trying to put everybody at ease,' I countered. 'Nobody has done anything wrong, that we know of.'

'Except maybe breaking into my mother's house overnight.' Arial dug out the paper we'd found under the windshield wiper and flattened it on the coffee table. 'And certainly threatening us.'

'That note was meant to help you,' Melinda said.

The woman was petite, not much bigger than Arial, and her voice was soft and melodic. She didn't look like a thief. Or an attempted killer, if that's where Arial was going with this.

'Did you want to "help" my mother, too?'

Yup, that's where she was going.

'I don't know what you're talking about,' Melinda said. 'I was hoping to speak to your mother at the wake. When she wasn't there, I went to the house with the rest of the attendees, hoping to get a moment alone with her there instead. Believe me, I was disappointed when I couldn't.'

Disappointed. It was an odd word to use.

'How did you know Ruth had died?' Arial, smart girl, didn't correct the misconception.

'Your trip to the funeral home,' Melinda said. 'I'm sorry for your loss.'

'You broke into the house last night after the police and fire department left,' Sarah said. 'What were you looking for?'

'I didn't break in,' she countered automatically, her face reddening a bit. 'The door around back was open.'

'The door around back was forced,' I corrected.

'Perhaps, but not by me.' She shoved a lock of dark hair behind one ear. 'In fact, I didn't go in. I barely got there when the fire department showed up.'

'This morning you're talking about?' I asked. 'Not yesterday.'

'Yes, this morning.' Melinda opened her purse and took out a paper of her own, slipping it under her coffee cup. 'I went there looking for proof.'

'Proof of what?' Arial's mouth had dropped open. 'That my mother's asphyxiation wasn't an accident?'

'Or that Edna had been killed.' I glanced sideways at Sarah. 'Sorry. Again.'

'Your . . .' Melinda seemed shocked. 'What are you talking about? I thought Edna Mayes died a natural death. And what are you saying about Ruth?'

'You tell us.' Sarah seemed to be losing her patience. 'You're the one skulking around, remember?'

'I wasn't skulking really,' she said, now just the tip of her nose bright red. 'More looking for a time I could talk to . . . well, first Ruth, but now I guess Arial.'

'You had plenty of opportunities to talk to Arial,' I pointed out. 'Even if Ruth wasn't at the funeral, Arial was. And you were parked in front of the house this morning *and* at the funeral home.'

'Where you deduced my mother was dead and left us a cryptic message.' Arial shoved the paper toward her.

'I just . . . well, I thought you were making funeral arrangements for Ruth. I didn't want you—'

'You didn't want us to cremate Ruth,' Arial said. 'Why?'

Melinda said something, but her chin was on her chest and her voice so soft I could barely hear her.

'Speak up!' Sarah snapped.

'DNA. You see,' she lifted her face and turned to Arial, 'I think I'm your sister.'

ELEVEN

'Half-sister, to be precise,' Melinda continued.

Looking at them side by side from across the coffee table, I had to admit there was a resemblance. Melinda's hair was darker than Arial's reddish-brown, but along the same lines. Build – both petite. And both very attractive, as evidenced by the stare of a young man passing through the lobby.

Sarah glared at the man. 'What are you looking at?'

The guy blinked twice and then wisely scurried away, rubbing his fashionably stubbly chin.

Sarah turned on Melinda. 'How old are you?'

'Twenty-eight,' she said.

'Three years older than me.' Arial was studying her face. 'Who is your father?'

'Jonathan Springbok,' Melinda said.

'And you think he's also Arial's father – why?' Sarah asked. 'Did he tell you he and Ruth had a relationship?'

'One-night stand,' Arial corrected. 'Or at least that's how the story was always told to me. One-night stand with some computer guy.'

Which was why Arial's name was spelled with an 'a' like the computer font, instead of an 'e' like the mermaid. It was Edna's little joke, according to Sarah, intended to remind Ruth of her indiscretion. Fun family.

' . . . Father was attending a tech thing at the Monterey Convention Center that December, almost twenty-six years ago,' Melinda was saying. 'Apparently it was part conference, part holiday party.'

'Would you have been there for the holidays?' I asked, turning to Sarah.

'The year Arial was conceived, I assume we're talking about? No, but Edna and Ruth were.'

Arial cocked her head to regard Melinda. 'Does your family live in Monterey?'

'No, we were in Portland at the time. My dad just flew down for the conference.'

'Does your "dad" know he got Ruth pregnant?' Sarah asked. 'Ruth must have told him about Arial.'

'No, and no.' Melinda shifted to face Arial dead on. 'I'm so sorry to spring this on you.'

'You could have picked a better time.' First Arial's grandmother dies, then her mother falls into a coma. And now a supposed sister appears out of nowhere? Even in a dysfunctional family, this was a bad week.

'I'm sorry,' Melinda said again, tears rising in her eyes as she pulled the paper out from under her coffee cup. 'But I just found out myself. When I read Edna Mayes Kingston's obituary in the local paper . . .'

Arial glanced at me and then back to Melinda. 'That's the article in the Carmel paper. I thought you live in Portland.'

'I lived in Portland as a kid. I went to school at CSUMB – that's California State University of Monterey Bay – and stayed there for a job.'

'Dad has a soft spot for Monterey?' Arial's tone dripped sarcasm.

'Dad is dead,' Melinda said, looking down at her hands. 'He never left Monterey that December.'

We were on our second press pot.

'Let me get this straight,' Sarah said. 'Your father died in a car crash the last day of the same conference that Arial was . . .'

'Conceived,' the fetus supplied.

'Crossing the street early the next morning to catch the shuttle to the airport,' Melinda confirmed. 'I was two, so obviously don't know first-hand, but my mom said she left me with my grand-mother and hopped on a plane to Monterey. They thought my father might pull through, but . . .'

'But he didn't,' I said after a second.

'Internal bleeding,' Melinda said. 'He died that same night, just hours after my mother got there. She told me later, much later, that she wished she hadn't made it in time. Because then she'd . . . never have known.'

'About me.' Arial had tears in her eyes now. 'I can understand that.'

'Not about you,' Melinda said, putting her hand on Arial's shoulder. 'Like I said, my father never knew that your mother was even pregnant – how could he? But he did confess to my mother that he'd cheated.'

'Deathbed confession,' Sarah said.

'He probably didn't want to die with it on his conscience,' I offered Melinda.

'So instead, he left my mother with a broken heart.'

There was that.

'Oh, God,' Arial said, rubbing her forehead. 'Are you sure about all this?'

'Honestly, no. My father told my mother that the young woman's name was Ruth and that her mother was some painter called Edna. Said he thought her last name was Pagrovian.' She smiled wryly.

'That's the name you used in the guest register at the wake,' I said.

'Yes, because I'm an idiot. I was making things up as I went, and it was the first thing that came to my mind. I didn't want to use my own name.'

'Though you had to use it here at the hotel,' I said. 'You needed a credit card, or at least an ID, to check in.'

'Of course I did,' she said, shaking her head. 'I guess I'm not very good at this. I don't even know what I hoped to accomplish. My mom is dead and my—'

'Your mom died recently?' Arial asked.

'About a year ago. That's when this all came out.' She smiled. 'Guess deathbed secrets must run in the family.'

'Not this branch,' Arial said. 'We take our sins to the grave.'

'There's something to be said for that,' Melinda said.

I was trying to understand. 'So your mom dies. You're feeling sad and a year later Edna's obit pops up in the local paper and you realize she's the painter your father mentioned – the mother of the woman he had the affair with. That's quite a coincidence.'

'It does sound like it,' Melinda admitted. 'But I guess it felt like unfinished business. I knew that my mother tried to find Ruth after my father died and—'

'Why?' I asked. 'Like you said, your father was dead.'

'Maggy is asking whether your mother wanted revenge,' Sarah said. 'It's the way her mind works.'

Instead of seeming horrified, Melinda looked thoughtful. 'I think it was natural curiosity. You know, who was this woman? What did she look like? Why would my father have been tempted?'

'I wonder if she ever found her,' Arial said.

'My mother – Joan was her name – was a shy person at heart,' Melinda said. 'I doubt she'd have had the nerve to confront Ruth, even if she did find her. But now that she and Ruth are both dead, we'll probably never know for sure.'

Ruth, not really being dead, might be able to tell us if she ever came out of her coma. But Melinda didn't know that.

'There was enough information,' I said. 'From what Jonathan told your mother, Joan should have been able to find Gretchen Mayes – mother of the painter Edna and grandmother of Ruth, the one-night stand – living on the peninsula.'

Arial seemed doubtful. 'It wasn't as easy to find people back then.'

In the stone age, apparently.

'Besides,' Sarah said, 'Edna and Ruth were living in Denver at the time, remember?'

Still. But I let it go. 'Who were the Pagrovians? Any relation to Edna?'

'No.' Melinda smiled, as she had when she'd mentioned the name in the first place. 'Ruth must have given my father a false name.'

'Like you did at the funeral home,' I said. 'But why Pagrovian?'

'I realized what it meant when I moved to the peninsula,' Melinda said. 'Pagrovians are what people who live in Pacific Grove call themselves.'

'I didn't remember that,' Sarah muttered. 'Probably because it's stupid.'

'Actually, I think it's kind of fun,' Arial said. 'More distinctive than Pacific Grovers certainly.'

'Certainly.' Melinda's smile got bigger. 'From Edna's obituary and what I've been able to piece together since, your grandparents – or I guess it would be your great-grandparents – lived there.'

'The Mayes family of Pacific Grove,' Sarah confirmed. I

noticed she didn't tell this supposed new relation that Arial had inherited the property.

'But you didn't tip to what a Pagrovian is?' I asked Sarah.

Sarah shrugged. 'Who pays attention to that stuff, especially when you're a kid. I just liked that I could bicycle all over and go to the beach.'

'The house is still there,' Melinda said, and colored up. 'I . . . uh, went by when I found the family name in the obituary.'

'What shape is it in?' Arial asked.

'Old, but a lot of houses in PG are like that. Historical,' Melinda said.

'Could you tell if somebody was living there?' Sarah asked. 'Hopefully somebody who's paying the taxes?'

'Maybe Edna took care of that,' Arial said. 'Or the trust.'

'We still need to get into Ruth's house to be sure and get the rest of what we need,' Sarah said. 'You don't want to fall behind in taxes, Arial, or they can attach the property.'

'You inherited?' Melinda asked her half-sister, eyes wide.

'You didn't say if somebody is living in the house,' I reminded her, since I didn't think Arial's inheritance was any of her business.

'Maybe,' Melinda said. 'Just be aware that whatever shape the house is in, it will be worth a fortune. Don't let somebody buy it cheap.'

'I won't,' Arial said, her eyes suddenly wary.

Sarah seemed on the same wavelength. 'What exactly do you get out of this little jaunt?' she asked Melinda. 'I mean, even if you and Arial are related through your father, you don't have a claim on anything here. Or in Pacific Grove, for that matter.'

'No, you're right,' Melinda said. 'In fact, if there's anybody who would have a claim, it's Arial. On my father's estate.'

That seemed an extraordinarily generous take on the situation. Though more than twenty-five years after his death, presumably her father's estate was settled.

'Not interested,' Arial said flatly.

'Fair enough,' Melinda said. 'But . . . aren't you the least bit curious?'

'About what?' Arial was still studying her. 'Having a sister?'

'Maybe you do, maybe you don't,' Sarah cautioned. 'We need proof, as Melissa's little missive points out.'

'Melinda,' I corrected automatically. 'I don't know if DNA is routinely taken at an autopsy,' I said, playing along with the 'Ruth is dead' thing, 'but I don't quite understand why Ruth's DNA is needed. We have Arial.'

'That's true. The two of us can just take DNA tests,' Arial said, hooking a thumb Melinda's way. 'Since there's no way that Ruth isn't my mother, presumably—'

'Saw you come out,' Sarah confirmed.

'Charming,' Arial said. 'Then if the test shows we're half-sisters, we know Melinda's father is my father.'

'That makes sense.' Sarah's head was cocked as she rubbed her chin. 'Beyond that, though, I was thinking we should take a trip west.'

I eyed her. 'To Pacific Grove?'

'Exactly. We need to tie up a few odds and ends at the house here first, but after that we can go meet the family.' Sarah tossed a toothy grin at Melinda that edged on menacing.

Melinda blinked. 'If you mean my father's side, they're in Portland. There's just me in Monterey.'

'No matter,' Arial said. 'I want to see the house anyway. Melinda can show us around, and you'll come, too, Maggy. Right?'

'Absolutely,' I said, having had no thoughts of it being otherwise.

'Great.' Even Melinda seemed to be jumping on the westward-bound bandwagon. 'Search for flights into Monterey, that's MRY. It's a nice little airport, otherwise you have to drive from San Jose or San Francisco – an hour and a half or two hours respectively. And that's if there's no traffic.'

'MRY, got it.' Arial was already busy on her mobile. 'Meanwhile, you want to see where you and I can get the DNA testing?'

'Sure, in-person or a kit?'

'Probably better if we can have it done at a lab here before we leave,' Arial said. 'But otherwise see if we can just get a kit at the drug store and send the samples in.'

'On it,' Melinda said, as Sarah and I exchanged looks.

Sarah leaned my way. 'Arial has taken to her supposed sister awfully quickly,' she said in a low voice.

'You have your doubts?'

She shrugged. 'Trust but verify.'

'Which the DNA test will do. Eventually,' I said. 'But I assume even the tests conducted at a lab could take a few days to process and get results.'

'Meanwhile, they're picking out matching sweater sets,' Sarah said, eyeing the two younger women.

'Jealous?' I asked.

'Maybe. Arial and I have always been close. She considers me the normal one in the family.' She eyed me. 'Hard as that might be for you to believe.'

'Given what I've heard about Ruth and Edna over the past couple of days, I must concur.'

'That's unusually kind of you,' Sarah said.

'Because I'm unusually kind,' I said, lowering my voice as I went to get out my phone. 'Listen, I know you're suspicious of Melinda. I am, too, but for a different reason.' I looked up. 'Why would she think we needed Ruth's DNA to prove paternity? Kids now know all about ancestry and DNA. She had to know it was Arial's we needed.'

'You're right – Ruth is no relation to her,' Sarah said, rubbing her chin with her thumbnail. 'She's irrelevant in the equation. Jonathan Springbok's DNA would be helpful, but that ship has long sailed, unless you want to exhume another body.'

'Again, no need,' I said. 'A DNA test should show the two girls have a fifty percent match, which has to be Jonathan Springbok, unless somebody else had sex with both Ruth and Joan.'

'Probably a long shot,' Sarah agreed. 'What are you doing?'

'I'm texting Pavlik to see if Kelly's people are done at the house. Maybe we can go over there right now.'

'Good idea,' Sarah said. 'About this trip. Do you think Amy will be OK with manning the fort alone for a few days?'

'Absolutely not,' I said, glancing sideways at her. 'And don't think I'm going to volunteer to stay behind.'

'I didn't.'

'Good. Because now I'm going to text Tien to see if she can

help out while we're gone. She told me the catering side is a little slow right now, so maybe she'd like the hours.'

'Another good idea,' Sarah said. 'It'll also assuage your conscience.'

'And yours,' I said.

'But I have to go to California,' Sarah said. 'Arial's my niece. You're just a hanger-on.'

'I am . . .' OK, maybe I was.

Arial looked up from her phone, apparently having been oblivious to us and our conversation. 'Think four days is enough? Today is Monday. We could fly out Thursday and come back Monday. Fares aren't too bad.'

'Once you get there, you won't want to leave,' Melinda warned, getting up. 'Do you know where the restroom is down here?'

'To the left of the revolving door,' I told her. 'Down that little hall.'

'Do you already have your return flight?' Arial called after her, as she hurried away. 'Or should I book four seats?'

But Melinda just held up a finger to wait, as she dodged incoming cross-traffic from the front door and ducked into the hallway.

'When you got to go, you got to go,' Sarah said.

'What are you?' I asked. 'Five years old?'

'You should talk, Maggy.' Arial's tone was chiding. 'Or, actually, you shouldn't. Melinda and I could hear practically every word you said.'

'We lowered our voices,' I protested.

'Thing is we're in our twenties, not our eighties,' Arial said. 'We can still hear. And speaking of being old, matching sweater sets haven't been a thing since June Cleaver.'

'Wow,' I said, my eyes wide.

Arial blushed. 'I'm sorry. I don't mean to be cruel, but—'

'No,' I said. 'I'm just impressed you know who June Cleaver was.'

'You don't have to have watched *Leave It to Beaver* to get the reference,' Sarah told me. 'Nineteen Fifties, stay-at-home mom, sweater sets, pearls.'

'Sarah's right,' Arial said. 'It's like Kleenex here and Hoovering in the UK. June Cleaver has transcended her original character.'

My phone pinged a text message. I picked it up. 'Pavlik says his people have finished with the crime scene and we can go in and look for Ruth's personal papers. He just wants a list of everything we take.'

'Crime scene?' Arial repeated. 'Is that literally what he called it? I thought Ruth's poisoning was an accident from the fire investigators' point of view.'

I held up the phone so she could see. 'He does say crime scene, but maybe he's talking about the break-in.'

'Maybe so.' Arial was chewing it over.

Pavlik chose his words carefully and meant what he said. Which was annoying at times, given my predilection to saying whatever came into my head. 'Melinda needs to tell Pavlik or Kelly Anthony that she was at the house this morning.'

'Why would she do that?' Arial asked. 'The door was already damaged, and she didn't go in. What good will it do to raise the issue?'

This from the one of us who just got off probation.

'I can't believe you'd say that,' her aunt snapped. 'She has to tell them because one of the neighbors might have seen her. If she doesn't volunteer the information first, she'll make herself look guilty.'

I shot daggers at my partner. '*Plus*, it's the right thing to do and it might help the police.'

'Of course. I meant that, too,' Sarah said. 'Policemen are our friends.'

Arial rolled her eyes. 'Exactly how will it help, Maggy?'

'It can bracket the time of the break-in, for one thing.'

'Not by much. From what Melinda said, she got there just before the fire investigators did.'

'We know from Kelly that was about eight,' I said, glancing across the lobby. 'We'll ask Melinda exactly what time she arrived.'

'To trip her up, you mean,' Arial said, getting up. 'I'll go check with her now, so I can book these tickets.'

As she left us, I caught a glimpse of flashing lights and turned to look out the front windows. 'Are those squad cars?'

Sarah stood up to see. 'Two. One with its lights on just pulled in and another one is already parked.'

'I wonder what's going on.' I started toward the revolving door.

Arial, coming out of the restroom hallway frowning, nearly ran in to me. 'Melinda's not in there.'

'Maybe the restroom was busy, so she went up to her own room,' I offered.

'Or maybe not.' Sarah was craning her neck to see the far reaches of the parking lot where we'd parked. 'The Toyota is gone.'

TWELVE

'We probably shouldn't jump to conclusions,' Arial said as we walked out to my car thirty minutes later. 'Melinda may have gotten a call and gone somewhere to take it. Or Maggy is right, and she went to her—'

'And her car just vaporized?' Sarah suggested. 'Good thought.'

'No, I—'

I put my hand on Arial's arm. 'The fact the sheriff's deputies took our cups and saucers for fingerprinting is a pretty good indication that they're looking for Melinda.'

'Maybe they want our prints for elimination,' Arial said. 'You know, at the house because of the break-in.'

'And tracked us down here to get them?' Sarah asked. 'Believe me, they have Maggy and mine. And yours, too, because you're a criminal.'

'That's hurtful,' Arial said.

'But truthful,' her aunt said. 'You pleaded guilty.'

'To being a dope, mostly,' Arial said. 'But I do get your point.'

'More dupe than dope,' her loving aunt told her. 'Did you see the police lights when you went to the restroom to look for Melinda?'

'What are you thinking?' I asked her.

'That Melinda probably went straight out the door and drove off in the Toyota. But why? That was before the police arrived.'

'The police car with the lights was pulling in as I went past the revolvers to look for Melinda,' Arial said.

'But there was another squad already parking in the lot,' I said. 'We saw it and maybe Melinda did, too.'

'But why should it spook her?' Arial said. 'She didn't do anything.'

Sarah waved for her to get into the front passenger seat. 'So she says. But for all we know, she has been feeding us a boatload of lies. Long-lost half-sister, my ass.'

I thought I saw Arial quickly swipe away a tear as I got into the driver's seat. The last twenty-four hours really had been a rollercoaster for the girl.

'You weren't very nice,' she told Sarah now. 'When you thought we couldn't hear.'

'Nice?' Sarah repeated. 'She's been stalking us, yet her feelings get hurt because we're debating why she left the anonymous threat on our car?'

Arial sniffed. 'It wasn't really a threat.'

'Listen,' I said, starting the car. 'We don't know anything at this point. I say we go to the house and dig around. See if we can find Ruth's will, any insurance policies, and especially the healthcare directive.'

'The hospital will need that,' Arial said. 'Especially with us out of . . .' She stopped. 'Is it all right for us to go?'

Sarah slid into the back seat and leaned forward. 'You heard the doctor this morning. There's nothing we can do but wait.'

'But if there's a change? Or if she—'

'Then they'll call and we'll fly right back.' She patted her niece's shoulder. 'But just to be sure, we'll double-check with the doctors. OK?'

'OK.' Arial seemed relieved.

'We'll also have to dig through Edna's drawer,' Sarah said, sitting back. 'We need to find anything on the house in Pacific Grove.'

'And the Monterey Peninsula in general,' Arial said, perking up. 'Who knows? Maybe Ruth tried to contact my father when she found out she was pregnant. She'd have no way of knowing he was dead.'

'If he's dead,' Sarah said. 'That could be another lie. And right now, I'm more concerned about the property taxes, to tell you the truth.'

'You worry about that,' I said, backing out of the parking space. 'Arial and I will deal with the less mundane. Like maybe Ruth had an address book. Or correspondence.'

'Twenty-five years ago,' Arial said. 'Probably no chance of finding anything electronic.'

'There were computers, you know,' Sarah said.

'My mother is barely computer literate even now,' Arial said.

I took a quick right onto a side road that would take us more directly to Ruth's house, bouncing over railroad tracks and potholes to get there.

'But assuming Ruth did have a computer then,' I said, over the whining from the back seat, 'the word-processing programs have changed a lot over the years. I still have Lotus and WordPerfect documents on floppy disks that I'll never be able to access.'

'So why do you keep them?' Arial asked. 'Museum exhibit?'

'They're memories, I guess.'

'Well, don't lose hope,' Arial said, softening. 'I think you can still get a disk reader that plugs into your computer. Once you have the document on your computer, I'm sure there are programs that can open them.'

'Or companies that can,' I said hopefully. 'Like the VHS tapes of Eric when he was little that I had converted to DVD.'

'And you'll want those on a cloud at some point, or a USB drive,' Arial said.

'There are still DVDs,' I said defensively.

'Mostly Blu-rays now,' Sarah said mildly. 'And my computer doesn't have a DVD drive, does yours?'

'Well, no,' I admitted.

'But back to the subject at hand,' Arial said, turning to me. 'Maybe the sheriff's department can pull Melinda's DNA from her coffee cup, in addition to her fingerprints.'

'Assuming that's what they wanted with the cups,' I said dubiously. 'I didn't know the two deputies who responded, and they weren't very forthcoming.'

'I noticed that,' Sarah said. 'Even when you pulled the "engaged to the sheriff" card.'

'That did seem to make them even colder,' Arial said, wrinkling her nose. 'Pigs!'

'That's not nice,' I told Arial. 'They're just doing their jobs.'

'No,' she said, pointing. 'There.'

'Oh.' I stopped to let a man lead two pet pigs, each probably weighing two hundred pounds and wearing pink harnesses, across the road. 'Sorry.'

'I haven't become a hardened criminal,' Arial said, giving me a sideways grin. 'Really.'

'Didn't even go in the slammer,' Sarah reminded me.

'I know.' I started up again with a wave to the man and his pigs. 'I just feel protective of Pavlik and the men and women he works with. It's not an easy job.'

'Absolutely,' Arial said. 'And I would never call them pigs.'

'I know you wouldn't,' I said.

'Flatfoots, maybe.' Arial sneaked a smile at me.

Sarah snorted in the back. 'Copper. Fuzz.'

'Fuzz?' Arial said.

'Coined back in the Sixties, I understand. Because they had short hair.' Taking a left, I stopped in front of the house. 'Looks like there's no one here.'

'There's crime scene tape across the front door now,' Sarah observed as the car idled. 'That's new.'

And suggested that it really was ruled a crime scene. Or they just wanted to keep nosy people out.

I decided to turn into the driveway. 'We'll go in the back door. I don't want the neighbors to report us ducking in under the tape.'

'I thought Pavlik said it was OK to go in,' Arial said, as we stopped in front of the garage door.

'He did, but he'll expect us to do it discreetly.' I led the way through the gate and to the back door. 'Good, they haven't secured this one yet.'

'Why good?' Arial said. 'Anybody could get in.'

Sarah pushed the door open with her shoulder. 'Be careful not to leave prints. I should have brought gloves.'

'It's already been fingerprinted,' I said, following her in. 'No need to tiptoe around.'

'Yet we snuck in the back door.' Arial closed it behind us. 'Which is hanging wide open because the cops didn't secure it. Or can't I say cops either?'

'Actually, "cop" is short for Sarah's "copper," which was derived from the fact they wore copper buttons in the day.'

'Fun fact,' Sarah muttered, glancing around. 'Where should we start?'

'Bottom drawer of Edna's dresser,' I suggested. 'We know there are papers in there and there was nothing in Ruth's drawers that I saw. You?'

'No,' Sarah said. 'Did you go through all the papers in the kitchen cabinet?' she asked Arial.

'Yes,' Arial called from Edna's room. She was already sitting on the floor in front of her grandmother's dresser, drawer open. 'No will or directives in the kitchen. But there's no lack of papers in here. Should we divvy them up?'

'Sure,' Sarah said, going to sit on the bed. 'You two go through them and divvy the important ones to me.'

'No way,' I said, nudging her to shove over. 'Edna was your mother. It's only right that you go through her private papers first.'

But Arial was already sorting. 'Looks like the farther down you go, the older the stuff is. Which I guess makes sense. She just dumped things in, probably, and never went through it.'

'That means Kelly's right that it's unlikely whoever broke in rifled through them,' I said.

'Unless they were careful and put them back in chronological order,' Arial said.

'Kelly didn't go through them as thoroughly as I would have expected,' Sarah observed.

I shrugged. 'They have a presumed accidental death or even suicide, so they wouldn't necessarily inspect everything.'

'What about financial statements?' Sarah said. 'If Ruth's death was a possible suicide, wouldn't they be looking for a reason?'

'There are easier ways to check finances than to go through stacks of old paper,' Arial reminded us. 'I mean, who prints out bank statements anymore?' She held one up.

I didn't answer that.

'I don't suppose you even own a file cabinet,' Sarah said to her niece.

'File cabinet? I don't even own a bed,' Arial said. 'Or a printer.'

'You keep everything important on your computer or phone,' Sarah said, shaking her head. 'What happens if your phone dies or your hard drive crashes?'

'I back up regularly. What happens if you have a fire?'

'I have fire sprinklers and my file cabinet is metal.' Sarah's eyes narrowed. 'What happens if the apocalypse comes and there's no electricity or internet?'

'Then we're both royally screwed.' Arial handed over a paper. 'This one looks important enough to scan and store on my computer. It has an official seal – a property deed, perhaps?'

Sarah held it so we both could read it. 'Yup, registered deed for the house and property in Pacific Grove, California. Like Cokely said, it's held in the name of Gretchen's trust.'

'Is that a good thing?' Arial asked. 'That it's in a trust, I mean.'

'Yes.' Sarah folded the deed and slipped it in her purse. 'Because as beneficiary of the trust, the property passes to you without probate.'

'Cool.' Arial handed Sarah a stack of papers. 'I think these are recent tax bills and maybe insurance.'

Sarah took them. 'Paid tax bills for both houses, thank God. And both homeowners insurance and earthquake insurance on the PG house are current.'

'There's separate earthquake insurance?' In the Midwest, our natural catastrophe of choice was tornado. They were destructive, but usually cut a narrower swatch of destruction than the hurricanes that afflicted both coasts. Earthquakes – the very ground crumbling under your feet and your home – was a whole 'nother level of disaster.

'I think California law requires that it's offered,' Sarah said. 'I'm just glad Edna took them up on it.'

'House keys,' Arial said brightly, jangling a set of three.

'Also good,' Sarah said, nodding. 'For which house, though?'

'Says "PG" on the tag,' Arial said. 'There are more bills for the California house here, too. And a monthly statement from a management company.'

'Again, thank you, Lord,' Sarah said, taking the stack to look over. 'They'll be looking after the property for a fee – usually a percentage of rental income.'

'It's currently rented?' Arial asked.

Sarah nodded. 'Seems so. The management company takes ten percent, and the rest of the rental income is a disbursement to the trust.'

'How much is that?' Arial asked.

'Three thousand dollars after the management fee.'

Arial blinked. 'It's renting for $3,300 per month. That is a great little moneymaker.'

'It is,' Sarah said. 'It's an entire house, remember. Two bedrooms, from what I can recall, and there's another building – a guest cottage – on the property. We'll get the lease from the managers if we can't find it here and see what the terms are.'

'I'll have to honor it, right?'

'Usually,' Sarah said. 'Unless it was a month-to-month rental. But then you still have to give sixty days' notice.'

'I wouldn't kick somebody out before the end of their lease, even if I could,' Arial said. 'Besides, three thousand dollars a month is a really nice income. Meanwhile, I could just stay on your couch, Sarah, and build up the bank account.'

Sarah raised an eyebrow. 'You could stay here, you know.'

'After you get the furnace fixed,' I suggested.

'It's very odd to actually own something,' Arial said, continuing her excavation of the drawer. 'I'm not used to having all these options.'

'Would you think of moving out to California?' I asked.

'Sure. I don't have anything to keep me here.'

'Thanks,' Sarah said dryly.

'You know what I mean.' Arial looked up to grin as she lifted the last pile of papers out.

I smacked my partner in the arm. 'Leave her alone. Kids are supposed to take off and fly on their own. You'll see that with Sam and Courtney before you know it.'

'They're practically gone already, between college and friends,' Sarah said. 'Any legal papers for Ruth? The directive or a will?'

Arial was sifting through. 'No, this stuff is much older.'

I caught sight of a folded piece of cream-colored writing paper that reminded me of the one I'd seen in the painting. 'What's that?'

Arial retrieved the paper and unfolded it. 'Part of a letter in Ruth's writing. Apologizing yet again for my birth, from the looks of it. No wonder Edna kept it in a special place.'

'Give.' Sarah held out her hand.

Arial held it back. 'It's OK, I'm not devastated or anything. It's not like I didn't know—'

'Give.'

Arial did.

'". . . ashamed and humiliated,"' Sarah read. '"But you believed me and took on a lifelong burden. I am so sorry."' Sarah passed the paper back. 'The first page is missing, but you're just assuming you're the burden?'

'Who else?' Arial was back to the stack of papers and pulled out a matching ivory envelope. 'No first page, but . . .' She was unfolding a yellowed newspaper article. 'It's from the Monterey paper the year before I was born . . .' She left off, reading.

'What?' Sarah was trying to see over her shoulder.

But Arial just waved her off and slid so her back was against the wall. She shielded the clipping as she read it, her lips moving. Finished, she put the clipping face down on the floor and slid it to her aunt. Her hand was shaking.

'What?' Sarah repeated, leaning down to get the clipping.

I just waited as she read it silently, her face going pale.

'What . . .' my voice cracked. 'What is it?'

Sarah held it up so I could see the headline: *Woman Sexually Assaulted in Pacific Grove.*

THIRTEEN

'No wonder my mother and my grandmother hated me.' Arial was holding both her hands up, palms out, as if to ward off the news. 'I'm the product of a rape.'

'If that's true, it certainly wasn't your fault,' Sarah said. 'And, setting your mother aside for now, you can be sure Edna didn't hate you or consider you a burden. She named you her heir.'

'Gretchen named me her heir.' Arial got up from the floor and Sarah and I slid apart so she could sit between us on the bed. 'Edna just gave me the house to piss off Ruth.'

'Is there a date on the letter? Or a postmark on the envelope?'

Sarah snorted. 'You think Ruth would have mailed it?'

Arial was nodding. 'That would have really ticked off Edna. "Why would you waste that postage when you're right here in the house?"'

Fair point, I guess, though I always loved getting cards in the mail from Eric, even when he was living home.

'So, no date on the letter,' I said, taking the newspaper clipping. 'But the letter is much newer than this clipping.'

Arial wasn't listening. 'I wonder if Melinda knows her father raped my mother.'

'It would explain why she was so hot on talking to Ruth,' Sarah said. 'Maybe she wanted to hear it from her.'

'Who would want to hear their father was a rapist?'

'We're getting ahead of ourselves.' I was reading the newspaper account, which was short on detail, as you'd expect with a sexual assault. 'The victim isn't named, of course. Only that she was visiting Pacific Grove for a conference and that the assault took place in Monterey. There's no way of being sure it was Ruth.'

'But look at her age,' Arial said, pointing. 'Eighteen. Which is how old my mother would have been when I was conceived.'

'Sure, but—'

'And the day of the assault.' Arial was tapping the newspaper now with her fingernail. 'Sunday, December twentieth.'

'And Arial was born nine months later on September nineteenth of that year,' Sarah said.

'You weren't in Monterey,' I said to my partner. 'But did Ruth or Edna say anything to you?'

'About Ruth being raped?' Sarah asked incredulously. 'Of course not. Don't you think I would have said something about it before now?'

'You might have wanted to protect me,' Arial said.

'I *would* have wanted to protect you,' Sarah agreed. 'That is, if I'd known. Which I didn't. I was at school in Madison and never heard a word about this.' She plucked the clipping out of my hand and waved it.

'But it was a few days before Christmas,' Arial said in a small voice. 'Wasn't campus closed?'

Sarah rolled her eyes. 'I had a boyfriend, OK? I didn't want to go home to Denver for the holiday *or* to PG with Ruth and Edna.'

'But they still went, of course.'

'Of course.' She was thinking back. 'That may have been the last time, in fact.'

'When did you find out my mother was pregnant?' Arial asked.

'Edna insisted I come home to Denver for spring break. By that time, Ruth was just starting to show, and my mother informed me that they were moving to Brookhills to be closer to me.'

'That's it? You didn't ask how it had happened?'

Sarah was usually up in everybody's business.

'Despite my repressive upbringing, I did know how babies are made,' Sarah told me.

'But Ruth was your younger sister,' I protested. 'Didn't you—'

'Give her a break,' Arial said. 'I'm sure the fact they were following her to Wisconsin after she'd escaped to college was what got Sarah's attention. It would have mine.'

'I had been so thankful to get away,' Sarah admitted. 'But to be honest, Madison is a good hour away from Brookhills, and I really didn't see much of them anyway.'

'They probably didn't get out much, hiding the bastard child,' Arial said. 'I'm sure that's why they left Denver in the first place. The shame.'

'Don't forget spawn of a rapist,' Sarah said, punching her in the arm.

Amazing what passed for comfort and reassurance in this family.

Arial rested her head on Sarah's shoulder. 'I guess it's a good thing to know, right? I mean, it answers a lot of questions.'

'It does?' I asked. 'Seems to me it demands more answers than it provides. Despite the dates and Ruth's age fitting, we don't know this story is about her. Or that it was Jonathan Springbok who raped her.'

'We do have Jonathan's deathbed confession,' Sarah pointed out.

'To cheating, not to rape,' I countered.

'And this is according to Melinda, who learned it from her mother,' Arial said. 'Joan might not have told her the whole story.'

'Thinking she'd spare her somehow,' I mused. 'After all, what good comes from Melinda knowing?'

Arial cocked her head, eyes narrowed. 'Would she have come looking for me, if she knew the whole truth?'

'Alternatively, if she did know, would she have just blurted it out?' Sarah asked.

'True,' I said. 'She had no way of knowing what your mother told you or didn't tell you.'

'How sensitive of her,' Arial said sarcastically.

'I thought you liked Melinda,' I said.

'That was before I knew her father was a rapist,' Arial snapped.

Sarah and I just kept our mouths shut.

'Oh, yeah,' Arial said, after a moment. 'Guess I have a glass house problem there, my father being a rapist, too.'

'It's not anymore her fault than it is yours,' Sarah said.

'We still need to go to Pacific Grove,' Arial said. 'Maybe the police there can tell us more about the investigation.'

'Melinda said her father was killed Sunday, the last day of the conference, trying to catch a shuttle off the peninsula,' I said. 'He may have believed the police were close.'

'There's no description of the suspect in the article,' Sarah said. 'No indication whether she knew him or not.'

'If they knew he was part of the convention group, the police might have kept it under wraps.'

'As she got older, Ruth did like to hang out downtown or at the hotels when we visited,' Sarah admitted. 'Meet people from all over the world.'

'You were in what year of college?' I asked.

'Second,' Sarah said. 'Ruth planned to start the next fall, but then she got pregnant.'

'I assume Edna wouldn't have let Ruth terminate the pregnancy?' Arial said it like she wasn't talking about her own life.

'No.' Sarah was shaking her head. 'And I don't know that Ruth would have, regardless. She always seemed . . . lonely.'

'So lonely that she had a rapist's child,' Arial said, standing up. 'That's pretty pathetic.'

'Not that child's fault,' I reminded her as I got to my feet. 'And we're getting ahead of ourselves. It may be that the investigation went nowhere after Springbok died, but it's also possible he was never named or implicated. Or that it wasn't Ruth who was raped. You're right that we need to go to California and find out more.' I started out the door.

'Right this minute?' Arial asked.

'What?' I turned at the door. 'Oh, no. I'm going down to the basement to check out the furnace.'

'And what do you think you'll find down there?' Sarah said, following me down the basement stairs.

'Signs that the cracked heat exchanger wasn't replaced,' Arial answered for me.

'Pavlik also said the venting was "incomplete,"' I reminded them.

Sarah frowned. 'That might mean the furnace was being worked on.'

I'd reached the furnace on one end of the concrete floor and now tapped on it. 'It looks pretty old. You're the handy one, Arial. Can you tell if the heat exchanger is cracked? Or if it's been replaced?'

'I may know the periodic table of elements, but I have no idea how to inspect a furnace.' She gave the exterior a once-over. 'I assume the heat exchanger is in there somewhere, but I'm not even sure what one looks like.'

Fine help she was, but at least I'd distracted Arial from the latest blow.

Turning my attention to the venting, I saw it was similar to that on my furnace. 'Well, there are two runs of white PVC venting. As I understand it, one would bring air in from outside and the other would vent . . .' I was looking for a word but gave up, ' . . . bad stuff out.'

Arial went to pick up an elbow piece on the floor. 'There's a piece left over.'

I touched one of the PVC runs to the outside wall. It shifted. 'I don't think the sections of PVC are supposed to be loose like this.'

'They're not.'

I recognized the voice from the top of the stairs. 'Pavlik?'

Footsteps down, and there was my man. He was wearing his buttery brown leather jacket. Which I loved almost as much as I did Pavlik.

I went in for a hug and snuggled into said jacket for a second before I stepped back. 'What are you doing here?'

'I'm looking for somebody,' he said, glancing around. 'Don't suppose you've seen your mystery woman, Melinda Springbok?'

'You mean my sister?' Arial said, and then shrugged. 'Or so she says.'

'How is that?' Pavlik said, his eyes darkening with interest. 'I assume you didn't know?'

'It was news to all of us,' Sarah said. 'Neither Arial nor I had ever seen this woman.'

'Or heard of her,' Arial added, 'until she showed up at Edna's funeral on Sunday.'

'Don't suppose you happen to know where she is now?' Pavlik asked. 'Her clothes are still at the Hotel Morrison, but she seems to have disappeared.'

'Why are you looking for her?' I asked. 'And how did you know she was at the Morrison?'

'I could ask you the same.' The sheriff had a gift for answering a question with a question. Or just not answering it at all.

'Keen deduction,' I said. 'First, it's the only hotel in town and, second, it's the only hotel where I had a prayer of extracting information from the management.'

A smile played at Pavlik's lips. 'We started with the Morrison based on your first point. We're pretty adept at the second, regardless.'

'Lucky you,' I said.

'We think Melinda must have seen the first squad pull in,' Sarah said, finally getting her name right. 'But we don't know why she's running.'

'Except that she told us that she was here at the house this morning,' Arial surprised me by volunteering. 'She said the door was already broken, but she didn't go in.'

'Only because she heard the fire inspectors arrive,' I added.

'This morning then,' Pavlik said, 'when the inspectors came back.'

'At eight and found the break-in, according to Kelly.' It had been a very long day.

'She told you she didn't enter the house,' Pavlik said. 'Yet we think we found her prints inside. We're confirming it now.'

'She lied again,' Sarah said. 'Told you.'

'You matched them to the fingerprints from her coffee cup?' Arial asked.

'Where—' I started, but Arial talked over me.

'Is it that big a deal, though? Maybe she didn't want to admit she came in and snooped around, looking for evidence of her parentage . . .' Arial stopped to ask me, 'Does the sheriff know the details?'

'No,' I said. 'But I'll get to that in a—'

The girl rolled her eyes. 'Like I said, Melinda says we're sisters – half-sisters. I'm the result of an affair or a rape, depending on who you believe.'

That got Pavlik's attention. And me in trouble. 'How could you not mention that?'

'To be fair,' Arial said, 'we just found out about the sister thing at the hotel, and the rape ten minutes ago upstairs. I'm sure Maggy will fill you in, because we can use your help when we approach the authorities in Monterey.'

'Monterey?' Pavlik was trying to keep up.

'California, remember? It's where the affair/rape took place,' I explained. 'Edna's parents had the house there, which Arial has now inherited. So we thought—'

'Thought you'd check it and Arial's parentage out,' Pavlik supplied.

'Exactly,' Arial said. 'You're very quick.'

'Thank you,' Pavlik said with a grin, his eyes playing at blue again. 'Maggy keeps me sharp.'

'I'd forgotten how nice he is,' Arial said, as Pavlik's phone buzzed, and he stepped away to answer it. 'And how cute.'

'He is on both counts,' I admitted, as Pavlik listened for a second and then rung off.

'We've got her,' he said, turning toward the stairs.

'You have Melinda in custody?' I was following him.

'No, I mean we have her for breaking and entering at the minimum.'

'But the door was apparently open,' Arial said. 'That's not breaking.'

'It is entering, though,' Sarah told her niece. 'Besides, she has to be lying again. If she didn't break the lock, who did?'

But I was thinking about something Pavlik had said. 'At the minimum?' I asked. '"Breaking and entering at the minimum"?'

'See those vents?' The sheriff chin-gestured toward the PVC pipes we'd been examining.

'They were not vented out last night when the fire inspector checked them. In fact, that elbow on the floor was connected and sent carbon monoxide upward toward the bedrooms. Since there are extensive cracks in the heat exchanger and the bedroom is directly above, he considered it the cause of Ruth Kingston's poisoning.'

'Shouldn't they have left them like that?' I asked.

'Who's "they"?' Arial asked.

'The fire inspectors,' I said. 'Pavlik's crime scene people needed to check for fingerprints and all, so they shouldn't have moved anything.'

'That's the thing,' Pavlik said. 'The PVC had been connected – albeit loosely, as you found – when the fire officials arrived this morning.'

'Meaning somebody did break in,' I said, 'but it wasn't to look for something.'

'It was to cover their tracks.' Pavlik started up the stairs. 'And we did check for fingerprints.'

The three of us left in the basement exchanged looks.

'That's where you found Melinda's?' I asked.

Pavlik turned at the top. 'I'd have thought so, but no. There are fingerprints on the venting, including the elbow. Most of them dusty and smudged, as you can imagine, but there are a few that look fresher. We're running them down now.'

'Then where . . .?' I was frowning up at Pavlik.

'Did we find Melinda Springbok's prints?' Pavlik said, seeming to weigh how much he should tell us.

'Please?' Arial asked.

'On the doorknob to your mother's room.'

'On the outside,' I said, climbing the stairs up to him. 'My fingerprints would be on that, too. I opened the door to find Ruth.'

'And if Melinda *was* nosing around this morning,' Arial said, 'it figures she'd open the door. Not because my mother had nearly died in that room, but because Melinda was looking for confirmation that her father was my father.'

'Only thing wrong with that,' Pavlik said, 'is that Melinda's print was under Maggy's.'

Oh, geez. 'She was in this house – and likely inside that room – yesterday, not today.'

'Correct,' Pavlik said. 'And—'

'Before we found Ruth,' Sarah finished for him.

FOURTEEN

'**B**ut why would Melinda try to kill Ruth?' Arial repeated. Pavlik had left and we were sitting on the steps of the back porch.

'Are you kidding?' Sarah demanded of her niece. 'Your mother accused her father of rape.'

'He's her father,' I said. 'I can understand why she wants to believe he's innocent.'

'She didn't even know him.' The girl was pinballing from accusation to defense and back again for pretty much all the characters in this little drama. 'What is she, a psychopath?'

'We thought a sociopath,' I said. 'But then again, maybe she's just completely lost. She never knew her dad, her mother drops this bombshell on her and dies, leaving Melinda alone. What is she supposed to do with it all?'

'Well, it's obvious, isn't it?' Arial snapped. 'Track down my mother and asphyxiate her.'

She was nearly as good at sarcasm as her aunt Sarah.

'Ladies,' Sarah said now. 'Let's think about this rationally. To have purposely asphyxiated Ruth, Melinda would have to have sneaked into the house *before* Saturday night and tampered with the furnace venting.'

'Also disabled the carbon monoxide detectors,' I said. 'And Pavlik didn't find her fingerprints on either. Though anybody could've handled the detectors when we'd thought Ruth's death was an accident. Which it could still be.'

Sheesh.

'We need to give the batteries to Pavlik,' Arial said. 'My prints may be on them from when I first wrapped them in the paper towels, though.'

'And I handled the doorknob,' I said. 'They can eliminate your prints and see who else handled the batteries.'

Arial sat up straight. 'None of this works if the heat exchanger isn't cracked, does it?'

'And how would Melinda possibly know that?' I said, seeing where Arial was going with this. 'Good question.'

'Maybe she saw the estimate in Edna's drawer,' Sarah said, 'and decided to stage an accident?'

'You're giving her an awful lot of credit,' I said. 'She's not a master criminal.'

'How do you know that?' Sarah demanded. 'Sociopath, psychopath—'

'Daughter of a rapist,' Arial added. 'But Sarah is right. Who knows how long the woman has been nosing around?'

'For all we know,' Sarah continued, 'she did go to church with Edna or work at the county senior center, like she told everyone.'

'There is no county senior center,' I reminded her.

'You know what I'm saying.' Sarah was losing her patience.

'I do,' I said. 'I'll see if Pavlik knows what day she got here.'

'Good,' Sarah said. 'Meanwhile, Arial and I will go—'

'You are not going to Monterey without me,' I said, standing.

'I was about to say we'll go visit my sister who's in a coma,' Sarah said, lifting her chin at me. '*Then* we'll go to Monterey. With you.'

'Great,' I said, pulling out my keys. 'Let's go back to Uncommon Grounds and book the flights.'

'No need.' Arial was tapping on her phone and now she put it into her pocket and stood. 'All done. We leave tomorrow, six p.m.'

'There's nothing to say Melinda Springbok is crazy,' Pavlik told me that night. 'She plans special events – weddings and things – in Monterey. No criminal record, not even a speeding ticket. But she does have some questions to answer.'

We were standing in the kitchen, eating leftover pizza at the counter.

'No sightings of her car?'

'A blue Corolla?' he asked. 'Way too many.'

'Were you able to find out when she flew in?'

'Friday night,' he said. 'So, if you want to stick with your *super-criminal cased the house and used what she found to plan the perfect murder* theory, I guess she would have had Saturday to do it.'

'Nearly perfect attempted murder,' I corrected. 'And it's Sarah's theory, not mine.'

Frank and Mocha were sitting on the floor in front of us, a pool of drool in front of each. I tore my crust in two and – giving the sheepdog the big piece, the chihuahua the small – got a dirty look from Mocha for my efforts.

'Sorry,' I told her. 'Got to maintain your girlish figure.'

She gave a grunt and stalked off, probably less because of my words and more because my plate was empty.

'You guys going to be all right while I'm gone?' I asked Pavlik.

'We will miss the gourmet meals,' Pavlik said with a grin, and leaned in to kiss me. 'But we'll survive.'

'Takeout menus are on the side of the refrigerator,' I reminded him. 'Do you think you can give us some help with the Monterey police?'

'You mean to find out what happened twenty-five years ago?'

'I know it's a long shot,' I said. 'The responding officers might not still be there, but they'd have records, right?'

'Right,' Pavlik said. 'And because I have a case here that involves Melinda Springbok, I can rightly ask some questions about her father, Jonathan.'

I had filled Pavlik in on the rape allegation. 'He does provide the connection between Ruth and Melinda.'

I was silent while Pavlik finished off his last slice of pizza, and then, 'There's no indication that Edna died anything but a natural death, is there?'

Pavlik did a double-take. 'Edna? No, she died of congestive heart failure. According to her doctor, they'd been expecting her to go any day.'

'But there was no autopsy.'

'You think somebody helped her along? That maybe Melinda made an earlier trip?'

I shifted uncomfortably. 'Probably not. She claims she only found out where Ruth was from Edna's obituary.'

Pavlik picked up the wine bottle and poured us each another inch. 'She apparently claims a lot of things. I think you're probably barking up the wrong tree about Edna. Why would Melinda want her dead?'

'Melinda wouldn't. But maybe it was a mercy killing?' I tried. 'Or a I'm-going-to-kill-you-before-you-change-your-will killing? Or a little of each?'

'Meaning you suspect Ruth, who is lying in a coma,' Pavlik said.

'Maybe.' I wrinkled my nose. 'She cleaned up that room – with bleach – and got Edna in the ground awfully fast. Maybe afterward she was wracked with guilt?'

'Before or after buying her new car?'

'After,' I said. 'Decidedly after.'

'And so tried to kill herself in the most convoluted – and unsuccessful – way ever?' Pavlik asked. 'And how do we account for Melinda's fingerprints on the doorknob in this scenario?'

'We don't.' I shrugged. 'I don't know how we account for it in any scenario, really. Maybe she came to see Ruth on Saturday and maybe this blast from the past – and the possibility that Melinda might tell Arial – was more than she could handle.'

'That's two maybes and a might in there,' Pavlik said.

'I know.' I sighed. 'And to be honest, I'm not sure Ruth loved Arial enough to care what she knew about her conception.'

'That's awful,' Pavlik said. 'Poor Arial.'

Yes, poor Arial. But as much as I liked the girl, I continued to have this niggling doubt.

Because Arial, of anybody, had the most to gain from both her mother and grandmother's deaths.

I couldn't say it out loud. Not to Sarah or Arial, of course, but not even to Pavlik. I didn't want to send him down that road.

So it was with some relief, anticipation and trepidation that I sat beside my murder suspect and her aunt the next evening, waiting for the portable ramp to be wheeled up to the plane for us to disembark.

From what I could see, Melinda had not been lying – for once – about the Monterey Regional Airport. It was a small airport, perhaps five gates, but no connected jet bridges. You got on and off under your own power, which was plenty pleasant given the moderate temperatures, even at nearly midnight.

'Must be sixty degrees out,' I said, pulling up the handle of my wheelie bag. At Sarah's insistence, we had no checked luggage. 'And not at all humid, like I'd expect in California.'

'This is the central coast,' Sarah said, waving me and my bag to lead the way up the lined path to the terminal. 'Much more like San Francisco than LA. Almost never humid, and the average daily highs vary about five degrees year-round.'

'Like around what?' Arial asked, trotting after her aunt.

'Like right around what it is now. September is the hottest month, if you can call it hot. It rarely gets above high seventies here, or below mid-forties.'

'Sounds like autumn in Wisconsin,' I said. 'Year-round.'

'Heaven,' Arial said, glancing around the starlit night. 'Is that a storm coming in?'

She was pointing toward a patch of sky no longer starlit and getting downright murky.

'Marine layer,' Sarah said, pushing into the terminal. 'AKA fog.'

'You just made it in.' The name tag on the smiling agent at the door read 'Marissa.' 'The ceiling is dropping rapidly. Last night and the night before, this flight from San Francisco was canceled.'

'Does that happen a lot?' We were on a peninsula poking out into the Pacific Ocean, so I guess it made sense.

'Tons, especially in the summer,' Marissa said. 'But September is one of our most beautiful months. Enjoy your stay!'

'She was so nice,' Arial said. 'We must look like tourists.'

'People are nice here,' Sarah growled as we wheeled past the now-closed TSA checkpoint. 'Almost irritatingly nice.'

'I didn't know you had a niceness ceiling,' Arial said, shooting me a grin.

'Then you don't know me very well.'

'Nice is good in Sarah World, unless it gets in her way,' I confirmed from experience.

'Like when the traffic light turns green and the car in front of you just sits there. Here, everybody is too nice to do anything.'

'What do you want them to do?' I asked as we exited the terminal.

She was pulling her phone out of her purse. 'Blow their horn first, of course. But here? They just sit through the whole damn cycle again until the idiot notices.'

'That's kind of refreshing,' I said.

'Kind of irritating. Now where's my car share app?'

'I've already ordered one,' Arial said. 'Bill is our driver and it's a . . . there it is.' Her mood had noticeably lightened as we distanced ourselves from Brookhills. And the go-ahead from Ruth's doctor for the trip probably didn't hurt.

'I like traveling with Arial,' I said, sliding into the back seat of the black SUV next to Sarah as Bill loaded the bags. 'She takes care of everything.'

'That's because I ordered a car in Chicago and it didn't come to the right place,' Sarah said. 'She doesn't trust me anymore.'

'We circled Union Station on foot trailing our luggage trying to find that ride,' Arial said. 'Only to have the driver cancel and charge us anyway.'

'Those were the early days of rideshare,' Sarah grumbled.

'Only for you,' Arial countered as Bill got in and punched up our destination. 'The rest of us had been using it for like five years.'

'Where are we going?' I asked. 'There's a tenant at the house, even if we did want to go looking at it at this time of night.'

'I booked a hotel room for the night,' Arial said.

'One room?' Sarah asked.

'Monterey Suites,' Bill kibbitzed with a smile. 'Nice place, and if you'd like a local recommendation, I'd go to Acme for coffee in the morning.'

'Acme?' I repeated.

'Acme Coffee Roasting, you'll find it online. It's in an old garage, just a few blocks down from the hotel. Larry's been there since 2005, first roasting coffee on site and now just serving it. Had to find a bigger place to roast.'

'We do love our coffee,' I said. 'In fact, we own a coffeehouse in Wisconsin called Uncommon Grounds.'

'Then you are going to love Acme,' he said, twisting around. 'Local watering hole – of the caffeinated variety. Suits, municipal workers, techies, cops, firefighters, retirees, field workers – you'll find everybody there at one time or the other during the day.'

'Watch the road,' Arial said, about to reach for the steering wheel.

'No worries,' Bill said, turning back in time to make a quick right into the hotel parking lot. 'We're here.'

The hotel had a queen-sized bed in one room and a pull-out couch in the other.

'I have dibs on the couch,' I said.

'Just because Sarah and I are related we have to share the bed?' Arial asked.

That and the fact that Sarah snored. 'There's no door between these two rooms.'

'Don't think so,' Arial was paging through a tour pamphlet. 'We should go to the Monterey Bay Aquarium tomorrow. I hear it's world class.'

'It is,' Sarah said, taking the booklet out of her hand, 'but we're here on business.'

'And detecting,' I added. 'Did you hear what Bill said about Acme?'

'Great local spot since 2005,' Sarah said, slinging her suitcase on the bed. 'It wasn't here last time I visited, but I'll take his word for it.'

'Hopefully he and his pals don't tell everybody who arrives about it.' Arial glanced at Sarah's suitcase and set hers on a chair to unzip. 'Or it won't stay local long.'

'You're missing the point,' I said. 'He said cops go there.'

'That's how to find the best restaurants in a city, too,' Sarah said. 'See where the squad cars are parked at lunchtime and—'

I was tossing the couch cushions across the room. 'While I applaud the pursuit of the best coffee and food in town, my thought is that we might be able to chat up a cop or two.'

'Have a thing for authority figures, do you?' Arial was grinning.

'Connections,' I insisted, tugging out the sofa bed. 'We meet somebody there and get a name. Then when we go to the station, we can say so-and-so suggested we see . . . whoever it is they suggest.'

'Somebody who was here twenty-five years ago?' Arial was sliding folded clothes into the dresser. 'They'll be ancient.'

'Just slightly older than Maggy and me,' Sarah said, sourly. 'Which side of the bed do you want?'

'Right,' Arial said. 'So, OK. Tomorrow we'll get up, go get coffee, chat up coppers and go look at my house.'

'I've got the name of the rental agent,' Sarah said. 'We'll stop in there, first. Introduce ourselves and find out about the tenants. When you're in the bed or facing it?'

Arial screwed up her face. 'What?'

'On the right when you're in the bed or when you're facing it?'

'Oh, in it,' Arial said, as her aunt tossed her suitcase in the corner and slid under the sheets on the appropriate side. 'Then can we go to the aquarium?'

'Let's get done what we have to first.' Pulling pillows out of the closet and placing them on the bed, I regarded the half-wall between the two rooms. 'That's not going to do much for sound, is it?'

Arial raised her eyebrows. 'She not only snores, she kicks in her sleep. Count your blessings.'

'She's your aunt,' I said.

'And your friend,' Arial retaliated.

'And right here,' Sarah said. 'Will you two shut up and come to bed? It's after one a.m. here, which is three a.m. our time. I'm beat.'

'Fine,' I said, switching off the main lights and sliding under the covers.

Arial got into bed and turned off her lamp.

A silence.

'Umm,' I said into the darkness. 'How are we going to get around? We probably should have rented a car.'

'I did,' Arial said with a weary sigh. 'For tomorrow morning. I didn't see the point in paying for an extra day.'

Another silence.

'Thanks, Mom,' I said in a small voice.

Sarah just growled.

FIFTEEN

'So where is this car you ordered?' Sarah demanded as we got off the elevator in the lobby the next morning. 'I need my coffee.'

'Acme is just a ten-minute walk from here,' Arial said. 'And the car rental just a fifteen-minute walk beyond that.'

'Perfect,' I said.

Sarah was less enthusiastic. 'Walk? Before I have coffee?'

'You've heard of incentive?' I asked, as we stepped outside. 'Which way, boss lady?'

Arial laughed. 'Sorry if I'm being bossy, but—'

I held up my hand. 'I'm grateful to have you be the laboring oar, believe me.' I threw a glance at Sarah, who was trailing behind us. 'Especially when the rest of the boat is so grumpy.'

'It's only fair, since she's related to me,' Arial said, pointing to the left and coming to walk beside me. 'Besides, I'm the reason we're here.'

A harrumph, from behind us. 'Yet I'm the one who has spent time here and know my way around.'

'Half a century ago, apparently,' I said. 'I'm sure things have changed. Besides, Arial is the one who's young and has the travel apps.'

Arial laughed. 'It's not exactly new technology.' She consulted her watch. 'Turn left here on Del Monte and then it's a right a few blocks up.'

'Great,' I said. 'So coffee, then car, and then what?'

'Catherine Smythe,' Sarah said. 'She's the management agent and I told her we'd be there about ten or ten thirty.'

'See?' I said, turning. 'You're pulling an oar, too.'

'Shuddup.'

'She's a bear without her coffee,' I said.

'Like you have to tell me?' Arial said, pointing for us to turn right now. 'I've lived with her.'

'Where is this place?' Sarah's head was on a swivel.

Arial gestured a left. 'Left here, then it's on the left.'

There was no mistaking the coffeehouse when we got there. Cream-colored brick building with an orange 'Acme Coffee Roasting' sign painted on one corner. A line of about ten people led up to the garage-door-like opening, where two espresso machines were going full tilt and a pour-over counter had four drip coffees going, as well.

On a bench on one side of the building a couple sat with their newborn in a carrier. To the other, people were scattered about, either waiting for their drinks or sipping on them. In the parking lot, a knot of people clustered at the back of a bright blue SUV. The vehicle's lift gate was open and one of the men was treating the three dogs sitting obediently inside to bits of a croissant.

'Wow,' I said, giving a smile to the man with the puppy croissants. 'This place is hopping.'

'Always is,' he said with a nod. 'Best coffee in town.'

As we got in line, I saw a police car pull in. 'Seaside,' I read on the side of the squad. 'Where's that?'

'We're in Seaside,' Sarah said, before Arial could. 'Monterey is a few blocks back the way we came.'

'Ah.' I was watching one of the police officers join the line, while the younger one joined two people who had already ordered. 'Suppose they might know the Monterey officers?'

'We will see,' Arial said, slipping out of line. 'I'll have a large nonfat latte.'

And with that, she was infiltrating the group.

'She's not shy, is she?' I said, watching her introduce herself. We stood for a while. 'Umm, would you mind if I go—'

'Suit yourself,' Sarah said darkly. 'Latte, on me, I assume.'

'You assume right,' I said, going to slip in alongside Arial.

'Hi,' I said generally to the group, which comprised the young officer, an older man in a tracksuit and a thirtyish woman.

'This is my friend, Maggy,' Arial told them. 'She and my aunt are helping me with my move here.'

'Arial just told us she's inherited the old Mayes house in PG,' the woman said, shaking hands. 'That's a really nice property. Needs work, of course, but most of the original houses in PG do.'

'Do you live in Pacific Grove?' I asked.

'Monterey, but the peninsula is a very small community, you'll find.'

'What Christine means,' the older man said, 'is that we're all up in each other's business.'

The woman – Christine, apparently – shrugged with a grin. 'Like I said, small town. Or cluster of towns.'

'Speaking of everyone knowing—' I started, but Arial interrupted.

'Officer,' she glanced at his badge, 'Norris—'

'Call me Ned,' he said.

Arial smiled her thanks. 'Ned was saying that his sergeant in the line there was with the Monterey police years ago, when my mother's . . . incident occurred.'

Like I said, not shy, and she didn't waste any time. Which I'd applaud, if she wasn't stealing my investigative thunder.

' . . . how are you finding it?' Christine was asking, 'I mean, you're moving halfway across the country and at the same time looking for your father. I'm not sure whether I'd be excited or frightened.'

'Not much frightens Arial,' I said, tossing a smile her way. 'Or so it seems.'

Arial cocked her head. 'I think fear and excitement are two faces of the same coin.'

'That sounds like the words of an old soul.' The police sergeant had joined us. 'Wise beyond her years.'

'Or a meme.' Arial smiled and stuck out her hand. 'I'm Arial Mayes Kingston.'

'Dan Sotherly,' the sergeant said. 'You're related to the Mayes of Pacific Grove, I assume.'

Everybody seemed to know this family. I glanced around to find that Sarah, having ordered, was standing off to the side, keeping to herself. Not one for chit-chat, our Sarah. At least not before full caffeination.

'She is,' Ned said. 'On your mother's side, right, Arial?'

'Yes, and her mother, who grew up here,' Arial said. 'Edna Mayes?'

'The artist,' the sergeant said, rubbing his face. 'This is a community of artists and writers, but those born and bred here, especially, stand out. Edna Mayes was one of them, at least until she up and got married. Moved away to Denver, I think.'

'Did you know her?' I asked.

'Not personally. She was more my parents' generation than mine. I did see her obituary last week. I'm very sorry for your loss.'

'Thank you,' Arial said, flushing. 'I didn't know that my grandmother was an artist or that she came from here until I read that obituary. But there's apparently a lot I didn't know about my family. My grandmother's death has set me on a bit of a quest.'

'We found letters and clippings in her grandmother's things,' I said, wanting to help. 'Things that Arial didn't necessarily—'

'I never knew my father, you see,' Arial explained. 'And it didn't really matter to me until my – air quotes – "half-sister" showed up at my grandmother's funeral.'

'Oh my God,' Christine said. 'If it wasn't all so sad, it would be a Hallmark movie.' She slapped a hand over her mouth. 'Sorry.'

'Right?' Arial was nodding. 'This woman about my age shows up and says my mother and her father had an affair. *But* we found a clipping hidden in my grandmother's things about a sexual assault at a conference right around the time I was conceived.'

'You think your mother was raped?' The woman gasped.

Arial spread out her hands. 'That's just it. I don't know anymore, so I came here hoping—'

'I know just who you should talk to,' the sergeant said. 'Retired MPD cop, who I think you'll find interviewed your mother.'

'How could you possibly know that?' I was astonished.

'Small town, remember?' Christine said.

The sergeant shook his head. 'Well, happily we don't have many sexual assaults, especially revolving around conferences and visitors. We take those things very seriously.'

'I can't believe you just bared your soul to a group of strangers,' I said to Arial as we walked away. With the retired cop's contact information, naturally, as well as that of the rest of the group.

'Strangers are just friends you haven't met,' Arial chanted, and then grinned. 'But really, they were all great. Dan, Ned, Nick, Christine. We're going to keep in touch.'

I had a feeling they would. 'You like it here,' I said to her as we joined Sarah.

'I do,' Arial said. 'I can't explain it, but it feels comfortable. Like home.'

'Because it is home, ancestorially, at least for part of your family.' Sarah handed her a latte. 'And I have to admit these lattes are damned good.'

'Yum,' I said, taking a sip of mine. 'They are. Is ancestorially a word?'

'Regardless, I do know what she means,' Arial said, going to shake a little organic cocoa on her latte. 'There's a certain . . . recognition. Which I know makes no sense at all.'

'No matter.' I set my cup on the round metal table attached to the center support of the coffee shop's awning. 'Where will that recognition take us next?'

'Well, Dan said he'd text Scott, that's the retired MPD officer, letting him know we'd be contacting him. That may take a while, so I say let's get the car and then go to the appointment Sarah set up with the rental agent.'

'We get to do something I say?' Sarah said, taking a final slurp of her latte and depositing the cup in the trash receptacle. 'Nice change.'

'It is, isn't it?' Arial said, this time slinging her own arm over her aunt's shoulders. 'Now I hope you have on walking shoes.'

'I thought you said it was a fifteen-minute walk,' Sarah complained, sliding into the passenger seat of our rental.

Arial was at the wheel, adjusting the seat to her liking. 'It was just short of a mile. Which would have been fifteen minutes if you weren't totally out of shape.'

'Don't talk to me about fitness. I'd like to see you stand on a hard tile floor for eight hours a day. Believe me, your dogs would be barking, too.'

'My what would be what?' Arial was now working on the mirrors.

'Your feet – aka dogs – would be hurting,' Sarah snapped. 'I'm surprised a veteran dog-walker like you doesn't know the expression.'

'Because I'm not a hundred years old,' Arial said. 'Bet even Maggy hasn't heard of that one, right Maggy?'

'Right.' I had slid happily into the back seat, just me and my latte. Let the two Kingston women duke it out.

'Liar,' Sarah said, and then, 'turn left here on Del Monte. It'll change names a couple of times, but we can take it all the way into Pacific Grove.'

'I know. I have it in navigation,' Arial said. 'Think we have time to run by the house first?'

'It's just a couple blocks out of the way,' Sarah said. 'So, probably.'

'Good.' Arial handed Sarah her phone. 'Can you just plug in the address as a stop?'

'Or I could just tell you where to go,' her aunt said.

'I know you're tempted,' Arial said with a sideways grin. 'But fine – oh, look! There's the turn-off for Cannery Row and the aquarium!'

'Cool,' Sarah said. 'Stay left.'

'But . . .' Arial was glancing back wistfully.

'I'd actually like to go, too,' I said, leaning forward. 'Cannery Row of John Steinbeck fame – wow. But Sarah's right that we need to do what we came here for first.'

'This is Wednesday,' Sarah said, 'and we have flights back on Saturday. We can go on Friday. For a while.'

Arial didn't bother to argue. I was sure she would simply do what she wanted regardless.

She was very much like her aunt. Only nicer.

'Straight,' Sarah snapped.

Arial had just pulled into the left-turn lane. 'What do you mean? The navigation—'

'Is wrong,' she said. 'Assuming you want to see downtown Pacific Grove and drive by the house, this is the simplest way.'

'Fine.' Arial signaled to pull back into the lane and a driver waved her in. 'See? Nice.'

'Ugh,' was Sarah's only response, until we came to a stop sign a few blocks further on. 'Left.'

Arial turned obediently and drove up a hill, coming to first one stop sign and then another. 'Lighthouse Avenue.'

'Turn left here.'

'This is so cute.' My head was swiveling. 'This is Pacific Grove?'

'Lighthouse Avenue in Pacific Grove,' Sarah said. 'The main drag.'

Restaurants and shops lined the street, not a franchise operation in sight.

'Is my house near here?' Arial asked. 'I've always wanted to live somewhere where I could just walk to dinner.'

'Take a right at the next corner.'

Arial turned. 'I asked—'

'Right there on the right,' Sarah said. 'That green house.'

Arial pulled over. 'That is so cute. Tiny.'

'Not that tiny by Pacific Grove standards,' Sarah said. 'That white building next to it is also part of the property – a guesthouse, my grandmother used to call it. We'd stay there when we came.'

'And the building beyond that?' I asked, craning my neck to see.

'Garage, but it was used mostly for storage the last time I saw it. I think it fronts on the alley on the other side.'

Arial put the car into park mode and swung open the door to step out. 'It does look bigger than the properties across the street. I mean, the size of the lots and all.'

'It's a double lot,' Sarah said. 'That's why it's so valuable. But it's also going to take some money to update, as you can see.'

The paint was peeling and the front steps sagging, but neither seemed to be dragging down Arial's spirits. She was on the sidewalk now. 'It is so cool. I'm going to go to the door.'

'No,' Sarah said flatly. 'We're going to the rental agent's office—'

But her niece was already there. 'Don't know if this old doorbell works. It's all painted over.'

She pressed it, stood for a count of two and then pounded on the door. 'Hello?'

The cycle was repeated. Twice.

'They aren't home,' I called to her.

'Or they're frightened to open the door to a crazy woman,' Sarah offered as an alternative.

'Fine,' Arial said, returning to the car. 'But I'm sure I heard motion in there.'

'You can't hear motion,' Sarah snapped. 'Now let's go. I don't like to be late.'

'You can too hear motion,' Arial started, and then glanced in the rear-view mirror to see me, my finger to my lips. 'Pick your battles,' I mouthed.

She nodded and started the car.

'I did tell the tenants about Edna's death,' Catherine Smythe told us. We were sitting in her office, the rental agent – a woman of about sixty – behind the desk and the three of us across the desk in front of a sunny window overlooking the street. 'It's a shame. They've only been in the house for a little over three months.'

'You said it's a month-to-month lease?' Sarah asked.

'Yes,' Catherine said, opening a file folder to select a sheaf of papers. 'Technically you're only required to give them thirty days' notice to vacate since they've been in the property for less than a year. But I'd suggest sixty days, if at all possible. Finding alternate living arrangements on the peninsula isn't easy or cheap, and the Bucks are such a nice young couple.'

'Sixty days seems only fair,' Arial said, reaching for the leasing contract Catherine was extending to her.

Sarah grabbed it first. 'Sorry, I'm a real estate agent myself, so I like to look over these things.'

'Of course,' Catherine said. 'I don't know how the State of Wisconsin compares, but California law goes to great lengths to alert tenants to their rights.'

'I can see that,' Sarah said, flipping through. 'This lease is practically the size of a phone book.'

'When they had phone books,' Arial whispered to me.

Sarah ignored her. 'It looks like Christopher Buck moved in June first?'

'Yes, he and his wife,' Catherine said. 'Prior to that, an elderly couple – friends of your grandmother's, I believe – rented it. Sadly, they're both gone now.'

I'd assume so, if they were friends of Sarah's grandmother and Sarah's mother had been eighty-four. People here lived into the triple digits?

'I'm sure Arial and Sarah know this' – actually, I wasn't sure at all – 'but when did Sarah's grandmother die?'

'Oh, it's been at least ten years now since Gretchen's death,' Catherine said. 'Ninety-nine. The Mayes always have been long-lived, I'm told.'

'Hope that streak continues,' Sarah muttered, still perusing the lease.

'Pardon?' Catherine said.

'Ignore her – she just reads aloud,' Arial said brightly. 'Is it possible to get in to see the house today?'

'Only if the tenants agree, I'm afraid,' Catherine said. 'Unless there's an emergency of some sort.'

I saw Arial's eyes shift – probably wondering what constituted an emergency and how we could orchestrate one. But she evidently decided on a different route. 'We're only here until Saturday, and in order to give them the full sixty-day notice, I'd want to see the property before I go. In fact, once I meet the Bucks, who knows? Maybe we'll decide to extend the lease.'

'Excellent thinking,' Catherine said. 'I'll text them right now and let you know what I hear back. Now if that's all—'

'I assume taxes and insurances are up to date?' Sarah asked. 'What about the condition of the house? Are there major repairs in the offing?'

'Taxes are fully paid. I think you'll find they're very low, since your family has owned the house since it was built in the early nineteen hundreds and there are limits to how much they can increase.' She turned to me. 'It's so people aren't taxed out of their houses, you see.'

'And when the property is inherited?' Sarah asked.

'Per Proposition Nineteen that went into effect a few years back, there will be some sort of reassessment and bump in taxes if you choose to keep the property. I have to tell you that it'll be a much smaller bump if the property is used as your primary residence.' This was directed to Arial. 'Which will obviously enter into your decision about the Bucks's lease.'

It certainly would. 'So, if Arial decided to continue to rent the property instead of living in it?'

Catherine actually grimaced. 'The property would be re-appraised and taxed at full market value. Which would likely mean an increase of tens of thousands of dollars in taxes.'

'Per year?' Arial's voice was a squeak.

'I'm afraid so,' Catherine said. 'You'll want to get the advice of a tax attorney, of course.'

'Of course.' Satisfied with the lease and the information, Sarah stood up, handing Catherine Smythe her card. 'Can you email an electronic copy of that lease to me?'

'My pleasure,' Catherine said, escorting us to the door. 'And I'll let you know as soon as I've heard back.'

'Geez,' I said, as we walked down the sidewalk to the car. 'Those property taxes.'

'It's a big deal,' Sarah admitted. 'I'd bet the taxes now are a few hundred dollars a year because they're based on the original price of the house. If that house is reassessed, the market value could easily be two million dollars and the taxes one percent of that.'

'But one percent of two million is twenty thousand dollars. Per year,' I said. 'Arial can't afford to pay that.'

But Arial had already recovered. 'No worries. I was already thinking about living here. This decides it.'

'You can't make a decision like this so quickly,' Sarah started. 'You could also sell the property. You won't pay capital gains because the cost basis will be stepped up at—'

'I'll miss you, too.' Arial punched her aunt in the arm and went around to get into the driver's seat, before letting out a happy sigh. 'So, where to next?'

SIXTEEN

'You know, this might be just the thing for Arial,' I said to Sarah as we crossed the street from the parking structure on Cannery Row.

'What?' Sarah demanded. 'A visit to the aquarium?'

'That, too,' I said, falling into step with her as we walked down the sidewalk to the Monterey Bay Aquarium. Arial, of course, was leading the way. 'Especially since Scott Holmes, the retired police detective, can't meet with us until tomorrow morning. Nor has Catherine heard from the renters. But I meant Arial moving here. Getting a new start.'

'Escaping her criminal past,' Sarah said sarcastically. 'You of all people know running away isn't the solution.'

'Me of all people?' I asked. 'What exactly have I run away from? And, I've lived in the environs of southeastern Wisconsin all my life, so if I did run, I sure didn't get far.'

'See?' Sarah said. 'Because you're smart. Divorce, business collapse – you didn't just take off.'

'You're babbling, you know,' Arial said, not bothering to turn around. 'Saying anything that supports your unsupportable point.'

'Which is what?' Sarah demanded.

'That nobody should go anywhere.' Arial, now at the entrance, turned.

'At least without you,' I added.

'I, personally, don't want to run anywhere,' Sarah said, pulling out her charge card and handing it over. 'I'm happy in Brookhills. With *my* family.'

Arial pursed her lips. 'Meaning Sam and Courtney.'

'Meaning you, too. If you don't abandon us.' Sarah took her card and receipt back from the cashier. 'Sixty bucks a person?'

'You should take out a membership,' I told Arial, holding up a brochure. 'Free admission, plus you'll be supporting this jewel of an aquarium.'

Sarah elbowed me hard.

Arial laughed. 'Come on. I want to see the anemones.'

'And the sea otters,' I said, reading the brochure. 'Ooh, there's a tidal pool in back, that—'

I got another elbow in the ribs.

'What an amazing aquarium,' Arial said as we strolled back out onto the sidewalk. 'I could have spent another four hours there.'

'Then I can only thank God it was closing time,' Sarah muttered. 'Fish is fish.'

I didn't bother arguing, but turned my attention, instead, to the pleasant Kingston. 'And all this, Cannery Row – you can just feel John Steinbeck's spirit, can't you?'

'And smell his fish.' Sarah sniffed.

'It doesn't smell like fish,' Arial said. 'But that reminds me. Where should we go for dinner tonight?'

'I'm thinking fish or seafood,' I said. 'How about the wharf? Maybe clam chowder in a sourdough bread bowl?'

Sarah made a face. 'Sounds a little touristy, don't you think?'

'We are tourists,' Arial said flatly. 'And I think it sounds delicious. Or maybe calamari steaks, sautéed in butter and lemon.'

'With capers?' I asked, as my phone dinged. 'I love pretty much anything done piccata.'

'Or,' Arial continued, glancing sideways at her aunt, 'I read about this great little Italian place just off Lighthouse in Pacific Grove.'

'Italian sounds good,' Sarah said, perking up. 'Who's the text from, Maggy?'

'Pavlik.' I finished reading and slipped the phone back into my pocket. 'He talked to the Monterey PD, but they couldn't tell him much about the hit-and-run that killed Jonathan Springbok. Dark blue or black sedan that Springbok said came out of nowhere, but it was early and barely light.'

'And never solved,' Sarah said.

'Dan said he'd ask Detective Holmes to dig up what he can on the accident, as well,' Arial said, pleased with herself. 'I told him it might be connected to the sexual assault.'

'Good girl,' Sarah said, stepping around the corner of the coffee shop to an open plaza on the bay. 'Let's get coffee and sit down by the fire pit here.'

'Wow,' I said, glancing around. 'This is breathtaking. Is it OK to sit here or does it belong to the hotel?' I nodded at an elegant cream-colored building opposite the coffeehouse.

'I'm honestly not sure,' Sarah said. 'But the plaza is public, so nobody is going to chase us away.' She sucked in a deep breath and then let it out slowly. 'I used to love coming here. It reminded me how lucky we were to live in such a beautiful place.'

Arial wrinkled her nose. 'But you didn't really. Live here, I mean. From what you've said, you were just visiting too.'

'Our grandmother lived here,' Sarah said. 'And our mother was brought up here. Ruth and I figured that made us locals.'

'The Mayes,' I said, sweeping my hand in a flourish. 'Does that also mean you could sit your butt by the fire pit, and somebody would get you your coffee?'

'I wish.'

'Well, you were very patient in the aquarium,' Arial said. 'So I will get the coffee. Latte, Maggy?'

'Please,' I said, starting to sit down and then popping up again. 'Want help?'

'No need,' Arial said. 'No doubt when they find out I'm a Mayes, they'll fall all over themselves to help me.'

I shook my head as I watched her walk away to the café. 'I love that girl.'

'Me, too,' Sarah said, with an uncharacteristic sigh. 'And this place.'

'Then why have you been so pissy?'

'Because my sister – love her or hate her – is in a coma, and I'm losing her only daughter . . .' she swept her arm, not unlike the way I'd done, ' . . . to all this.'

'I'm sorry about Ruth, but coming in second to "all this," as you put it, isn't half bad. This is your family home, after all. This is where you spent your summers. You should be thrilled Arial will be keeping it. In fact, I would think you'd want to spend a lot of time out here. She'll need your help.'

After I said it, I wanted to smack myself. I needed Sarah's help, too.

She read my face and laughed. 'See how it feels? But no worries, I'm not going to relocate here. For one thing, Arial—'

'Thank you for this,' Arial's voice said, and we turned to see her coming toward us, trailed by a young man carrying a cup tray.

'How does she do it?' I asked, turning to Sarah. 'It's like she makes best friends everywhere.'

'Her mother was like that, too,' Sarah said, her head cocked, remembering. 'And then somehow . . . the light went out.'

'The rape?' I asked, lowering my voice.

'And a lifetime with my mother. I swore I'd never let it happen to Arial.'

'It hasn't. She has you. And now it's time to let her go.' I raised my voice as the two twenty-somethings approached the table. 'Such service – thank you!'

'Matt insisted,' Arial said, her cheeks a little pink. 'He's from Michigan.'

'Right down the road and across the lake from us in Wisconsin,' Sarah said dryly.

'I came here for school and never left,' the rusty-haired young man said. 'I hear Arial is moving here, too. You're going to love it,' he said, turning to her.

'Yes,' Sarah said, staring at her smiling niece. 'I guess she will.'

We had dinner that night at the little Italian place in Pacific Grove that Arial had mentioned.

'I'm going to come visit you just to go to La Mia Cucina,' I told Arial, collapsing on the sofa bed in our hotel suite. 'That's the best lobster ravioli I've ever eaten.'

'Same for the marsala,' Sarah said.

'The sand dabs, too,' Arial said. 'Weren't the owners, Paula and Mike, sweet? And Richard, our waiter. Do you know he's from New Zealand?'

Sarah and I exchanged grins. 'There she goes again,' I said. 'Making friends everywhere.'

'And from everywhere,' Sarah added.

'But of course,' Arial said, seeming surprised. 'If you're not open to new people, new experiences, what's the point?'

I groaned. 'I find your enthusiasm both inspiring and exhausting.'

Somebody's phone dinged.

'Mine,' Arial said. 'It's Catherine. We can go over to the house at noon tomorrow. The Bucks won't be there, but they'll leave the doors unlocked.'

'Is that wise?' I asked.

'Maybe not,' Sarah said, 'but it's done here more often than not. And don't get me started on locking cars.'

'I know PG is a small town, but . . .'

'It's a small town that thinks it's an even smaller town,' Sarah said. 'And you wait, Arial. Not only does it seem like everybody knows everybody, but they've dated them.'

Arial settled onto the bed and tucked her legs under her. 'Small pool, huh?'

'With no room for jealousy,' Sarah said. 'At least that's how it was way back when. Your grandmother used to say . . .'

They were still talking and laughing as I drifted off to sleep.

SEVENTEEN

The next morning we swung by Acme for coffee before heading to so-called New Monterey to see retired MPD detective, one S. Holmes.

'So why *New* Monterey?' I asked, getting into the back seat with my latte.

'Because it's not as old as Old Monterey,' Sarah said, taking a sip from one of the two to-go cups in her hands.

Arial took pity on me. 'From what I've read, downtown Monterey is considered "Old Monterey" because some of it dates back to the 1700s.'

'Seventeen-Seventy,' Sarah said, handing me back a to-go cup. 'Here.'

'I already have one,' I said.

'Chai latte for Detective Holmes,' Arial said.

Great name for a detective. 'How do you know what he likes to drink?'

'Dan,' Arial said. 'I texted to thank him for connecting us and asked.'

'She *is* good,' Sarah said, turning back around to face front for the short drive.

'Cute neighborhood,' Arial said as she pulled up in front of a small adobe house and got out.

'It is,' Sarah said, joining her on the sidewalk.

I was still in the back seat. 'Can somebody open the door? My hands are full.' Thanks to my partner.

Arial obliged. As I climbed out with the two lattes, I looked north. 'Is that the bay I see down there?'

'It is indeed,' a male voice said. 'You have to crane your neck a bit to see it from the kitchen window, so the realtor termed it "glimpses of Monterey Bay" when we bought the place.'

'It's beautiful,' Arial said, putting her hand out. 'I'm Arial Kingston.'

'Scott Holmes,' the tall man with dark hair graying at the temples told her. 'And, please, no Sherlock jokes.'

'S. Holmes. Didn't even occur to me,' I lied, handing him a cup. 'This is for you.'

'Acme,' Holmes said. 'Thanks.'

'Sergeant Sotherly told me your drink of choice,' Arial said. 'This is Maggy Thorsen.'

'And I'm Sarah Kingston,' my partner told him, holding out her own hand. 'Arial's aunt.'

'And another Mayes, I assume,' Holmes said. 'You bear quite a resemblance to Edna Mayes – when she was young, of course.'

Sarah blushed. Maybe it was the allusion to her being young, or at least younger than her now deceased mother.

'Edna is . . . was my mother,' she said. 'As I'm sure you worked out, you're being a detective and all.' She giggled.

Arial's eyes widened as we exchanged looks. A giggling Sarah was a rare and somewhat unsettling occurrence.

But Holmes was handsome, and my partner had a soft spot for men who had pistols in their pockets.

'Oh, sorry,' the detective said, catching me looking at his sidearm. 'I just finished cleaning it and was taking it back to the house to lock up when I saw you pull in. Didn't think it was the best form to meet you holding a gun.'

'Good call,' Sarah said. 'Though I once saved Maggy's life with a Smith and Wesson 649.'

'Great little snubbie,' Holmes said. 'Three fifty-seven magnum?'

'Yup. A little heavy but fits nicely in a purse.' Sarah blushed again. 'Not all of us have pockets.'

Bonding. My partner was bonding with the detective.

'A holster is safer than either,' Holmes said, slipping out the gun. 'Digging into a purse or pocket to get—'

Arial cleared her throat.

'Sorry, sorry,' Holmes said with a grin. 'I don't get much chance to talk weaponry these days. Should we go sit? I think Mary made some scones this morning.'

'Oh, I didn't think to bring your wife a coffee, too.' Arial edged through the door after him, blocking Sarah, whose face had fallen. 'That was really rude of me.'

A short stack of file folders sat at one place at the table, a plate of what looked to be raspberry scones in the center. Holmes gestured for us to sit. 'Mary is my daughter and she's already off to school anyway. Not that she drinks coffee.'

Sarah slipped into the chair to the right of the file folders. 'Not even Acme?'

'Just the hot chocolate. She's nine.'

That shut Sarah up.

'Are those the files on Jonathan Springbok's accident?' Arial asked, gesturing to the folders.

'Vehicular homicide,' Holmes corrected, sitting down in front of the folders. 'And also your mother's sexual assault complaint.'

'Thank you,' Arial said.

'Thank Dan Sotherly.' He flipped open the jacket cover. 'Let's start with Springbok. It was early Sunday, December twentieth – just before seven. Springbok was hit when he crossed the road in the middle of a block and at a blind curve to catch his shuttle which was due at seven.'

'The driver didn't stop.' Arial was leaning forward, trying to read upside down.

Holmes flipped the folder around for her. 'It's possible that he had been out all night and was over the legal limit.'

'No witnesses,' Arial said, looking up.

'None other than the victim, himself, who died later that day. Springbok told the responding officers that the car was a dark sedan and came out of nowhere. There were no skid marks, no indication that the driver attempted to brake.'

'Could it have been deliberate?' I asked.

Holmes did a double-take. 'There was no reason to think so at the time. Do you know something we don't?'

'My mother was raped that same weekend,' Arial said.

'I took her statement. But you think they're connected?'

'We do,' Arial said. 'Jonathan Springbok confessed to his wife—'

'On his deathbed,' Sarah injected.

'That he had cheated. A quote,' Arial made air quotes, '"one-night stand" with a woman named Ruth – the daughter of Edna, a Pacific Grove artist.'

'Your mother.' He rubbed his chin. 'You think this one-night stand Springbok confessed to was actually the rape that Ruth

Mayes reported? But why would the man lie at that point? He was dying.'

Arial shrugged. 'Maybe he convinced himself it was consensual.'

'Or was just too chicken-shit to admit what he'd done,' Sarah said.

'But if you think there's a connection, what are you saying?' Holmes asked. 'That Springbok's death wasn't an accident?'

'I don't suppose he could have thrown himself in front of the car?' I suggested. 'You know, riddled with remorse?'

Arial gave me a sad smile and shook her head. 'What Maggy is trying not to say is that my mother could have killed him.'

I glanced sideways at Sarah, thinking that if Ruth had been raped and then committed murder, it certainly could have taken that light out of her eyes.

Holmes had flipped open the other file. 'The date of Ruth Mayes's sexual assault was Sunday, December twentieth.'

'As was the vehicular homicide,' Arial said, tapping the file in front of her.

'That makes sense.' I frowned, craning my neck to see Holmes's folder. 'If Ruth was raped early the morning of the twentieth, that—'

'But she wasn't,' Holmes said, re-reading the file. 'She reported the assault on Monday, December twenty-first, and stated that she met this man in the bar around nine on Sunday night. She suspected he slipped something into her drink but refused a drug test.'

He looked up. 'I remember that. I assumed that either she was afraid something else would show up in her blood or she'd gone up to his room willingly before the assault and didn't want to admit it in front of her mother.'

'Either or both could be true, I guess,' Sarah said. 'I doubt Ruth was above the occasional party drug.'

Arial cleared her throat. 'Either way, though, the man couldn't have been Jonathan Springbok. He was hit by a car Sunday morning and had already died by the time Ruth was raped that night.'

'So what does this mean?' Arial said as we got into the car. 'My mother was raped by somebody else?'

'Or had the time wrong,' Sarah ventured. 'Or the date.'

'Hardly something you'd forget, is it?' But you might lie about it. If you had a reason to. 'The assault report wasn't filed until Monday, Holmes said.'

'Which tallies with her being raped the night before,' Arial said, pulling away from the curb. 'House next? It's nearly noon.'

'Definitely,' I said absently. 'What did Holmes say? That he had the impression Edna was the one who had insisted Ruth file a report?'

'And Gretchen. That wouldn't be unusual, would it?' Arial said. 'Plenty of rape victims have to be encouraged to report.'

'It especially wouldn't be unusual for Edna and Ruth,' Sarah said.

'Did Ruth always do what her mother told her?' I asked curiously. 'I can't imagine you were as easily controlled.'

'I wasn't,' Sarah said. 'And Ruth wasn't either, early on. The more I think about it, the more I think that night in December changed her life. Made her . . .'

'Into a doormat?' Arial asked, and then sighed. 'I guess.'

'It's sad that she never got out from under your grandmother's thumb,' I said. 'Not even after Edna died.'

'Out of the frying pan and into the coma,' Sarah said.

'Is there anything—'

'No,' Sarah said before I could ask. 'Nothing new from the hospital.'

Silence, and then Arial said, 'I turn here, right?'

'Right. Left.'

'Gotcha. I think.' Arial turned left and drove down the block to the last house. 'Twelve noon on the dot.'

Switching off the engine, she turned toward us. 'I'm really excited to see the house.'

'I don't blame you,' I said, climbing out. 'So, let's put all the rest of this out of our heads for now.'

'Absolutely.' Sarah draped her arm over her niece's shoulders and pulled her close to give her a noogie on the top of her head. 'Let's go see your new home.'

As we had been told to expect, the front door of the little green house was unlocked. I tried the buzzer as Sarah swung open the door. Nothing. 'Put "get the doorbell fixed" on the to-do list.'

'That will be a minor item on a very long list,' Sarah said, stepping into the front room of the house. 'Not much of anything has been updated, at least since the last time I was here.'

'Which was when you went away to college,' I said, stepping back so Arial could precede me into her new house. 'You'll excuse me if I point out that a lot of things could have changed since then.'

'That was the last time I spent a summer here,' Sarah said. 'But I was in the house most recently when my grandmother died.'

'Ten years ago, then,' Arial said, looking around at what was undoubtedly the main room of the small house. 'Oooh, hardwood floors.'

That would need sanding, but I had to admit they were lovely. Narrow old-fashioned planks, mostly even. In the corner of the room was a fireplace. 'Is that operational, you think?'

'There's a note here to the tenants,' Sarah said, reading a sticky note taped to one side. 'Says not to use it, which is probably why they've put candles on the hearth instead.'

'You'll want to—'

'Have it checked out,' Arial said, with a grin. 'And I'll put refinishing the floors on the list as well, no worries. Assuming I have the money.'

'Depending on what happens with Ruth, you could sell the Brookhills house for working capital,' Sarah said, going to look out the window to the side yard. 'But you also might want to consider renting out either this or the guesthouse while you're living in and renovating the other. Give you an income.'

'That's right, there's a guesthouse,' Arial said, coming to the window. 'That white building.'

I joined them. 'And that building that backs up to it is the garage, you said?'

Arial was levering herself closer to the window, craning her neck to see. 'Would I be able to combine the two? They seem to be just feet apart.'

'You could, but it's filled with junk,' Sarah said. 'If I were you, I'd clean it out and use it for its original purpose, a garage.'

'Why?' I asked. 'I mean, this isn't Wisconsin, so no snow to shovel in the winter.'

'Yes,' Arial said. 'Why not just park on the street like every-body else seems to?'

'Everybody else pretty much has to,' Sarah said. 'Because they don't have garages, or they've converted them to living space. A garage – maybe even a two-car garage, by the looks of it – raises the value of the property.'

'But she's not selling it,' I reminded the real estate agent.

'Even so,' Sarah said, raising her chin. 'And don't forget car week.'

'Car week?' I repeated.

'Monterey Car Week, featuring Concours d'Elegance in Pebble Beach, among other events. Thousands of car lovers descend on the peninsula and all of them—'

'Are looking for indoor parking for their babies,' Arial finished. 'I've read about it.'

'They also need a place to stay, which is another way to go with the guesthouse,' Sarah said. 'Short-term rentals.'

'There are two bedrooms, one bath in this house?' I asked, poking my head around the corner. 'Kitchen here.'

Arial followed me in. 'Pink and black tile.'

'Told you nothing's been renovated,' Sarah said, nodding at the chipped sink which held a single dirty knife and fork.

'You'll want to gut this,' I said, unable to help myself. 'I mean, eventually.'

'I don't know, I kind of like it.' Arial was running her hand over the tile countertop. 'Retro.'

'One woman's retro is another woman's mildew-attracting grout lines,' Sarah said, turning up her nose.

'But—'

'I'm sure you'll be able to modernize it, without ruining the character,' I assured her.

Sarah was opening the cabinet doors. 'Dishes in here.'

'Probably the tenants,' I said. 'Should you be snooping? They were nice enough to let us in while they were gone.'

'And therefore, should expect some snooping.' Arial was inspecting the heavy oak kitchen table. 'Think this is theirs?'

'Place was rented furnished,' Sarah said, closing the last cabinet door and going to the refrigerator. 'Must be young. They have kale.' She pulled out a container and sniffed it. 'And chai.'

'Or old and healthy,' Arial said lightly. 'Bedrooms?'

Sarah closed the fridge door and pointed toward the main room. 'Hallway to the left of the fireplace.'

Arial led the way, throwing open the first door on the right. 'Oh, look! Matching tile!'

We were in the bathroom. And, yes, the black and pink tile surrounded a pink tub. And topped the cabinets. I couldn't think of anything else to say except, 'Retro.'

'Right?' Arial said delightedly.

'Hmm. Maybe I'm wrong.' Sarah had the doors to the bedrooms open. 'The tenants aren't young.'

'Why do you say that?' I asked.

'They sleep in separate rooms,' Sarah said, pointing toward the unmade beds in each room.

I stepped into one of the rooms. 'So what? Maybe they work different shifts. Or one of them snores.'

'Frank snores and you still sleep with him,' Sarah pointed out.

'Frank is my sheepdog.' Mocha snored, too, but her chihuahua snores were mostly covered up by Frank's sheepdog snores. 'And Pavlik doesn't.'

'Yet you all happily sleep together,' Sarah said.

'After a fashion.' That 'fashion' being that Pavlik and I woke up every morning with aches and pains from contorting ourselves around our furry bedmates. 'Anyway, what's your point?'

'Just—'

'The bedrooms are a fair size,' Arial said, poking her head into each. 'Let's look at the guesthouse. Is there a back door?'

'Through the bathroom.'

Arial blinked. 'That's weird.'

'Sand,' Sarah said. 'We were supposed to shower off when we came back from the beach.'

I guess that made sense. 'How far is the beach?' I asked, following them through the bathroom and out a door I'd assumed was a closet.

'Maybe five blocks,' Sarah said.

'There's a shower out here, too,' Arial said, pointing at a jerry-rigged hose set-up.

'No hot water, though,' Sarah said, leading us to the guesthouse. 'At least in my time.'

'Hope this is unlocked, too.' Arial was trying the knob. 'Damn.'

'It's possible the tenants don't have use of it,' Sarah said, shading her eyes to look in the window.

'Well then, Catherine should have given us the key,' Arial said, her lower lip jutting out for just a second before she brightened. 'Oh, wait!'

'For what it's worth,' Sarah said, rubbing a little grit off the window, 'there's one bedroom and the kitchen is more—'

But Arial had the door open. 'The PG keys, remember?' She was dangling the set we'd found in Edna's room.

'Smart girl for remembering to bring them,' I said.

'I should have remembered them yesterday,' she said, moving into the guesthouse. 'We could have looked then.'

'Illegal to go in without the tenants' permission,' Sarah reminded her.

'Right, right, right,' Arial said, darting from door to door. The set-up wasn't unlike the main house, but no fireplace in this room and the kitchen was more kitchenette than kitchen, with a two-burner stove top and no oven.

'Glad they continued the theme,' I said, running my hand over the pink and black tiles.

'Probably got a deal,' Sarah said.

'The bedroom and bath are really small,' Arial said, having apparently finished her whole-house inspection. 'If we could steal just a little space from the garage . . .'

'It's pretty run-down,' Sarah said, leading the way back out the door and around to the adjacent building.

'I'll say.' Arial's eyes were wide as she took in the weathered wood structure. 'Looks like Swiss cheese.'

'Termites,' Sarah said, sidestepping a pair of stinky metal trash cans. 'They're pretty common here. You'll probably want to tent the whole property.'

'And fumigate it?' I asked. 'Is that safe?'

'Not for the termites,' Sarah said. 'But you won't find a sales contract that doesn't have a stipulation for some kind of exter-mination and termite repair.'

'*Not selling it*,' Arial and I chorused.

'I'll ask Catherine if the property was tented before the new renters came in,' Sarah continued, ignoring us. 'This may just be old damage.' She pulled on the door into the garage and held out her hand to Arial for the keys. 'It's locked.'

'Why would you bother locking this, of all things?' I asked. 'Looks like you could blow on the garage and it would fall down.'

But Sarah had the door unlocked and swept her hand toward Arial. 'Want to go in first?'

'*Now* you show manners?' I asked, as Arial stepped in.

'Let her take on the termites,' Sarah said. 'Probably earwigs in there, too. And, of course, spi—'

'Guys?' Arial's voice came from inside. 'There's a car in here.'

'Somebody actually put a car in a garage?' Sarah asked. 'Wonder of wonders.'

I ignored her, stepping in and blinking in the dark.

'No light switch I could find,' Arial said, raising the light on her phone. 'But look at this.'

'Can't look at anything with that light in my face,' Sarah said, shielding her eyes. 'What—'

'This.' Arial turned the light toward a car-sized shape covered by a tarpaulin.

She lifted the front corner nearest us, revealing a very old, very dusty but distinguishably dark-colored sedan. With extensive front-end damage.

EIGHTEEN

'Ford Escort,' Arial said, circling around to the back of the car as she pulled off the rest of the tarpaulin and dropped it on the floor of the garage. 'Is it old enough to be . . .?'

'The one that ran down Jonathan Springbok?' I asked. 'It could be. If—'

'The Escort was made in the 1981 to 2003 model years,' Sarah interrupted. 'This is a 1996.'

I regarded Sarah. 'You recognize it?'

She hesitated and then nodded. 'The color is "aubergine."'

'Eggplant?' I said, squinting. 'I guess that would fill the bill as a dark-colored sedan.'

'I remember because it was a rare factory color when Gretchen got it.'

Apparently Sarah had been into cars, even back then.

'It was Gretchen's?' Arial said. 'I was expecting you to say Edna's. Or Ruth's.'

'It's a long drive from Brookhills, Wisconsin to Pacific Grove, California,' Sarah said. 'We would fly in and use my grandmother's car while we were here.'

'Could the Escort have been stashed in this termite-infested garage all these years?' I asked.

'It's entirely possible,' Sarah said. 'My grandmother was in her late seventies then and had glaucoma. She'd walk most places – or take her bicycle – rather than drive.' She nodded at a rusted beach cruiser with a white wicker basket, leaning against a wall.

'I guess that would explain her not seeing the human-sized ding in the front bumper,' Arial said, coming back to the front. 'And the blood.' She took another look. 'Or is that rust?'

'Let's not get ahead of ourselves,' Sarah said. 'Jonathan was run down on Sunday morning and died that night. Later that night, Ruth said she was drugged and raped by an unknown man. So she couldn't—'

'"Ruth said" being the key words,' Arial said. 'Melinda might not be the only one lying here.'

'We're saying Ruth lied about when she was raped.' After all, who was alive to contradict her?

'Well, wouldn't you?' Arial asked. 'Otherwise, she'd be handing the police a motive for killing Springbok.'

'She never named him in the rape,' Sarah pointed out.

'She wouldn't, would she? He was dead at her hands.' Arial touched the car. 'Or her grandmother's bumper.'

But something didn't fit. 'Then why did Ruth report the rape at all?'

Sarah and Arial exchanged frowns.

'Gretchen, probably,' Sarah said finally. 'If she got wind that her granddaughter was assaulted, Gretchen would have been on the phone to the police. It's like the woman had a hotline, called them for everything, including the neighborhood cats padding through the back yard.'

'At the time she called, she couldn't have known Ruth ran down Jonathan. Or she wouldn't have called, right?'

'Probably not,' Sarah said. 'But if Ruth subsequently broke down and told Edna and Gretchen what she'd done, they may have conspired to say she'd been raped Sunday night, rather than Saturday night. Kingston women do tend to stand together.'

'Not in my experience,' Arial muttered.

Her aunt raised her eyebrows.

'Except for you and me, of course,' Arial amended.

Sarah sniffed.

'The report wasn't filed until Monday,' I said. 'So, let's say your daughter or granddaughter comes home Saturday night and says she was raped and . . .' I stopped, thinking. 'You say Gretchen didn't drive much, but what about Edna? Could she have taken out Jonathan for raping her daughter?'

Sarah hesitated and then nodded once. 'Wouldn't put it past her. She'd consider it divine retribution.'

'But it doesn't change anything date-wise,' Arial said. 'To deflect suspicion, they still would have to distance the rape from the accident.'

'Vehicular homicide,' I reminded her as my phone signaled a text. 'Hmm . . . Pavlik says they've managed to isolate a couple of fingerprints – two different people – on the PVC venting for the furnace.'

'Do they know whose?' Arial asked.

'No, but one is quite a bit smaller than the others.'

'Melinda?' Arial asked.

'I don't—' Another ding. 'Well, that's weird. He says to be careful.'

'Why's that?' Arial asked.

'Because apparently Melinda Springbok has a brother. He—'

I was interrupted by the crash of the garbage cans outside.

Arial was out the door like a shot. As Sarah and I followed, we caught sight of the girl making a flying leap onto the back of a dark-haired man.

'Whoa,' I said, when we caught up. 'That's action hero kind of stuff.'

'I'm calling the police,' the man said, still pinned with Arial's knee on his back. 'What are you doing in my yard?'

'You're the tenant?' Arial said, crawling off. She stuck out a hand. 'I guess I'm your landlord.'

'Catherine Smythe said she had your permission for us to inspect the property,' Sarah said, switching into real estate mode. 'This is Arial Mayes Kingston, and I'm her aunt Sarah Mayes Kingston.'

Apparently we were making use of the family name all of a sudden. 'And I'm Maggy Thorsen,' I said, holding my own hand out to help him up. 'No middle name.'

'I'm very sorry,' Arial said, brushing him off. 'You must be Christopher Buck.'

I frowned, studying him. 'Christopher Buck?' I repeated. 'Are you sure it's not Springbok?'

He backed away like I was a crazy woman. 'No, of course not. Why?'

'You shaved your stubble, but you're the guy who passed through the Morrison lobby when we were talking to Melinda. I remember because you did kind of a double-take when she and Arial were sitting side by side.'

'Double-take?' Sarah repeated. 'Looked more like ogling to me.'

The man was holding up both hands, backing away. 'I have no idea what—'

'Oh, give it up, Christopher.' A car door opened on the street and Melinda Springbok emerged.

NINETEEN

'Let me get this straight,' Sarah said, as we sat down across from the Springboks/Bucks at the kitchen table. 'You two are the tenants.'

'Brother and sister, not husband and wife,' Arial added. 'Which explains the separate bedrooms.'

'But why did you rent this place?' I asked. 'It certainly isn't a coincidence.'

'Not at all,' Christopher said, having brushed off the dirt and regained his dignity. 'As I'm sure Melinda has told you, we've been looking into our father's death. We thought this place might give us some answers.'

His tone was icy, so I turned my attention to Melinda. 'You made it out of Brookhills without being brought in for questioning?'

'Chris was waiting by the car at the Morrison. We went straight to the airport and took the first standby seats we could get heading west.' She leaned forward. 'But I don't understand why the police came looking for me in the first place. I haven't done anything.'

'Your fingerprint was on the doorknob to Ruth's room,' Arial told her.

'So what?' She sat back. 'I told you I was inside the house Monday morning, looking around.'

'You have trouble keeping your lies straight,' Sarah said. 'Maybe you should write them down.'

Melinda hesitated and glanced at her brother.

'You said the fire investigators arrived and you never went into the house,' Arial told her, sliding a notebook out of her pocket. 'I did write it down.'

I was impressed. 'Problem is,' I told Melinda, 'your print was under mine, and I touched that knob Sunday afternoon when we found Ruth. That means yours had to be left before that.'

'You can tell us, or you can tell the cops,' Sarah snarled, sounding like something out of a TV show.

Melinda rolled her eyes. 'Fine. Chris and I may have been in Brookhills before this weekend.'

Sarah frowned. 'When was this?'

'In June,' he said. 'We met with Edna then.'

Arial's eyebrows went up. 'You saw my grandmother? Why? To ask her if she knew your father had raped my mother?'

'Or if she knew your mother had mowed him down in the street and left him for dead,' Christopher retorted.

'That—'

'You've just seen the car.'

Hard to argue with that. 'What did Edna say?' I asked.

'An eye for an eye, I think were her exact words.'

'Sounds like my mother,' Sarah said. 'And while Chris and Edna were chatting, Melinda, what were you doing?'

She stuck her chin in the air. 'Nosing around. Ruth's room, the garage, even tried the attic but I couldn't open it.'

That must have been one long conversation between Christopher and Edna. 'You said you found out where Ruth and Edna were from the obituary.'

'I lied.'

Now there was a surprise.

'It wasn't hard to put it together from what my mother told us,' Christopher said. 'Woman named Ruth, mother a local painter. All we had to do was Google it.'

Like I said.

'Makes sense,' Sarah said. 'Smart of you to find a way to nose around this house. From the looks of it, nothing has changed since my grandmother died.'

Maybe it was Sarah's conversational tone or her praise, but Christopher seemed to thaw a little. 'That's because I told the property manager not to bother updating the place after the old couple renting it died. I hoped we'd find something left behind, but I was shocked when I saw the car in the garage. I rented the house on the spot.'

'I suppose the police wouldn't have had reason to look for it here,' Arial reasoned. 'And from what Sarah says, my grandmother didn't drive anymore. Did you have it tested? I thought I saw blood on the front.'

'We thought the same thing,' Christopher said, leaning forward. 'Checked it with luminol. It's rust.'

'We think they may have washed the car before putting it away,' Melinda contributed.

'Why didn't you call the police?' Arial asked.

'Because we wanted to know more. That's why we went to see your grandmother,' Christopher said.

'Did you tell her about finding the car?' I asked. 'I assume you'd already found it.'

'We had, but no, we agreed Chris wouldn't tell her,' Melinda said. 'We figured if she knew we were the tenants, she'd kick us out and dispose of the car.'

I leaned over to Sarah, who was on my left. 'When was it again that Edna told you she was writing Ruth out of the will?'

Sarah nodded significantly. 'June.'

I cleared my throat. 'So after Edna died, you thought you'd go straight to the horse's mouth?'

Christopher and Melinda exchanged unsure looks.

'You intended to ask my mother directly if she killed Jonathan?' Arial asked.

'Yes,' Melinda said. 'Edna was obviously protecting her. With Edna gone, we thought Ruth might cave.'

'Of course, we also knew that Edna could have been driving the car,' Christopher continued. 'Or even your great-grandmother. With both of them dead, we thought Ruth might tell us the truth.'

'Murderous lot,' I murmured. 'These Kingston women.'

Arial rolled her eyes and then turned back to her tenants. 'I ask again, why didn't you just go to the police? They could do DNA on the inside and the outside of the car.'

Christopher's brow was wrinkled in surprise. 'You want us to catch your mother? Or grandmother?'

Don't forget great-grandmother.

'Neither of them was exactly kind to me,' Arial said. 'My being a bastard and all.'

'But the only motive for the hit-and-run was the supposed rape of your mother,' Melinda said, putting her hands in her lap. 'We knew about that and, like Christopher said, we wanted to know more before we raised all that with the police.'

'I bet you did,' Sarah said. 'But you did raise it with my mother?'

'More like she raised it with me when I said they had an affair,' Christopher said, his eyes wide. 'Kept screaming liar, liar, liar and quoting the Bible. Scared the hell out of me.'

'I almost fell off the chair I was standing on to pry open the attic hatch,' Melinda said. 'I thought the woman was either going to kill us or have a heart attack, so we ran.'

'She could be scary,' Arial said.

'And had a bad heart,' I added.

Melinda's eyes were huge. 'I looked up the Bible verse she recited. It's Psalm fifty-eight, verse three. "The wicked are estranged from the womb; they go astray from birth, speaking lies." Totally creeped me out.'

'So what? You waited until she was dead to come back and talk to Ruth?' I asked. 'That's pretty creepy, too.'

'Maybe, but we were too late,' Melinda said. 'Thanks, by the way, for letting me think Ruth was dead all this time.'

'How did you find out she wasn't?' Sarah asked.

'I called the hospital on a hunch,' Christopher said. 'They wouldn't give me any information, of course, just referred me to the family.'

'Which they wouldn't do, obviously, if she'd never made it to the hospital,' Melinda snapped.

'We didn't owe you any information,' Arial said. 'Given all your lies.'

'I assume she's still in the coma?'

Arial didn't answer.

'Well, we can still call the police about the car,' I said. 'Find out the truth.'

Christopher shrugged. 'Everyone involved is either dead or in a vegetative state. What good will the truth do now?'

What good indeed?

Back at the hotel, I called Pavlik to tell him we'd seen both of the Springbok siblings and that they'd been inside the Kingston house in June.

'Pavlik confirmed that Melinda's fingerprints do not match the ones in the basement,' I said, clicking off. 'He also says that with what he has now, he can't compel Melinda or Christopher to return to Brookhills.'

'It would be nice to have Christopher's prints to compare with the other set on the PVC,' Sarah said. 'I should have just grabbed a dirty glass when we were in the house.'

'There were no glasses,' Arial said, digging into her pocket and coming up with knife and fork. 'But I got these.'

'That's my girl,' Sarah said.

'You also scored big with your notebook,' I told Arial. 'I didn't realize you were writing things down.'

'On paper? You got to be kidding me.' She took the pad out of her pocket, and I saw it was in actuality a sea life book from the aquarium.

I should have known. 'Well, it worked regardless.'

'Thanks,' she said, going to the closet for a plastic dirty clothes bag to wrap the fork and knife. 'Should we go to the police here?'

I frowned. 'Good question. But getting Christopher's finger-prints off stolen silverware is probably best done in Brookhills.'

'Assuming you can talk Pavlik into it,' Sarah said. 'But I think Arial means about the car.'

'The vehicular homicide is a Monterey police matter,' I said. 'And maybe PG, since the car is located there.'

'But you agree that we should alert them,' Arial said. 'I get what Melinda and Christopher said about nothing really to be gained, but—'

'Yeah, I have to admit I didn't quite understand that,' Sarah said. 'It was their father who was killed, after all. Wouldn't they want some closure?'

'Their rapist father,' Arial reminded her. 'But . . . it almost feels like they're hiding behind that, doesn't it? All of a sudden, they don't want to pursue the truth.'

'Maybe they did something in Brookhills they don't want to come out,' I suggested. 'They were both in Ruth's house in June, but we have only Melinda's word that fingerprint on Ruth's doorknob was left then.'

'Ruth didn't normally close that door when my mother was alive,' Sarah said. 'In case Edna called.'

'It was closed when I found Ruth, though,' I said.

Sarah shrugged. 'She changed her habits, I guess.'

'As proven by the purchase of the car and even turning on the heat this early,' Arial said.

And look how that turned out. 'Maybe she closed the door to keep the heat in.'

'Or the carbon monoxide,' Arial said. 'We have way too many theories going on simultaneously.'

I would agree with that. 'We also only have Melinda's very questionable word that she or Christopher weren't in the house this trip.'

'Which is why we're going to check Christopher's prints against the larger prints on the venting.' Arial was frowning. 'But do you really think they'd go as far as trying to kill Ruth?'

'If they believe she killed their father,' I said, with an apologetic shrug. 'Your father.'

'My father the rapist.' Arial rolled her shoulders and groaned. 'OK, first things first. Or first thing that we can do from here. Should I call Holmes and tell him about the car?'

'He's retired,' Sarah pointed out. 'Shouldn't we call your friend Dan instead?'

'Different department and Dan referred us to Holmes,' I said. 'Retired or not, he's familiar with the case and will know who to talk to about the car.'

'I'm not sure what they'll get off it,' Sarah said. 'Ruth or Edna's prints or DNA in the car will mean nothing. They both drove it, along with Gretchen.'

'They'll have to dig up Edna's prints,' I said, as my phone pinged.

'No pun intended,' Sarah said, throwing me a sidelong grin. 'Unless you mean it literally.'

'Not this time, I hope. But Pavlik will need to find her fingerprints in the Brookhills house and send them on to the Monterey PD, I assume.'

'Ruth did a real number on that room with the bleach and the paint,' Arial said, as I turned my attention to my message. 'But there will be prints and DNA on the things in the dresser, I'm sure.'

'As far as the outside of the car is concerned,' I said, putting down the phone, 'there might be some trace of Jonathan Springbok, even if Melinda is right and it was washed.'

'Ruth and her bleach again,' Sarah said. 'But if Jonathan Springbok's DNA is still on the Escort, at least there will be plenty of offspring to compare it to.' She gave Arial a wolfish grin.

Arial rolled her eyes. 'Whether there's evidence on that car or not, we still have to get it out of there. I'm not living in that place with a murder weapon in my garage.'

'You should talk to Maggy,' Sarah said. 'She manages fine with corpses littering the neighborhood. Just steps over 'em and presses on.'

'You're way too chipper,' I told Sarah as another message from Pavlik came in.

'She is,' Arial said. 'Why's that?'

'Because as far as I can see,' Sarah said, 'our work is done here. Time to go home.'

'It's Thursday,' Arial protested. 'Our flight is Saturday, which gives us tomorrow to—'

'I'm afraid Sarah is right,' I said, putting down my phone again. 'We should change our flights and head back.'

Sarah's eyes narrowed and she gestured at the phone. 'What did Pavlik say?'

'They've matched the larger of the fingerprints, so it's not Christopher after all. Turns out it's the J of JM Services.'

Arial cocked her head. 'The company that did the estimate for the furnace work? That's not surprising, is it? Their technician would have examined the furnace and the venting before they wrote the estimate in March.'

'True, but Pavlik's people had trouble running down the company. No electrical or plumbing license.'

'I can't imagine they're the only unlicensed contractor in Brookhills,' Sarah said. 'In fact, I can assure you they're not.'

Arial's forehead was wrinkled. 'But if they couldn't find the company so the guy could provide his prints, how did they match them to the ones on the furnace?'

'That's exactly the question to ask.' I threw a triumphant look at Sarah. 'He was in the system.'

'For being unlicensed?' Sarah demanded. 'I doubt it. Even if he was, they couldn't compel him to provide fingerprints for an offense like that.'

'But they could for burglary. And, get this, his partial print also appears on the forced back door.'

'He's the one who broke in?' Arial said, puzzled. 'But nothing was stolen.'

'Melinda showed up,' Sarah reminded her. 'Maybe she disturbed him.'

'And the fire investigators, in turn, disturbed her,' I said. 'At that point he probably just gave up and took off.'

'But who is "he"?' Arial said impatiently, flopping down on one of the beds. 'And why does it mean we have to go back tomorrow?'

'He is Jackson Morris.'

'Jackson.' Sarah's forehead was wrinkled. 'That . . .'

'Bernie and Caron's Jack-of-all-trades, as you called him.' I held up the photo Pavlik had sent me. 'Look familiar?'

'He was at the funeral, too,' Arial said, taking my phone. 'He was talking to Charles Cokely.'

'Very good,' I told her. 'I couldn't put it together when we saw him in his work coveralls at the Morrison.'

'He told me he worked for Edna.' Sarah snatched the phone away from her. 'And I guess he did. You think he was casing the joint to rob it?'

'Maybe,' I said. 'I texted Pavlik that Jackson was working at the Morrison and they're bringing him in. You do want to be there, don't you?'

'I certainly do,' Sarah said. 'Arial?'

'Yes?' The girl was still sitting on the bed, tapping on her phone. She set it down. 'Just changed the flight to nine a.m. tomorrow. We'd best get packing.'

TWENTY

'You stole these,' Pavlik said, holding up the plastic clothes bag with the fork and knife in it.

We were in Pavlik's office at the sheriff's department. The sheriff sitting behind the desk, Sarah and Arial in the guest chairs across from him and me, standing.

Arial squirmed, making the faux leather chair give off a fart-like toot. 'Not really stole. Borrowed.'

'Arial owns the house,' Sarah said. 'And it's rented furnished—'

'And fully equipped with linens and dishes and all,' Arial contributed, though I wasn't sure we'd verified that actually was true. 'Which means it's really my silverware.'

'But Christopher Buck's fingerprints,' Pavlik said darkly. 'Which you stole.'

Sarah gave a little snort. 'Even his name isn't his.'

'Actually, it is,' Pavlik said. 'He changed it legally from Springbok. And, tenant or not, he—'

A tap on the door and a deputy stuck his head in. 'The Egans are here.'

'Might as well send them in,' Pavlik said. 'The more the merrier.'

The deputy stepped back and Caron, a short, freckled-face brunette and Bernie came in.

Arial hopped up. 'Take my chair, please.'

Sarah groaned and started to stand as well. 'Fine. Sit.'

'No need,' Bernie said, waving her down with a grin. 'You sit, Caron.'

She did, the gaseous chair letting out another squeal. 'Oops.'

Pavlik shook his head. 'I need to get new chairs. But thanks for coming in, you two. I assume you've confirmed that the man we have in custody identified himself as Jackson Morrison.'

'We did,' Caron said, frowning. 'Are you saying that isn't his real name?'

'It's close, but no,' Pavlik said. 'It's Jackson Morris – no relation to the hotel family.'

'I should have checked,' Bernie said, shaking his head. 'That's on me.'

'But he was so nice,' Caron said. 'And he knew so much about the hotel.'

'He apparently does his homework,' Pavlik said. 'Then he goes into a home or, in your case, hotel, posing as a workman of some type and ingratiates himself.'

'We certainly fell for it,' Caron said. 'The man could do pretty much anything.'

'Probably because he's done pretty much everything, or at least pretended to,' Pavlik said, turning to Sarah and Arial. 'We matched his fingerprints to the written estimate for the furnace repair.'

'JM Services is Jackson Morris,' Sarah said, chewing on that. 'But doesn't that mean he could have left his fingerprints in the basement back in March when he did the estimate?'

'That would be his defense, I'm sure,' Pavlik said. 'But luckily for us he had something on his thumb – maybe a burn or a blister – so we could tell which of the prints was made on the same day, specifically on that ninety-degree elbow you picked up, Arial.'

Arial's head snapped back. 'You can't be saying that the smaller print Maggy said you'd found was mine? You were there. You saw me—'

'I saw you pick it up,' the sheriff said, 'and we could eliminate your prints because they're on file.'

'Criminal,' Sarah mouthed at her.

Arial ignored that. 'It also wasn't Melinda's, Maggy said. Though she was with Christopher when he came in June.'

Pavlik frowned. 'Maggy told me. I can't believe we missed that.'

'Two different names?' I suggested. 'You'd just found out about Christopher, so I assume you made any inquiries using his legal last name, Buck. You weren't looking for a Springbok.'

'We should have been. We're supposed to be the professionals.' Pavlik's eyes were dark. 'But thank you for the information.'

I loved it when he talked that way. 'No ID on the other smaller fingerprint, then?'

He shook his head.

Caron's face was screwed up. 'What fingerprints? What are you talking about?'

'Jackson broke into my mother's house,' Arial explained. 'The morning after she was asphyxiated. Or I guess it could have been sometime during Sunday night into Monday morning.'

'Did he steal something there, too?' Caron asked.

Too. 'That vase Bernie said had been taken,' I said, the light finally dawning. 'That was Jackson.'

'Wait,' Sarah said, leaning forward. 'I thought that was just cheap hotel décor.'

'Not so cheap, as it turns out,' Bernie said. 'The vases dated back to the opening of the hotel.'

'There was more than one taken?' I asked.

'One from each floor, where they hadn't already been broken or stolen over the years,' Caron said. 'Five, at about eight hundred dollars apiece.'

Sarah whistled. 'Who leaves four thousand dollars' worth of vases standing around for people to steal?'

Bernie started to gesture toward Caron and then thought better of it.

Caron's eyes narrowed. 'It's history,' she hissed. 'Our history.'

'You think Jackson stole them?' I asked, hoping to relieve – or at least redirect – Caron's ire.

Pavlik nodded in the affirmative. 'When you told me Jackson was working at the Morrison, we went to pick him up.'

'We thought the sheriff's department was responding to our call about the vases,' Caron said.

'Sirens wailing,' Bernie said. 'It did seem a bit much.'

'Your tax dollars at work,' Pavlik said, with a grin.

'The one vase going missing seemed accidental,' Caron said, ignoring the men. 'But I told Bernie we had a master thief at work when they all were gone. We had no idea it was Jackson.'

'Did he admit taking them?' I asked.

'They were in the back of his truck when we picked him up,' Pavlik said, standing up. 'He's in the interview room now, so thank you again for coming in.' He was ushering us to the door. 'We'll be in touch.'

'Could . . .' I started, but was drowned out by the cacophony of voices.

'Did he tamper with the furnace?' Sarah asked. 'Why?'

'I'm going to do an inventory,' Caron was saying, 'see if anything else is missing.'

'You'll dust the silverware for prints, right?' Arial asked, flashing Pavlik a smile on the way out. 'Oh, and . . .' She was digging in her pocket and came up with a baggy which now held the batteries. 'Can you do these, too? I found them in Ruth's trash and meant to give them to you.'

'Of course you did,' Pavlik said, taking the bag. 'Maggy, can you hold back a sec?'

'Sure,' I said, and then to Sarah in a low tone, 'I'll talk to you later, OK?'

Sarah gave me a knowing look as Pavlik closed the door behind them.

'Does she think we're going to make out?' Pavlik asked, giving me a workplace-appropriate welcome-home kiss. Sarah, Arial and I had come directly to the station from the airport. In fact, my luggage was still in Sarah's car, which presumably would be leaving with her and Arial.

'No, she thinks I'm going to ask you if I can sit in on Jackson's interview.'

'To which the answer is no,' Pavlik said, giving me another quick kiss before letting me go. 'But you can observe.'

'Deal,' I said, going back in to kiss him.

'No quid pro quo in this office.' He warded me off. 'And Kelly Anthony will be with you in the observation room.'

'Understood.'

When Pavlik turned the knob on the first door in the hallway, I continued onto the next. Kelly was already in there and looked up.

'Pavlik said I could observe,' I told her.

'I know,' she said. 'You met this guy?'

'Greeted would be more appropriate,' I said. 'He came to Edna's funeral, told Sarah he had done work for her. Then I saw him again, but couldn't place him, at the Morrison.'

She nodded, switching on the audio as Pavlik sat down across from Jackson Morris.

'I don't know what you're thinking,' Morris said, 'but I didn't cause that lady's CO poisoning.'

'You're saying that you're a thief but not an attempted murderer?' Pavlik asked.

'Murder?' He'd gone white. 'If she died of carbon monoxide, that's an accident. Negligence at most.'

'Negligence,' Pavlik repeated. 'As in the heat exchanger was cracked and the furnace not vented out?'

He held up his hands. 'The lady was too cheap to have it fixed. That's not my fault.'

'Fixed by you,' Pavlik said, flipping open a file. 'Who's not even a heating contractor. Fat lot of good that would have done.'

'I told her she shouldn't use it. I—'

'Who did you tell? Ruth Kingston, the victim?'

'No, no – I never even met her. It was the old lady.'

'Edna,' I whispered to Kelly. 'Ruth may not even have known.' She shushed me.

'How did you leave it then?' Pavlik asked. 'Aren't you supposed to disable the thermostats or something, so the furnace can't be accidentally switched on?'

'I unplugged it,' he said. 'I'm sure I did.'

'Sure you did,' Pavlik said, and made a note. 'And the venting?'

'The furnace was exhausted to the outside in March when I left it,' he said. 'But not glued in real well. I would have taken care of that if they'd hired me—'

'Bullshit, you would have,' Pavlik interrupted.

'No, really,' Morris said earnestly. 'It was all down when I came back, so I . . .' Morris trailed off, realized he'd said too much.

Pavlik pounced. 'Exactly when was this? Before or after Ruth Kingston was in a coma?'

The man sat forward. 'Listen, I tried to get back into that house, but—'

'But to rob it, not to fix anything, right?' Pavlik flipped a page in the file. 'Five burglary charges. Only one stuck because people seem to find you likeable.'

'Well, yes. I guess so. I—'

'I don't like you.'

'That shut him up,' Kelly said.

Me, I wasn't sure shutting somebody up was the aim of an interview. 'Ask him what he wanted to steal.'

Kelly looked around. 'Who are you talking to?'

'Myself, I guess.'

Pavlik shifted in his chair. 'Just what did you have your eye on at the Kingston house? From everything I've seen, you do your research. Case the joint, get in under whatever guise you decide on and then steal what you've targeted. What was it that caught your eye?'

'A painting,' Morris said. '*Trompe-l'œil* by the old lady herself.'

Pavlik glanced up at the mirrored observation window.

'I knew it,' I whispered. 'I knew her paintings must be valuable.'

'What happened?' Pavlik asked.

'That is so smart,' I said to Kelly. 'Just leaving it open-ended like that.'

'I didn't get it,' Morris said.

'That's a lie,' I told Kelly. 'I think he took it off the wall above Edna's dresser but ditched it in the garage when either you or Melinda interrupted him. I saw it there.'

Kelly stared at me for a two-second count and then pulled over a notepad to jot a note. 'Stay here.'

She went out and to the other door. I heard a knock and she entered, passing the note to Pavlik.

The corners of Pavlik's lips tilted up as he read it.

He set it down. 'That's not true, is it, Jackson? You did take that painting off the wall in Edna Mayes's room.'

Morris didn't answer.

Pavlik watched him for a tick and then shook his head. 'I don't see you as a murderer. But . . . you know, if we don't know why you were there, what else can I assume?'

'Again, with the murder.' Sitting back, Morris crossed his arms. 'I should ask for a lawyer.'

'You are absolutely within your rights,' Pavlik said. 'We already have you on burglary, though. Vases – pricey, but I assume not nearly as valuable as that painting. After all, you broke into a house where one woman had died, and another was asphyxiated just to get it. That painting had to be worth a bundle. How much? Ten thousand? Twenty?'

'Thirty-five if it was a genuine Mayes.' Jackson was shaking his head. 'It must have been a copy though.'

'How do you know?' Pavlik asked. 'You some kind of expert?'

'I know enough that the paint shouldn't be wet in places on like a forty-year-old painting.'

'He stuck his finger in it,' I said. 'That's what you all thought was a blister or something on his thumbprint.'

Kelly did a long stare again and, with a sigh, made another note and passed it to Pavlik.

This time he nearly glanced back at me behind the window before he turned to Jackson. 'You got paint on your thumb. We have your print with evidence of that on the vent work in the basement. What were you doing? Covering up your crime?'

'I didn't kill anybody,' our burglar nearly shouted. 'The second lady, the daughter, was already in the hospital when I broke in. I just figured I'd make sure the . . . um, the venting and all didn't implicate me. You know, in the accident.'

'So you vented the furnace back out,' Pavlik said. 'Had one piece left over though. That's a little sloppy.'

'The elbow? That didn't belong there, so I just tossed it to the side. There was no need for the exhaust to go up vertically. It was a straight horizontal run out the window vent.'

I frowned and glanced at Kelly.

'What?' she asked. 'Another note?'

'No, just thinking.'

'So you fix the venting, conscientious contractor that you are,' Pavlik said. 'What did you do with this worthless painting?'

'I'd carried it to the basement before I realized it was a fake,' he said. 'When I heard somebody try the front door, I grabbed it and snuck up the stairs and out the back before they could come around. Stashed the painting in the garage.'

'Why not just leave it in the basement?'

'I didn't want anybody to realize I'd been there. Or wonder how the painting had gotten there.'

Yet he left it in the garage.

'You do know the fire department checked the furnace first thing once the gas was cleared,' Pavlik said. 'We knew the heat exchanger was cracked and the vents weren't connected the night before you broke in.'

'So . . .'

'So all you did is draw attention to yourself.'

'Well, in my defense,' Jackson said, drawing himself up, 'I did really go there to steal the painting.'

'Idiot,' Kelly and I muttered simultaneously.

TWENTY-ONE

'Jack-of-all trades, maybe, but pretty much an idiot at breaking and entering,' I said. 'Jackson Morris needs a new trade.'

'I'm sure they'll assign him one in prison,' Pavlik said.

We were sitting in lawn chairs in the back yard, watching the sun set. From the frigid temps of a few days ago, the weather had taken a warm turn – as it often did in September – making it downright pleasant to sit outside without a parka.

I did pull my light jacket closed though, against the fall breeze. 'I think he sees himself as a sort of gentleman burglar, like Pierce Brosnan in *The Thomas Crown Affair.*'

'When he's really more Joe Pesci in *Home Alone.*'

'Exactly.' I patted my lap. 'Want to come up, Mocha?'

The chihuahua gave me a disdainful look and jumped up on Pavlik's lap, circling twice before settling.

'She hates me,' I said.

'Absolutely not,' Pavlik said. 'She just loves me more, while Frank favors you.'

Frank, on the ground in front of me, caught my eye and grunted.

'Sadly, you don't fit on my lap,' I told him.

He sighed and laid his head back down.

Peace descended on our family for a moment. And then, of course, I had to break it. 'You only have Morris on theft.'

Pavlik raised his eyebrows. 'And burglary at the Kingston house.'

'But he didn't end up taking anything. The painting is in the garage.'

'He's confessed to entering the house with the intent to steal the painting. That's the definition of burglary. Plus, we have a number of other robberies I think we'll be able to tie him to.'

'Sorry, I didn't mean to diminish what you've done,' I said. 'But Ruth's accident is still . . .'

'An accident?' Pavlik said. 'Personally I think Jackson was negligent, leaving the faulty furnace functional in the basement and the venting off. But whether that's criminal?' He shrugged.

'Did you believe him when he said the furnace was unplugged and vented outside when he left it in March?'

'Maybe it was, maybe it wasn't,' Pavlik said, as Mocha got up and kneaded his thigh like a cat before curling up again. 'Either way, he was unsure enough to check it when he went in to steal the painting.'

'He saw the fire department arrive Sunday along with the rest of the funeral-goers,' I said. 'It wouldn't take much to find out what had happened. Sophie and Gloria were there, so it was probably all over social media.'

'They do like to be in the know,' Pavlik said.

'And let everybody else know that they're in the know,' I agreed, leaning down to give Frank a scratch.

'What?'

'What what?' I said, straightening up.

'You're not happy,' he said, studying my face. 'You'd like Ruth's asphyxiation all wrapped up in a nice little package, along with the burglaries.'

'No, well, maybe. But if Jackson Morris is telling the truth – the furnace was unplugged and the venting was in place, at least minimally – then somebody had to undo that.'

'He said Ruth wasn't there when he inspected the furnace,' Pavlik pointed out. 'Maybe she didn't realize the extent of the furnace problems and plugged it in when the temperature started dropping.'

Flipped on the thermostat and, when she didn't get heat, went downstairs and found the furnace unplugged, so she plugged it in. 'But what about the venting? Wouldn't she have noticed it was down?'

'She might not have realized what the PVC was for. Most people see a furnace and they only think of it heating and blowing hot air into the house, not what happens to the by-products of the combustion.'

Made sense. But, 'Arial did say that Ruth didn't go into the basement.'

'Probably true when she could have Arial do it instead. But once she was gone,' he shrugged, 'needs must.'

Needs must. We did what we had to. I sat upright. 'Are you checking those fingerprints?'

'On your stolen silverware?' Pavlik said. 'Yes, but it's not really necessary, now that we know the fingerprints on the elbow belong to Jackson Morris.'

'Do me a favor anyway,' I said, getting up. 'Check those and the batteries Arial gave you. Plus, the furnace plug.'

'Already in progress,' Pavlik said. 'As for the plug, I'm assuming we'll find Morris's along with the others you'd expect.'

'If Ruth's are on it, it'll prove you're right and she went down there to plug the furnace back in,' I said, dangling the 'you're right' carrot. 'Do you even have her and Edna's prints? The Monterey police will want them when they go over the car.'

'Of course. We needed them for elimination purposes.' He nudged Mocha to hop down and got to his feet. 'I'm going to order delivery. Chinese or pizza?'

I weighed my hunger for knowledge with my plain ol' hunger. 'I have to run out, so order whichever you want.' I stood on my tiptoes to kiss him. 'I'll eat your leftovers when I get back.'

'Want me to go with you?' he asked.

'I'm just going to check something,' I said, ducking into the house to get my purse. 'And I don't want to get you into any trouble.'

'With myself?' Pavlik asked. 'You're not planning to break and enter, are you?'

'Of course not,' I said, dangling the car fob. 'Why?'

'You have a nitrile glove hanging out of your jacket pocket.'

I stuffed the blue glove in. 'No worries. Sarah and Arial have keys.'

Unfortunately, Sarah and Arial were otherwise engaged.

'Ruth's condition was unchanged when we stopped by the hospital after leaving you at the station,' Sarah told me on the phone. 'But they just called and want us there now.'

'Oh, I'm so sorry,' I said. 'I don't suppose you can—'

'I'll put the keys in the mailbox,' Sarah said. 'And you're welcome.'

'Thank you,' I said to a dead line.

The house was dark when I got there, of course, but it was the garage I was interested in first.

Parking in the driveway, I skirted the house and went through the gate into the back yard to try the garage door. Somebody had turned the lock on the door, but happily the second key on the ring unlocked it.

I stepped in and flipped on the garage light. The Forester was still there, of course, but I was interested in the painting on the other side of it.

Belatedly, I realized I should have checked with Pavlik in case the painting had already been taken in for evidence.

It hadn't, thankfully. But I could see that it would be, since Jackson Morris's paint-smudge thumbprint was plainly visible on the frame. I slipped my gloves on.

Gingerly turning the painting around, I sniffed. 'Does smell awfully fresh for an old painting.' I was talking to myself, but then I had dogs so that wasn't unusual.

'Can't see well enough in here,' I said. 'Best take it inside.'

I carried the painting by the frame to the back of the house, setting it down to pull on the door. Damn. The damaged door had finally been nailed shut, meaning the keys would do me no good.

Undeterred, I circled to the front door and let myself in, moving through the main room into the kitchen.

Setting the painting carefully on the table, I switched on the overhead light and leaned down to examine the *trompe-l'œil* letter on the dresser.

There was a thick stroke of blue on the dresser scarf. 'Not wet wet,' I said, examining the paint. 'But certainly not painted decades ago.'

The blue seemed like a mistake, a rectangular splotch of paint to perhaps cover up something else. I got out my phone and used the flashlight to examine the faux letter. I could just make out letters and numbers in black. I used the phone to take a photo so I could enlarge it.

'Psalm fifty-eight, verse three,' I read on the expanded photo. That was the verse Melinda looked up. The one Edna had quoted to Christopher.

I Googled it, as Melinda had. 'The wicked are estranged from the womb; they go astray from birth, speaking lies,' this translation read.

I took another photo, this one of the blue, and saw there was black intermingled and what looked like two horns. 'Well, I'll be damned.'

There was just one more thing I needed to check here. Edna's bedroom closet.

As I got into my car, I called Pavlik. 'I don't suppose you got those fingerprints back yet?'

'How could you know that?' he asked, his mouth full. 'Results and Thai arrived at the same time.'

Mmm. I loved Thai. But the game was afoot. 'And?'

'The Basil Beef is delicious, and the fingerprint results are not unexpected. The fork—'

'Not interested in that,' I said, starting the car. 'The batteries?'

'Boring. Just Ruth and Edna,' Pavlik confirmed, sounding a little hurt. 'Also on the plug, along with Morris, as we suspected.'

'I'm right,' I said. 'But there's no way to prove it, with Edna and Ruth dead.'

'Ruth isn't dead,' Pavlik said. 'She's—'

'In a coma, I know. But Sarah and Arial were just called to the hospital. I'm sure—'

'She's regained consciousness,' Pavlik said. 'Sarah just called to say her mother wants to talk to me.'

I was a little hurt my partner hadn't called me. 'Are you going there now?'

'I am,' he said. 'Soon as I finish swallowing.'

'Meet you.' My phone pinged a text, as I hung up.

From Sarah: *Come to the hospital. Ruth wants to confess.*

I ran into Pavlik in the hospital corridor and sniffed. 'You got Pad Thai, too.'

'Among other things,' he said. 'Do you know what this is all about?'

'Sarah's text says Ruth wants to confess,' I said.

Pavlik frowned. 'Confess what? That she tried to kill herself? Or . . .' His face changed. 'Maybe you were onto something when you asked whether Edna's death was suspicious.'

'Maybe, but I kind of doubt it,' I said, as we turned the last hospital corner into the room. 'I think it's a much older crime.'

Arial and Sarah were on either side of the bed. Ruth was sitting up at a forty-five-degree angle, a nurse fixing a cannula under her nose for oxygen.

'She just snapped out of it about an hour ago, they said,' Sarah said, moving to Arial's side of the bed so we could get closer.

'A miracle,' the nurse said. 'We've taken out her breathing tube.'

'Thank you,' the patient mumbled in a low tone. 'Privacy?'

'Of course,' the nurse said, giving the cannula a last tweak.

'I'm very glad to see you're doing better,' Pavlik said, as the door closed. 'Was there something you needed to tell me?'

'Yes, I—' Ruth was convulsed with a coughing fit.

'Sorry,' she said, as she caught her breath. 'But I need to tell you—'

The coughing again.

'I think I know what you want to say,' I said, stepping closer. 'I'm Maggy Thorsen, Sarah's friend and Arial's too.'

'The detective,' she said breathily. 'You . . . you know?'

'I think I do,' I said. 'And you can correct me if I go astray, OK?'

She nodded.

I turned to the rest of the assembly. I didn't wish Ruth ill, but I was glad I was getting my big reveal. 'This all dates back to the day Arial was conceived, Saturday, December nineteenth.'

'So not the twentieth,' Arial said.

Ruth shook her head and pointed for me to go on.

I did. 'Ruth met a man named Jonathan Springbok at a conference in Monterey and went up to his room.'

'Where he raped her,' Sarah injected impatiently. 'We know this.'

My eyes met Ruth's and I shook my head. 'I don't think she was raped.'

'But that was the night before Jonathan was run down . . . oh.' Arial's eyes were big.

Ruth's eyes, for her part, were brimming with tears.

I continued. 'I think the sex was consensual. I even think that, in that intoxicating moment, Ruth might have believed she'd found the one.'

'But "the one" was married,' Sarah said.

'That was the problem,' I said, turning to Ruth. 'He told you, didn't he?'

She nodded. 'After . . . he said I had to leave. That he was flying back to his wife and kids the next morning. He made me feel like a . . . a . . . slut.'

The last word was barely audible.

'So you pulled on your clothes and ran,' I said. 'Ran home and maybe your mother—'

'She was there,' Ruth said, pulling herself up a bit. 'And my grandmother. I was a mess, tears running down my face. Edna said . . . she said I smelled like . . . sex.'

'So, you told them you'd been raped,' Arial said. 'Did you also tell them that you'd run the man down in a fit of jealousy?'

Ruth was shaking her head, back and forth, trying to speak.

I held up a hand. 'May I?'

She nodded.

'First of all, I don't think Springbok necessarily lied about being married. I think he just didn't say.'

'Lie of omission.' This was the first time Pavlik had spoken.

'Yes,' I said, watching Ruth for any signals I was wrong. 'I also don't think Ruth killed him. I think it was Edna.'

TWENTY-TWO

'Edna took revenge on Springbok,' Sarah said, mulling it over. 'An eye for an eye. It wasn't out of character.'

'How did she know what he looked like and where to find him?' Pavlik had his notebook out.

'I . . . told . . . her,' Ruth said.

'If he was taking the Monterey shuttle to the airport,' Sarah said, 'it would be on a schedule. Pickup on the corner across from the hotel.'

'Exactly,' I said. 'And it was a very early shuttle, which was why Springbok was so hot for Ruth to leave.'

'Meaning there were no witnesses,' Arial said.

'Then Edna,' Sarah took up, 'believing her virgin daughter has been raped . . .' She lifted her eyebrows at Ruth, who flushed.

'Not a virgin, I assume?' I asked Ruth.

Ruth shook her head.

'Edna, the avenging angel, mows down the man, comes back and stows the car in Gretchen's garage,' Sarah said. 'Bet they didn't say a word about it.'

Ruth shook her head. 'But I knew.'

'And at that point,' I said, 'how could you change your story?'

A single tear slipped from Ruth's right eye as she shook her head.

Arial reached down and took her hand as Ruth began to sob hoarsely. 'Is this why you tried to kill yourself? But why now? This is all in the past and it wasn't your fault. I mean, not really.'

But Ruth was shaking her head. 'Accident.'

'No,' I told her. 'Because your mother found out you lied, didn't she?'

Ruth's head dropped, but she finally nodded.

'Christopher saw Edna in June,' I said. 'He told her about Jonathan's deathbed confession – about cheating, not rape. I think it started Edna thinking.'

Ruth didn't move, didn't meet my eyes.

'She quoted a psalm to Christopher—'

'Psalm fifty-eight, verse three,' Arial said, sitting on the edge of Ruth's bed. '"The wicked are estranged from the womb; they go astray from birth, speaking lies."'

' . . . talking about . . . me,' Ruth managed.

'She wrote you out of her will that same month,' I said. 'And I believe she started plotting her revenge. Or, as she probably looked at it, some sort of poetic justice.'

'What are you talking about?' Sarah was staring at me.

'Ruth had lied to Edna, causing Edna to kill Jonathan. Edna lived with what she'd done all those years—'

'A burden,' Arial said to her mother. 'Your letter said something about a burden. It wasn't me.'

'No, never you,' Ruth said. 'Never, ever you.'

'You wrote that letter, apologizing,' I continued, 'but she never forgave you. Not really.'

'She was . . . hard, but . . . how could I blame her?'

'You told a lie, because you couldn't tell her the truth,' Sarah said. 'She's the one who killed a man.'

'And nearly killed her own daughter,' I said.

'What are you talking about?' Now it was Pavlik asking.

'We considered the possibility that Ruth's near miss was an accident, or a suicide attempt, negligence by Jackson or even a murder attempt by Melinda or Christopher or even Arial.'

'We did?' Pavlik asked.

'Well, I did,' I admitted. 'Sorry, Arial.'

'No worries,' she said, her eyes wide. 'But go on.'

'What we didn't consider was a murder attempt by Edna.'

'Because she was dead,' Sarah said. 'Duh.'

'I think she set this whole thing in motion before she died. Knowing she was going to die.'

Pavlik cocked his head. 'Justice, as you said?'

'Delayed justice,' I said. 'According to you, Edna's fingerprints were on the new batteries that were removed and thrown away as well as the plug for the furnace.'

Pavlik raised his hand like we were in class. 'I didn't have a chance to tell you. After we talked, I had her fingerprints compared to the small one on the PVC elbow.'

'It was a match,' I guessed.

'What's your theory?' Sarah asked. 'Edna, knowing the heat exchanger on the furnace was cracked—'

I held up a hand and turned to Ruth. 'Did you know that?'

She shook her head mutely.

'OK, go on,' I said to Sarah.

She was still staring at me. 'You think Edna set some sort of posthumous trap for my sister?'

'Yes. Obviously, she wasn't plotting this in March, when the estimate was done. But I believe she took advantage of the furnace that she'd been told was dangerous and had been unplugged. Sometime when Ruth was out, she went into the basement and knocked down the PVC that would have vented most of the toxic gases out, replacing it with a single elbow – the one we found on the floor, with her fingerprints on it – going up.'

'Toward the bedrooms,' Pavlik said. 'Not a sure way to kill somebody.'

'No, nor were the batteries she took out of the carbon monoxide detectors. None of these actions, alone, would necessarily cause Ruth's death. But together?' I shrugged.

'But how could she have known Ruth would turn on the furnace *after* she herself was dead?' Pavlik asked. 'She could have killed both of them. Or even after she died, how could she be sure Arial wouldn't be there?'

'Because she knew I would never stay there with my mother,' Arial said, squeezing her hand. 'Sorry.'

Ruth patted her hand.

'And as for turning on the furnace while Edna was alive,' Arial continued. 'That would never happen.'

'Edna's heart was failing,' I said. 'The doctor had given her weeks to live and, though Edna had outlived the original estimate, she could feel that the end was coming.'

'Weaker,' Ruth said, nodding.

'It's September,' Arial said. 'Even if Edna hadn't died last week, she could be fairly certain she wouldn't make it to November.'

'What's November?' Pavlik asked.

'Thanksgiving,' Sarah said. 'When Edna was alive, we never turned on the furnace until Thanksgiving, no matter how cold it got. We always hated that.'

'Which is why Edna knew Ruth would turn it on the first cold night after she died,' I said.

'Freedom.' Ruth laughed, sending her into another coughing fit.

'Is that also why you closed your bedroom door?' I asked when she'd caught her breath.

She cocked her head.

'It was closed when I found you,' I told her. 'I understand you normally kept it open so you could hear Edna.'

'The smell . . . bleach, paint.'

'From Edna's room,' I said, understanding now. 'The smell bothered you.'

'And this is important why?' Sarah asked quizzically.

'It's not,' I said. 'It was just a missing piece, not a smoking gun.'

'That's because there is no smoking gun,' Pavlik said regretfully. 'No hard evidence.'

'No,' Sarah said, thoughtfully, 'because Edna wouldn't want that. She'd already killed a man and lived with that knowledge. She wanted a situation where Ruth's own action – own selfishness, she'd think of it as – caused her death.'

'Poetic justice, as you say.' Arial shook her head. 'I'm surprised she didn't leave a note.'

'Take some credit for it,' Sarah said. 'I was thinking the same thing. It is sort of genius.'

'She did leave a note of sorts,' I said. 'It was in the painting.'

'The fake that Jackson left in the garage?' Pavlik asked.

'It's not a fake,' I said. 'The paint was wet because Edna added to it. Remember the paints you found on the shelf in the closet?' I asked Sarah.

She nodded. 'And, as Ruth said, there was the strong smell of oil paints in Edna's bedroom. But what did she add?'

'In the painting there was a letter on the dresser. She added a Bible citation on it. "Psalm fifty-eight, verse three" – the same verse she quoted to Christopher.'

'And directed at me,' Ruth said.

'Also addressed to you,' I told her. 'Your name had been added to the envelope in the painting.'

'Wow,' Arial said with a shudder. 'Could she get any creepier?'

'Actually, she could.' I punched up the photo I'd taken of that section of the painting and handed it to her.

'What am I looking at?' she asked, squinting.

'The blue rectangle,' I said. 'Enlarge it.'

Arial did, staring at it, before raising her head to stare at me. 'It's a battery.'

I nodded. 'A nine-volt battery, like the ones she took out of the carbon monoxide detector.'

'My mother killed a man.'

Sarah, Pavlik and I had moved away from the bed as Arial sat with her mother.

'What will you do?' I asked the sheriff.

'About Edna?' he asked. 'That's a good question. I mean, given what we know, it's a very plausible theory, but—'

'There's no hard evidence,' I said.

'And unless Ruth wants to press posthumous charges,' Sarah said, glancing at her sister, 'what's to be gained? Edna is dead.'

Christopher had said something similar about the car that killed his father. 'What about Jonathan Springbok's murder?'

'That will be up to the Monterey police,' Pavlik said. 'They already have the Escort. If there's still blood evidence on it, maybe it will confirm Ruth's story.'

'Her word isn't enough?' I asked.

'From what she's said . . .' He broke off. 'Or – more precisely – what Maggy has said, and Ruth has nodded to, she wasn't there.'

'So my mother killed a man and nearly killed her own daughter and is going to get away with it.'

'She is dead,' I offered.

'There is that.'

It was late that same night and Pavlik and I were on the couch, finishing off the Thai food.

'Arial took her mother being a pathological liar and her grand-mother a homicidal maniac pretty well, don't you think?'

'As well as can be expected,' Pavlik said. 'She was being pretty nice to Ruth, all things considered. Do you think she'll be staying in town now?'

'Rather than fleeing to the Monterey Peninsula?' I asked, nabbing a shrimp from the Pad Thai. 'Not a chance. She told me she's out of here next week.'

'I can't say I blame her. This place doesn't hold many good memories for her, except for Sarah and you, of course.'

'And Sarah will be devastated,' I said. 'The upside is we have a really nice place to go visit.'

'Because it's all about us.'

'It is,' I said, with a grin. 'But it is a beautiful place, and I think Arial will do very well there.'

He set his plate on the coffee table. 'You know she was right there with you, spinning theories as you were doing your big reveal. She wouldn't make a half bad detective.'

'But not as good as me,' I said, snuggling back into his arms. 'Right?'

'Of course not,' he said, rubbing his stubbly chin on the top of my head. 'But . . .'

'But what?'

'She *is* a whole lot younger.'

I smacked him. Lovingly, of course.